A New Valhalla

◊ ◊ ◊

A New Valhalla

A New Valhalla

a novel

by
mike whicker

a Walküre imprint

This is a work of historical fiction

ISBN: 978-0-9995582-1-8

printed in the United States of America

A New Valhalla

For

Gary Whicker

A New Valhalla

The Erika Lehmann Spy Series

Book 1: *Invitation to Valhalla*
Book 2: *Blood of the Reich*
Book 3: *Return to Valhalla*
Book 4: *Fall from Valhalla*
Book 5: *Operation Shield Maidens*
Book 6: *Hope for Valhalla*
Book 7: *Search for Valhalla*
Book 8: **A New Valhalla**

Other books by Mike Whicker:

Proper Suda (a novel)
and
Flowers for Hitler: The Extraordinary Life of Ilse Dorsch
(a biography)

All books are available in print copy from Amazon.com, bn.com, and electronically from Kindle. Signed copies are available from the author for shipping.

Author welcomes reader comments
Email: mikewhicker1@gmail.com

A New Valhalla

Prologue

The fiend in his own shape is less hideous than when he rages in the breast of man.

– Nathaniel Hawthorne, 1835

July 1942
Berlin, Gestapo headquarters
8 Prinz Albrechtstrasse

A large man wearing a black porkpie hat tilted toward the right side of his head entered the room.

Axel Ryker sat down heavily in the chair facing Heinrich Himmler's desk. Ryker, a repatriated German from Lithuania, was a man called upon by Himmler from time to time for "special" tasks. Ryker possessed several qualities that augmented his usefulness to Himmler and the Gestapo. He spoke fluent Russian (his native tongue), acceptable Slovak and Czech (most speakers of Slovak had few problems with the similar Czech), and German. Ryker even managed to stumble his way through English, although his English consisted of a strange mixture of Russian, Czech, and German accents.

He could also snap a man's neck as easily as a chicken bone, which he had proven on more than one occasion. For Axel Ryker, liquidation and torture were job skills honed sharp, and sometimes even pleasant diversions.

Ryker was a full six-feet tall (probably a little more) with a wide, heavily muscled torso, a shaven head, and dark, pitiless eyes. His protruding brow gave him a caveman countenance. Adding to his already grisly genetic features was a nose that had been broken but never properly repaired, and two noticeable scars on his face. The nose was a souvenir from the twenties, courtesy of a pipe swinging communist who crept up on him during a street brawl. Ryker was a teenager at the time.

To frighten women and intimidate men, Axel Ryker simply had to enter the room.

Yet Ryker was no mindless automaton dusted off only during the Gestapo's murder and maim hour. In addition to his impressive language skills, Ryker possessed an innate craftiness, including an almost supernatural ability to discern when someone was lying to him. These qualities allowed him to ferret information when others failed.

A week ago, Ryker had been in Budapest investigating a break-in at the Rumanian embassy. Some sensitive papers detailing Nazi plans to arrest a popular, but pro-resistance, Catholic priest in Oradea had been stolen. Ryker was ordered to Budapest to take over the case. His first task would be the apprehension of the embassy thieves; his second the eventual arrest of the priest.

A suspect in the burglary, under torture, had failed to implicate others. That is until Ryker had the man's wife and four small children brought in. The youngest child was still nursing, the oldest not yet seven years old. As the family stood in front of the bleeding, half-conscious father, Ryker transferred the infant from the mother's arms to the oldest child, took out his Mauser and shot the woman through the head in front of her husband and children. Ryker was preparing to do the same to the children, one by one, when the man gave Ryker the information he sought on condition the children be released. The man's associates were arrested and the papers recovered before they could be circulated. Ryker had all the conspirators shot, of course. The parentless children were released on the streets of Budapest. Axel Ryker kept his promises.

Ryker did not complete his mission. The Rumanian priest had yet to be disposed of when Ryker was recalled to Berlin by Gestapo chief Heinrich Müller on Himmler's orders.

That was six days ago. Himmler handed Ryker a photograph of a blonde woman. She appeared to be in her mid-twenties.

"Who is this?" Ryker asked.

"Her name is Erika Lehmann," Himmler answered with disdain. "She works for the Abwehr and Canaris has sent her to America on a mission in a city called Evansville. It's in the American state of Indiana. You're going to America, Ryker. Find this woman and cancel her."

Chapter 1

Denver, Colorado, USA
Saturday, 03 April 1948

The sun had sunk behind the Rocky Mountains three hours ago.

A wet snow of huge flakes blustered through the street lights on Federal Boulevard when the blonde woman walked through the door of the *Loro Rojo.* The snow had yet to stick on the streets. The past few days had been warm for this time of year in the Mile High City, but the woman figured the snow would eventually have its way with the pavement by the time she left. Her drive back to her apartment would most likely be a slow one.

The *Loro Rojo's* sign befitted its name. A hand drawn painting of a red parrot on the door greeted patrons as they entered—greeted or warned them to think twice about entering, it was hard to tell from the bird's stern look.

The bar would be categorized as a dive by most people's standards. The *Loro Rojo* was not particularly clean, its restrooms were a disaster, and the bartender gave the impression that he hadn't bathed in a fortnight. Most of the conversing in the bar was done in Spanish. The clientele was made up exclusively of Mexicans except for the blonde who had been showing up every Saturday night for the past three weeks. The only other women in the bar were Mexican, or Mexican heritage, prostitutes.

The blonde came in on Saturday nights to play the pinball machines and darts with the drunken clientele who, in their inebriated state, laid down silly bets. She was especially good with darts and always left with a sizeable profit. Last week she won over $75—much more than the prostitutes made in a night.

Nothing out of the ordinary happened until she was halfway into her third game of darts with a man who was losing badly.

That's when another drunken man walked up behind her and grabbed her buttocks.

Chapter 2

Washington, D.C.
FBI Headquarters
Sunday, 04 April 1948

Being Sunday, Chris Singleton had been at his apartment in Arlington when the phone call came. The nature of the call was such that it caused him to bolt out of his door wearing blue jeans and T-shirt, not wanting to take the time to change into a suit. He used the siren and detachable roof light on his unmarked 1946 Pontiac as he raced to FBI Headquarters located in the Department of Justice building on Washington's New York Avenue.

The Pontiac's tires screeched as Singleton came to a stop in a no-parking zone in front of one of the building's side entrances. The guard recognized the FBI agent, so he mentioned nothing about his illegally parked car as Singleton sprinted past.

Instead of wending his way through the corridors to the main entrance area and waiting on the slow elevator, Singleton dashed up the much nearer side entrance steps to the third floor where the FBI offices were located.

When he got to that floor, he quickly walked past several receptionists and lower-ranking FBI personnel seated in cubicles. Finally, he reached Harry Fallon's personal secretary. She saw him coming and said, "Go on in, Agent Singleton. Agent Fallon is expecting you."

"Damn! You got here in record time, Chris," Fallon boomed after Singleton entered his office. "Have a seat." Fallon was Singleton's immediate boss.

Singleton didn't wait to be seated. "You told me on the phone that Sarah Klein's fingerprints had shown up on the radar. Talk quickly, Harry." Singleton then sat down across from Fallon's desk. Sarah Klein was a German spy who conducted a mission in the United states during the war. The FBI also knew her by the name 'Erika.' They were not sure which name was her real name and which one was an alias. Perhaps both names were an alias—they simply didn't know.

"The police in Denver, Colorado, arrested a woman last night. They felt her story to be sketchy, so they sent her prints to us. Our guys pulled up a match to your favorite German spy in Evansville, Indiana, whose prints you logged during the war. She's being held in the Denver County jail."

"What for? Why was she arrested is what I mean," said Singleton.

"Something that seems pretty silly. She got into a melee at some dive bar in the Latin section of Denver. She injured a couple of men, including a Denver vice squad cop working an undercover case at that bar. I asked the Denver cops for a second set of prints and it came back the same. It seems she is indeed your Sarah Klein, or at least the woman who used that name in Evansville during the war."

"That's good work by our print guys, making the match overnight." Singleton knew many times it took days to find a match in the FBI files as all the prints had to be searched by hand.

"It speeds things up knowing the prints are a woman's," Fallon said. "There is a small fraction of female prints in the files as compared to men."

"Requesting permission for a special flight to Denver that will depart right away," Singleton stated.

"Granted. So you don't have to wait around Washington, I'll have our Denver field office work up the paperwork to have this woman turned over into your custody. Bring her back here, Chris. She's responsible for Charlie's death."

Chapter 3

Washington, D.C.
CIA Headquarters on E Street
Monday, 05 April 1948

Al Hodge had been at work less than an hour when Army Major Sheila Reid entered his office. Hodge was director of counter intelligence for the recently formed CIA, an organization that went into official operation less than a year ago. Yet Hodge was no novice when it came to the clandestine world. He and his boss, Leroy Carr, who now served as the deputy director of this new intelligence agency, had worked together throughout the war when they served with the now disbanded OSS.

Major Reid was Leroy Carr's executive assistant, but Carr was currently in London at a weeklong conference at White Hall between high-ranking officials of the CIA and their counterparts with the British MI-6. During Carr's absence, Reid reported to Hodge with any matters of importance.

"Good morning, Sheila," Hodge greeted as he closed a folder he had been reading.

"Morning, Al." The trio of Carr, Hodge, and Reid put formalities aside and addressed each other by first names when no one else was present. "We have a development with Erika."

Hodge grunted and rolled his eyes. "What has she done now?"

"She got herself arrested and is in jail in Denver."

"Dammit! I told Leroy he was making a mistake sending Lehmann to a city weeks before her mission was to begin. When Lehmann has too much time on her hands she's going to cause trouble. How many times does this have to happen before we learn?" Hodge and Carr were best friends, but as is allowed between best friends, both sides could be honest with one another. Hodge wasn't saying anything to Reid that she hadn't heard him say to Leroy Carr.

"Leroy wanted to give her enough time to acclimate to a strange town before the mission began. Knowing streets and how to get around is important if you have that time available before a mission begins. You know that, Al. It was sound strategy on Leroy's part."

"There's no such thing as sound strategy when it comes to Lehmann." Hodge quipped. "Anyway, what's done is done. What did she do *this time* to get arrested? Tell me it's something other than shooting someone or smashing up a bar."

"Well, actually, it's the latter." Sheila went on to tell Hodge what she had learned about the incident, "But that's not our main problem, Al. The Denver police sent Erika's fingerprints to the FBI."

Hodge stared at her. "When did the FBI find out about her?"

"Yesterday."

"Jesus! Singleton has been looking for her since the Evansville incident in '43. I guarantee you he's already on his way. Hell, he might already be in Denver." The FBI's Chris Singleton had never given up the search for the woman he knew as 'Sarah Klein' or 'Erika'. The CIA knew this because Singleton had asked for their help in locating her. Singleton reasoned that the Nazi spy was probably out of the country. The FBI's mandate focused on operations within the United States. For help in foreign lands, Singleton had little choice other than to ask the OSS during the war, and now the CIA, for help.

Hodge continued, "We have to get in touch with Leroy. What time is it in London?"

"Five hours ahead of us," Sheila answered."

Hodge looked at his watch. "It's mid-afternoon there. Leroy is probably in meetings. Don't interrupt him in a meeting. The Brits have also been trying to locate Lehmann since the caper she pulled there during the war when she worked for the Nazis. The boys at MI-6 will know something important is afoot and ask questions if Leroy leaves a meeting to answer a phone call. Leroy wouldn't tell them anything but there's no sense in putting him on the spot. You might have to leave a message at his hotel but get in touch with him and fill him in on what you know. I'll get an emergency Air Force flight to Denver from Andrews. Tell Leroy I'll call him as soon as I get there and I find out the real skinny on what's going on."

5

[same morning—Denver]

Chris Singleton's plane touched down at Denver's Stapleton Airport an hour ago. Two FBI agents from the Denver field office picked him up and took him directly to the county jail.

After a brief meeting with the warden, he was led to the women's cell block where he now stood in the corridor outside a cell holding a blonde woman sitting on her cot. She looked up, rose, and walked to the bars. She looked Singleton up and down then focused on his face.

Before Singleton had said a word or pulled out his badge, she volunteered, "I remember you."

Chapter 4

The Bridge

[Flashback to 1943]
Washington, D.C.

Forty minutes, maybe fifty, Chris Singleton waited until J. Edgar Hoover and an entourage of six men entered the room: three wore gray suits, the others military uniforms. Besides Hoover, the only person Singleton recognized was General William J. "Wild Bill" Donovan, the director of the OSS. Singleton rose and stood while Hoover introduced the others: two military intelligence supervisors, an OSS big shot named Leroy Carr, and a couple of FBI higher-ups. Singleton had written the reports and related the story of last Saturday night ad infinitum, but Hoover insisted on hearing it in person so Singleton was flown to Washington.

Hoover took the middle seat while the others divided up equally on the long side of the oval table. Young Chris Singleton sat conspicuously alone, opposite and facing the men.

"Of course, I have read your report, Agent Singleton," Hoover began. "The other men here have done likewise, but I ordered you to Washington because I wanted you to be on hand to personally answer any questions about the events of this Saturday past."

"I understand, sir," Singleton said.

"To begin, give us your rundown of what happened last Saturday." Hoover looked at the papers in front of him. "Start from the time the principals arrived at the meeting location."

Singleton began: "Agent Pulaski, myself and two of my men, Agents Stuart and Buecher, were stationed inside the nightclub. Agent Pulaski and I, because he felt the two of us might be recognized by one or both of the principals, watched from behind a curtained office window where we could see into the nightclub. Agent Pulaski kept the room we were in dark and we peered out of the edge of the curtains. Outside the club, Agent Falasco had assembled a large contingent of agents to establish roadblock capability in both directions on the highway that passes by the premises—out of sight, of course—including a team of agents on the Kentucky side of the bridge that crosses the Ohio River south of the club."

"The male suspect, we refer to him as 'Ivan,' entered the nightclub at 2010 hours, fifty minutes before the scheduled rendezvous. Initially, Ivan took a seat at the bar but after a few minutes moved to a table. The woman agent, we're calling her 'Erika' now, arrived at 2035; she spotted the man and joined him at his table."

Hoover held up his hand to stop Singleton. "The name 'Erika' comes from the woman herself?"

"Yes," Singleton nodded. "It is the name she claimed was hers during the break-in at the engineer's home the previous night."

"Wild Bill" Donovan broke in. "I saw that in your report. That certainly is a strange kettle of fish. In your report you state this engineer, Mayer, claims this German spy broke in and drugged an FBI agent just so she could tell this Mayer guy that she had succeeded in getting his relatives released from a concentration camp?"

"That's Mayer's story, General," Singleton confirmed.

"Then she shoots him for good measure?"

"She knew the engineer would try to capture her, sir."

The men behind the table looked around at each other.

"Go on, Agent Singleton," Hoover ordered.

"Agent Pulaski preferred to not make the arrest inside the nightclub if possible. The place was crowded and Pulaski worried about innocent bystanders. The two suspects talked for fifteen minutes before they rose and left the nightclub. We followed the suspects out, and it was outside in the parking lot where we attempted to make the arrest." Singleton paused for a moment to see if there were any questions. None were asked so he continued.

"As it states in my report, I was the first to approach the suspects along with Agent Pulaski who was a half-step behind me. I withdrew my identification and showed it to the suspects. The male, *Ivan,* immediately produced a handgun and pointed it in my direction and fired." Singleton paused for a moment and collected himself.

"I had my gun drawn but everything happened so quickly. Agent Pulaski knocked me out of the way, and he himself was hit by the bullet. Ivan fired two more shots in our direction but we—Stuart, Buecher, and myself—were able to find shelter behind some parked cars. I raised my gun and was about to return fire, when Ivan grabbed a bystander—a young woman who had just walked out of the club. He used the woman as a shield. We held our fire; Ivan forced the hostage into an automobile. The female suspect, Erika, also jumped into the same car. They sped from the parking lot with the man behind the wheel."

"This is when you radioed the road blocks?" Hoover asked.

"Yes," replied Singleton. "The first thing I did was check on Agent Pulaski, of course. He sustained a gunshot wound to the abdomen and was bleeding profusely but was conscious. I then ordered Agent Stuart to alert the road block people, and I ordered Agent Buecher to call for an ambulance. But Agent Pulaski insisted we help him into a vehicle and take out after the suspects. With the nature of Agent Pulaski's wound, I didn't think this was a good idea from his standpoint. I told him we had notified Falasco and the road block people and they would pick up the suspects. But Agent Pulaski would not calm down. He kept insisting his wound was not that bad, and he ordered us to pursue the suspects."

"What was the time frame," one of the military people asked, "from the gunshot to the time you pulled out in pursuit?"

"Less than one minute," Singleton answered the inane question, "probably forty-five seconds.

"The suspects headed south, away from the city and toward the bridge that crosses the river to Kentucky. Buecher drove our car and quickly closed on the suspect's vehicle. By the time we were on the bridge we were no more than one hundred yards behind them. I knew we had them when I saw the flashing red lights at the far end of the bridge. The Kentucky side of the bridge was completely barricaded with cars while Falasco, who was with the men north of the nightclub, ordered those cars to follow and set up a barricade at the Indiana side on the bridge. The suspects were completely trapped on the bridge."

"So," Hoover interrupted, "let's make sure everyone is picturing this correctly. It ended up being just your car, and the car driven by the suspects, on the bridge with both ends of the bridge blocked from escape."

"That's right, Director." Singleton confirmed. "Agent Pulaski, who I was trying to attend in the back seat as best as I could, ordered Buecher

9

to radio that there was a hostage situation and to maintain the barricade but not to pursue onto the bridge."

"I have a question, Agent Singleton," grilled the OSS man introduced as Leroy Carr who accompanied Donovan. "We have no eyewitness reports on the events that took place on the bridge from Special Agent-in-Charge Falasco or any of the other men from the Bureau. Why is that?"

"The bridge is a mile long, sir," Singleton remarked, "and it was after dark."

"Go on, Singleton," Hoover nodded.

"Again, I estimate we were about a hundred yards behind the suspect's car, both doing about ninety miles an hour on the bridge. When Ivan spotted the barricade at the other end he slammed on the brakes and spun to a stop. That's when the door opened and the hostage was thrown out."

Hoover shuffled through papers until he found what he looked for. "I see from your report the hostage claims the female suspect—this *Erika*—opened the car door and threw her out of the automobile?"

"Yes, Director, that is what the hostage claims. The hostage testified that the man, *Ivan,* ordered *Erika* to kill her, but instead *Erika* opened the door and threw her out of the car."

Singleton continued, "After the hostage was ejected from the car, the car headed back in our direction toward Indiana. I guess they were hoping the north end of the bridge wasn't blocked yet. With our headlights on bright and shining directly on the car as it came toward us, we saw what we thought was the female suspect fighting with the male as he tried to drive the car. That was just before the car swerved violently and crashed into the bridge guard rail."

"The car door opened, and the woman *Erika* fell out of the car. The man *Ivan* followed her out on the passenger side. I could see then that they were indeed fighting. The man punched the woman and she flew back against the guard rail. This is when he picked up a gun one of them had apparently dropped during the fight. We were all out of our car and had taken cover by this time. When I saw the man level the gun at the woman I fired two shots. The guy staggered for a second and dropped the gun but he didn't go down. Instead he went after the woman again."

"Where did you hit the suspect?" Hoover asked.

"I hit him with two solid shots in the torso," answered Singleton. "It was unbelievable the guy didn't drop." Singleton took a breath and went on.

"*Erika* began climbing the outside metal work of the bridge and *Ivan* went after her. I ordered them to come down and surrender but both ignored my orders. She went up much more quickly than he did and I got the impression she purposely slowed a couple of times to allow him to catch up, staying just high enough over him to stay out of his reach."

Donovan interrupted, curious about how Singleton could see all this in the dark.

"Stuart kept the car's spotlight trained on them," Singleton stated.

Donovan nodded and Singleton restarted.

"When they were finally near the top of the bridge's metal work, the woman produced a dagger then jumped down onto the back of the man. From where we stood it looked like she then buried the knife in his throat. He lost his grip and they both fell off the metal work. Together they plunged past us and down to the river. It was a long fall—over one hundred feet, but there was enough moonlight to enable us to watch them hit the surface. The woman still clung to the man's back when they disappeared into the water. We saw neither suspect surface, but within thirty minutes Agent Falasco had a Coast Guard runabout and a couple of Sheriff's Department motorboats conducting a searchlight sweep of the river."

"No bodies were found that night?" Donovan asked.

"No," confirmed Singleton. "Dragging operations began at dawn on Sunday. The man's body was dragged up Monday afternoon a mile down river."

"Any news on the woman's body?" Hoover jumped in.

"An hour ago I called Agent Falasco in Evansville for the latest. We still have not retrieved the woman's body."

Donovan: "What are the chances, in your opinion Agent Singleton, that the woman could have survived the fall?"

11

"Not likely. It would be hard to survive the fall for anyone. After a fall from that height, they would have entered the water at over sixty miles an hour."

"But still it could be possible to survive," Hoover frowned.

"Yes, anything is possible," Singleton conceded. "That's why we still have an APB out for the woman. The local police tell me bodies of drowning victims in that river are sometimes not recovered for weeks or even months. With undertows, cross currents, and underwater debris that can entrap a body and hold it under, I'm told bodies are sometimes never recovered. Nevertheless, the APB will remain in effect."

When Singleton finished, some of the men looked down at papers on the table, others looked at Singleton. Apparently, no one had any more questions. Hoover spoke to the committee.

"Despite some rather bizarre happenstance to accompany this case, gentlemen, I feel we must count our blessings. The stolen tellurium and several rolls of microfilm were recovered from the trunk of the male suspect's automobile. These highly classified materials were in the hands of the enemy for three weeks. To have recovered them is certainly reason for celebration." Hoover turned to Singleton. "Agent Singleton, you have every reason to be pleased with your work."

"Thank you, Director, but it was Charlie Pulaski who should get the credit for this case. Pulaski was the only one who felt the woman would return to Evansville. Pulaski's the one who uncovered the leads that eventually cracked the case." Singleton paused to collect his thoughts. "Not to mention he saved my life by taking a bullet intended for me."

"Of course, Agent Singleton," Hoover agreed. "What are the plans?"

"I'm flying back to Evansville this evening and accompanying Charlie's body to Chicago tomorrow for burial Friday."

"It was a shock when Falasco called last night to tell us Agent Pulaski passed yesterday," Hoover said. "We were all praying he'd make it."

Singleton said nothing.

"I will be there for the funeral in Chicago on Friday, of course," said Hoover. The FBI director asked the other men if there were any more questions for Singleton. When there were none Singleton was dismissed.

"Just one last reminder, Agent Singleton," Hoover warned as Singleton made his way to the door, "none of this reaches the newspapers."

Chris Singleton nodded and closed the door behind him.

Chapter 5

[Back to Present Day]
Denver, Colorado
Monday, 05 April 1948

Chris Singleton had handed over the proper paperwork to the jail warden for the prisoner to be remanded into his custody, and just twenty minutes after he arrived at the Denver County jail, he left with Erika Lehmann, her hands cuffed behind her back. The two Denver special agents who picked up Singleton at the airport drove Singleton and his prisoner downtown to the Denver FBI field office located on the fourth floor of the Federal office building where they would conduct her initial interrogation.

The interrogation room was similar to many in local police stations—a stark room with no windows. A wooden table and some chairs served as the entire décor. Before they entered the room, one of the field agents removed the cuffs from behind her back and put them back on so her hands were in front of her. There were papers she would have to look over.

Singleton took her into the room and the field agents stayed outside in the corridor. He told her where to sit. The 6'4" FBI agent took the chair opposite her across the desk. A folder rested on the table in front of him.

"As I told you at the jail, my name is Chris Singleton. I've already showed you my identification. I'm a special agent with the FBI stationed in Washington. Let's start with what we know about you." A handsome, fit man, Erika judged the FBI agent to be around thirty years in age. "We know during the war that you conducted an espionage mission for Germany against our country at the Naval Shipyard in Evansville, Indiana. That was in 1943." Singleton didn't have to refer to the folder; he was in Evansville at that time trying to chase her down.

"I knew I recognized you," the good looking blonde interjected. She smiled at him, which enraged him, but he moved on.

"You used the name *Sarah Klein* in Evansville. Later, testimony from Joseph Mayer, the scientist who ended up being your mark, told us you had revealed to him that your name was Erika. That was right before you shot him."

"I purposely shot him in the leg only so he couldn't chase me. I had no intention of killing him and I didn't."

"So, is your name really Erika?

"Yes."

"What's your last name?"

"None of your business."

"Okay, have it your way," Singleton snapped. He opened the folder and withdrew two sheets of paper that were paperclipped together. "This is a copy of your extradition papers. I'm taking you back to Washington where you'll be charged with the murder of an FBI agent in '43. Charles Pulaski was my partner. It doesn't matter if you sign the papers or not; I'm taking you to Washington."

She picked up the papers and briefly looked them over. "Don't I get a lawyer?"

"No. Not until we get you back to D.C."

She nicely handed the papers back to him. Singleton arose, walked to, and opened the door.

"Agent Helms," Singleton said to one of the agents standing nearby. "Please have someone go to the Brown Palace Hotel and collect my things—room 621. I'll arrange a flight to Washington for me and the prisoner to fly out as soon as possible. It might take a few hours to arrange things or it might even take until tomorrow morning. Please take the prisoner back to the county jail and we'll pick her up when we're ready to fly out."

Singleton said no more to the woman as he went back to the table, picked up the folder, and stormed out.

◊ ◊ ◊

The field agents left with the woman to return her to the county jail. Singleton stayed at the field office and went about the process of arranging a flight. He finally secured a C-47 from Lowry Air Force Base just outside Denver but the aircraft was undergoing routine

15

maintenance and it would be tomorrow morning before they could leave. Singleton would have to take his luggage back to the hotel.

The last thing on his agenda was to have the head agent in charge of the Denver office sign a paper that would release the prisoner into his custody. He opened the folder to retrieve that paper. It was then that he noticed the paperclip that had held the papers he handed to the woman was missing.

Singleton bolted out of his chair and raced out of the room.

Chapter 6

Denver, Colorado
Next day—Tuesday, 06 April 1948

Al Hodge had flown out of D.C. at four o'clock this morning. Picking up the two hours in time difference from the East Coast to the Rockies, that put the wheels down in Denver at 11:00 a.m. after the nine-hour flight. His Air Force Electra sat down at Lowry Air Force Base just outside Denver.

Hodge's first item of business was to check in with the base commandant, Major General Herbert Curry. The general ordered his aide to assist Hodge with a billet and procure him a car and driver.

The last information Hodge had was that Erika Lehmann was being held at the Denver County jail, so that's where he directed his Air Force driver to take him. The Jeep had a canvas canopy but that did little to ward off the cold.

"My nuts are ready to fall off," Al commented as they drove down Colfax Avenue. "What's the temperature here, Private?"

"It's nineteen degrees, sir."

"Nineteen degrees in April. What the hell?"

"I've been stationed here for nearly two years," the private said. "It's like that here this time of year because of the altitude. The temperature swings, especially in the spring, can be tremendous. I've seen three feet of snow fall one day and the next day you can be outside in shorts and a T-shirt. Two days from now, it's liable to be 75°. It's always hard for the weather people to predict because of the altitude and the Chinook winds that sweep down from the Rockies."

As they drove west into Denver, Hodge could see the majestic snow-capped Rocky Mountains that rose high toward the heavens just west of the city. The private, a personable young man, noticed Hodge looking at the mountains.

"Some of those peaks are over 14,000 feet high. I've been up there on the high roads—tough to breathe up there, not a lot of oxygen."

The Jeep pulled up in front of the jail entrance just before noon. So the young man wouldn't have to wait outside in the cold, Hodge took him inside and had him sit in the waiting area while Hodge inquired at the desk. He used his fake I.D. identifying him with the U.S. Department of Justice. The desk sergeant told him that the woman who admitted her name was Erika but wouldn't divulge a last name had been picked up yesterday by the FBI.

"They still have her?" Hodge asked.

"As far as I know," the cop replied.

"Can you give me the name of the agent who she was released to?"

The sergeant shuffled through some papers. "An Agent Singleton."

Shit! Hodge thought to himself. *He's the guy who has been looking for her since '43.* Even worse, Singleton knew he was CIA. The Justice Department I.D. would be worthless.

◊ ◊ ◊

Hodge told the private to take him to the Federal Building. When they arrived, Hodge double-timed it inside. Again, he left the Air Force driver in the waiting area. The sign by the elevator told Hodge the FBI offices were on the fourth floor.

Hodge stepped off the elevator and asked the nearby receptionist if Agent Singleton was in. She made a phone call and found out he was indeed in the building.

"Agent Singleton," she said into the phone. "This is Dolores at the front desk. A Mr. Albert Hodge is asking to see you." After hanging up the phone she said to Hodge. "Agent Singleton will see you right away." She directed Hodge where to go.

When Hodge entered the office, Chris Singleton stood up and circled around his desk to shake his hand. "Please have a seat Mr. Hodge. It's been a while since we've seen each other."

Hodge sat down. Singleton, instead of going back around his desk, sat in the chair next to Hodge. As soon as Dolores had called him and mentioned Hodge's name, it set off red flags in the FBI agent's mind. But he would let the CIA man talk.

"What brings you to the Mile High City, Mr. Hodge?"

"Agent Singleton, let's not play cat and mouse. You know why I'm here."

"The woman Erika," Singleton said. "Is that her real name?"

"Yes."

"And her last name?"

"I can't tell you that."

"That tells me you know her last name, and all those requests I made to you and Mr. Carr since 1943 to help locate her overseas were lies. I take it she works for you."

"Yes, and I need her released into my custody. The only paperwork I have on me now is for her release from the county jail, which is where our reports told us she is being held. I can have the necessary paperwork for her custody exchange from the FBI to the CIA by tomorrow morning."

"May I ask what your plans are for her, Mr. Hodge?"

"Again I'm sorry; I can't tell you."

"Well, then I'm sorry to remind you about something you already know. The FBI has final authority to hunt for fugitives within the borders of the United States. You can go to the State Department, the Department of Justice, or to the White House but you'll be wasting your time. The only person who could agree to turn over this case to the CIA is my boss, Mr. Hoover. I'm sure you know Mr. Hoover. What do you think your chances are of convincing him to do that?"

"What do you mean by 'fugitive'?" Hodge asked.

"The prisoner escaped yesterday afternoon while being transported back to the local jail. Director Hoover has placed me in charge of the task force to find her and bring her to justice for her crimes against our country during wartime. You and your CIA will not interfere."

"How did she escape?"

"She used a paperclip to get out of her cuffs and escaped while being driven back to the jail."

"Was anyone hurt?" Hodge asked. The last thing the CIA needed were additional charges against their top female spy who already had several hanging over her head.

"The agent sitting beside her in the back seat of the car has a sore jaw and his gun was taken from him. She held the gun on the driver and

19

forced him to pull over but he wasn't hurt. Injured prides are their worst wounds."

[a telephone call to CIA headquarters in Washington]

"Major Reid here," spoke the voice at the other end in D.C.

"Sheila, this is Al. I have to get in touch with Leroy in London. I'm spending the night at the Air Force base here in Denver." Hodge gave her the phone number of the guest housing room the base commandant had assigned him. "Tell Leroy to call me as soon as possible. I'll stay in my room until I receive his call."

◊ ◊ ◊

The call from London came that afternoon, just a couple of hours later, because it was evening in England and Leroy Carr had returned to his hotel.

"Hi, Al. What's up?" Carr said from London.

"We're up shit creek, Leroy. The FBI got to Denver before us."

There was a pause at the other end. Hodge didn't wait for a response. "Singleton, the FBI guy who has been dogging us about her since our OSS days got to her first but she escaped."

"Escaped!?" Leroy Carr thundered at the other end. *"How did they get her in the first place?"*

"Typical Lehmann. She got into a brouhaha at some dive bar. There were two Denver vice cops in the place conducting a sting operation because heroin was being sold by some scumbags who frequent the place. Somebody grabbed Lehmann's ass and all hell broke loose. The vice cops had to give up their cover and arrest Lehmann for her own safety because guns and knives were being drawn by several of the clientele. The Denver cops were livid that a sting they had been working on for months was blown. Even though all the local cops had her for was disorderly conduct they wanted to keep her behind bars as long as possible to teach her a lesson. Unfortunately for us, the Denver gumshoes sent her prints to the FBI and then Singleton took over. To make a long story short, Lehmann escaped—no surprise there—and now Hoover has placed Singleton in charge of finding her."

"Can you work with Singleton?"

"He's a sharp guy, Leroy, and I have my doubts he wants to work with us. He knew right away that we have been lying to him for the past five years. And you know Hoover; he had a grudge against the OSS and it continues to this day with the CIA."

An even longer pause from London.

"Leroy, are you still there?" Hodge said into the phone.

"I'm still here, Al. I'm just thinking." After a briefer pause Carr said. *"Stay put in Denver, Al, and keep working with Singleton in any way you can. These meetings with MI-6 are supposed to be over by Thursday. I'll fly home right away. I should be in Washington Friday. I can be in Denver by Saturday if things aren't resolved by then. Lehmann isn't going to let the FBI find her, but maybe she'll call Sheila for extraction and you can bring her back to D.C. and save us a lot of trouble."*

"Lehmann saving us a lot of trouble," Hodge laughed. "Leroy, you're the world's greatest optimist."

[just before midnight]

Chris Singleton had worked late while going through FBI personnel files deciding on agents he wanted on his task force. He didn't leave the FBI Denver headquarters until 9:30 that evening. He arrived back at his hotel at ten, took a shower then went to bed. He lay awake for an hour with a busy mind and finally decided to get up and go down to the hotel lounge for a late beer.

Singleton sipped his Coors in deep thought. That the CIA had shown up was only one concern among many. *Erika* could already be out of the state or possibly even out of the country by now on her own accord. Or, perhaps she had contacted her CIA overseers and they had spirited her away. All these thoughts had kept sleep at bay and the reason, despite being dog-tired, that he now sat in the hotel bar.

Just after he ordered his second beer, a woman suddenly sat down on the bar stool next to him.

She looked at him and smiled. "Hello, handsome. Buy me a drink. I'll have what you're drinking."

She was the woman he pursued.

Chapter 7

Denver—Brown Palace Hotel bar
Late night—Tuesday, 06 April 1948

Chris Singleton's first impulse was to reach for his gun.

"Don't bother Agent Singleton. You left your service pistol in your room as well as your handcuffs."

"How did you find me?"

"First of all, I'm sure you're planning to overpower me—a strong man against just a woman. I wouldn't recommend that. Unlike you, I *am* armed and I have no qualms about using weapons."

"How did you find me?" he asked again.

"You told me where you were staying when you opened the door of the interrogation room and instructed your colleagues to pick up your belongings at the Brown Palace. And of course, you gave them your room number. About ten minutes ago I knocked on your door several times. When I failed to get an answer I thought perhaps you were down here. And here you are."

"But you broke into my room first," Singleton said.

The woman shrugged and handed him his wallet. I thought you might need this to pay for your drinks, and mine."

"I put my drinks on a tab and pay for them when I checkout. Why are you here? You know I'm looking for you. Why pay me a courtesy call?"

"Nice photos in your wallet. Is that your mother and father?"

Singleton had had it and glared, "If you think you're leaving here tonight a free woman, you're insane. I don't care what type of weapons you have. You killed one FBI agent, my partner Charlie Pulaski; you'll have to add another one to your belt if you think you're going to walk out of here."

Now it was the woman's turn to get incensed; she got the bartender's attention. "Sir, a beer for me and another for my friend."

"What brand of beer?" the barkeep asked her.

"Whatever he's having. And we'll be moving to a table."

She rose abruptly and headed toward a small table in the corner of the bar. Singleton downed the small amount of beer left in his glass and followed her.

The Brown Palace was considered the swankiest hotel in Denver, named after the Titanic disaster survivor, the 'Unsinkable' Molly Brown, who was a Denver native. The lounge was overtaken by highly polished dark cherry wood walls and ceiling. Tables were covered with snow-white linen, sparkling crystal goblets, and real silverware. The utensils with Molly Brown's initials engraved on the handle where made of pure silver forged from silver mined in Colorado.

As soon as they sat down, she said sternly, "I didn't kill Agent Pulaski and you know it. That's why I want to talk to you and it's the reason I'm here tonight. That's a false story kept alive by the FBI since 1943. You were there in Evansville. You saw who shot your partner in the club's parking lot that evening. And you saw that same man try to kill me on the bridge over the Ohio River that night."

They stopped for a moment when the waiter dropped off the beers. She took both beers and sat them in front of her. "At least tip the man, Mr. Singleton. You have your wallet now."

Singleton looked down and took out a dollar from his wallet while she pushed one of the beers across the table toward him.

"What you said makes no difference," Singleton asserted after the bartender left. "Both of you were enemy agents working against the United States during a world war. You and this man, whoever he was, share equal blame in the eyes of wartime law."

"He was there trying to kill me."

"First of all, who is *he?*"

"His name was Axel Ryker; he was Heinrich Himmler's top Gestapo henchman."

"Why was he trying to kill you, a fellow Nazi?"

"It's complicated."

"And your name?"

"My real first name is Erika."

"Since you refuse to identify yourself with a last name, let's get to the marrow of this. I know you work for the CIA. Al Hodge showed up here in Denver. Yet if you think that's going to save you you're sadly mistaken."

"Al Hodge is here in Denver?"

"He came to my office this afternoon," Singleton said before he picked up his second beer and took a generous swig.

"Good night, Agent Singleton," she said and patted his hand.

Within just a few seconds everything went black for Chris Singleton.

Erika Lehmann stood and shouted in a panic, "Someone help me, please! My husband has passed out."

The bartender and a couple of customers rushed over. As they attended the unconscious man, his *wife* mysteriously disappeared in the confusion.

Chapter 8

Denver, Colorado
Wednesday, 07 April 1948

Chris Singleton woke up in Denver General Hospital three hours after being drugged with Nembutal. He cursed that he didn't see it coming. She had to have added the drug to his beer when she distracted him to reach into his wallet and tip the bartender. The doctors wanted to keep him for several more hours but he would have none of that. He walked out of the hospital at just before four o'clock in the morning.

[Eight o'clock that morning]
Erika knew Sheila Reid would be in her office in Washington (it was ten o'clock in the morning in D.C.). Sheila was one of the CIA agents codenamed the Shield Maidens, and Erika trusted her. Even though she was Leroy Carr's assistant, and an Army major who never shirked her duty, Erika knew Sheila would never betray her.

"*Major Reid.*"

"Hi, Sheila."

"*Erika!*" Sheila exclaimed in D.C. "*Where are you?*"

"I'm still in Denver. I'm calling from a pay phone inside a pharmacy."

"*Al is out there looking for you.*"

"I know. An FBI man told me. I got myself arrested."

"*We know all about it. Another bar fight. Good grief, Erika.*"

"I know. It was stupid of me. Where is Al staying?"

"*The Air Force base.*"

"Get in touch with him and tell him I'll meet him for dinner tonight at seven o'clock at Gaetano's Restaurant." Erika spelled the restaurant's name for Sheila. "It's on the corner of West 38th Avenue and Tejon Street."

"*Are you still living in that apartment we got you in Golden?*"

"Yes, but I'm not going back there until after I talk to Al. Sheila, do you have any idea why I'm out here in Denver in the first place? Leroy told me nothing other than spend some time getting to know the city."

"No, Erika. I don't know any more than you do about the assignment. Leroy did mention that he would bring you back to Washington for your mission briefing when the time was right. That's all I know. It seems to be very hush-hush."

[same time]
Al Hodge had just sat down in Chris Singleton's office. To Hodge, the FBI agent looked a bit bedraggled, as if he had had a hard night.

"I'm here to offer an olive branch, Special Agent Singleton," Hodge began. "We're hoping the CIA and FBI can work together on this case."

"Why would the FBI want to do that, Mr. Hodge? And how can I believe anything you tell me after being lied to for five years by first the OSS and then the CIA?"

Hodge knew he was backed into a corner. "Ask me anything you wish. I'll tell you the truth."

Singleton smiled and leaned back in his chair. "Okay, let's start with something simple. Is *Erika* her real first name?"

"Yes."

"What's her last name?"

"Lehmann."

"How does she spell that?"

Hodge spelled it as Singleton wrote it down. "Who is she?"

"Do I have the FBI's promise that all information is top secret?"

"Yes."

"Lehmann was an operative for the German Abwehr during the war. I think you already know that she was a German spy. Late in the war, she renounced her allegiance to the Nazis when Himmler had her father killed and then shortly after that she found out the truth about the horrors going on in the concentration camps. Since late 1944 she has worked for the United States and completed several successful assignments that have benefitted our country."

"Why is she in Denver, Mr. Hodge?"

27

"That is one thing I cannot tell you, Agent Singleton. I'm sure you understand. You would not be able to tell me of an ongoing FBI operation."

"So why are you here? What are you asking of the Bureau?"

"Just back off for now. I will keep you informed of anything I'm at liberty to confide to you as we move along. In return, the CIA will owe you and the Bureau a favor."

"Not going to happen, Agent Hodge. She's complicit in the murder of my partner in Indiana whether she pulled the trigger or not. In addition, there are charges against her in Cincinnati for the murder of a man, an assault on another man, and the brutal attack of a woman who she crucified to a wall. Her prints were found at the scene and there were witnesses who supplied a description that matches her exactly. For God's sake, what type of person is the CIA willing to go to bed with?"

"The men and the woman in Cincinnati were convicted felons who were raping and abusing two innocent women. Lehmann stepped in and saved them."

"First, I guess killing a perpetrator and causing serious bodily harm to the others would definitely dissuade them. I'd say they got what was coming to them except your track record for being truthful with me is less than sterling. I don't believe you."

Hodge interjected quickly, "It's the truth."

Singleton said, "Unfortunately, I have no way of knowing if it's the truth after your agency lied to me for five years. And none of that negates my partner's death. The answer is no, Agent Hodge. The FBI will stay on the case and we'll work alone without the 'help' of the CIA. When we find this *Erika Lehmann,* if that name is not another lie, she'll be prosecuted by the Justice Department, and I assure you she won't escape next time."

[7:00 p.m. that day]

Gaetano's Restaurant opened one year ago in the northwest section of Denver referred to by many, including the newspapers, as Denver's "Little Italy." Founded by the Smaldone family, Denver's infamous organized crime family, Gaetano's served authentic Italian fare. Erika had eaten here before during the month she had been in Denver.

The dining area was on the first floor, right off the street corner. Upstairs, in what was formerly an apartment but now converted to a poker den and offices, the Smaldone's gambling, bookkeeping, and loan-sharking endeavors were managed. The Smaldone family controlled the sports gambling in the Denver area including college football (professional football had yet to secure widespread interest) as well as horse racing and boxing. In the converted upstairs apartment, high-stakes poker games took place every night except Sunday and Friday during Lent. After all, the Smaldone's were Italian and Catholic.

When Al Hodge entered, Erika was sitting at the bar. It was no surprise to Hodge; Erika had a habit of sitting at the bar with the men. She spotted him and picked up her drink. "Hello, Al." She then led him to a booth.

After they sat down, Hodge said, "Start talking."

"Yes, I messed up. I'm sorry. The bar fight was my fault. I overreacted, but if those undercover cops hadn't been there nothing would have come of it."

"So that's your excuse? You overreacted? You know the Denver cops are very pissed they were forced to blow an undercover sting because of you. They thought you were in danger."

Erika laughed. "I was in danger from a bunch of drunken Mexicans. That's funny."

Hodge's face grew dark. "I'm glad you think it's funny, Aryan Princess."

"Al, don't accuse me of a racial remark because I'm German. I know the great number of Mexicans in this country are good, hard working people. I'm just stating a fact. That bar's customers are nearly all Mexicans and many get drunk in there on the weekends. German's get drunk and make fools of themselves, too. So do Americans."

"Whatever," said Hodge. "You do know your hot temper now has us all behind the eight ball."

"I said I was sorry. What else do you want from me?"

A young waiter appeared. Neither Erika nor Al Hodge had yet looked at the menu.

Without asking Hodge, Erika told the waiter, "Mirko, I'll have another brandy. My friend will have a Scotch on the rocks. I know you have Laphroiag." She knew what Hodge normally drank. "And we'll both have spaghetti and sausage."

When the waiter left, she said, "The linguine and clams here are also very good, but the spaghetti and Italian sausage you have to try. They make their own pasta and even their own sausage and it comes with a side of fried green peppers and some fantastic bread rolls baked here each morning."

"Cut the crap, Erika. This mission is probably over for you. Leroy will be back in the States on Friday and plans to be here in Denver on Saturday. Now we have this FBI guy, Chris Singleton, on our ass. Let me tell you, he's smart and he's a bloodhound. He doesn't give a rat's ass about any CIA mission. He's determined to hunt you down and turn you over to the Justice Department. You know what that would mean."

"I don't even know what the mission is, Al. The only thing Leroy briefed me on was to come to Denver and spend some time learning the city. What's this all about?"

"None of your business until Leroy decides to tell you. And all that probably means nothing now that you opened the window for the FBI to find out that you're still alive and in the States."

"Singleton doesn't know where I'm staying, and I'm using a false name at the apartment in Golden. He won't find me."

"I wouldn't be so sure of that, Erika. Like I said, this guy is sharp. You and I are going to stay at a flea bag motel on Alameda Avenue until Leroy gets here Saturday."

Mirko delivered Hodge's whiskey and told them the meals would be out shortly. Just then Hodge saw an intimidating-looking man enter the restaurant with two men following behind. He looked to be about 40. His hair was full and with very little gray. The man spotted Erika and walked over to the table.

"Hello, Erika," he said.

"Ciao, Checkers."

He looked at Hodge. "Who's this joker?"

"This is Al, a friend of mine."

"A friend of yours?" He looked at Hodge. "Sorry, Al, no disrespect." He reached out his hand and Hodge shook it. "Who is your waiter?" the man asked Erika.

"Mirko," Erika answered.

"Tell him your dinner and drinks are on me tonight."

"Thank you very much, Checkers," Erika said.

The man nodded and walked away, followed by the two other men. They disappeared up a stairway to the room above.

"Who the hell is that?" Hodge asked.

"His name is Gene Smaldone, but everyone calls him Checkers. This is his family's restaurant. The Smaldone family controls much of the organized crime in Denver—gambling, bookmaking, loan-sharking, all that sort of thing."

Hodge looked at her for a moment. "What is it with you, Lehmann? I figured you would have had enough of mobsters after the assignment in Cuba with Anastasia, Bugsy Siegel, Meyer Lansky and that ilk. Can't you ever frequent any respectable places? Why does it always have to be gangster dens or dive bars, like the one you got your ass arrested in last weekend?"

"Wait till you try the food, Al."

Hodge stared at her. "You've been a pain in my ass ever since I first laid eyes on you, Lehmann. For the life of me I don't know why Leroy puts up with your shit."

Mirko delivered their dinners and Erika dug in, ignoring Hodge's last remark. She broke open a roll and spread a generous amount of butter, then handed it to him.

"You have to try these rolls, Al. Here, I buttered one for you."

Chapter 9

Denver
Next day—Thursday, 08 April 1948

After they left Gaetano's last evening, Hodge took Erika to a motel on Alameda Avenue called the Shangri-La. Despite its patrician name, it was a flea bag, but Hodge knew it would be a good place to lie low until Leroy got back from London and made his way to Denver. Not trusting Erika to not sneak out and get herself in more trouble carousing around at night, Hodge rented one room with twin beds.

Last night, when they were finally ready for bed, Erika took a shower then walked out of the bathroom naked. Hodge had waited for her to finish so he could take his shower.

"Lehmann, put a towel on for Christ's sake." It was not the first time he had seen her naked. Whether coming out from a bath or changing clothes, she seemed to take some delight in embarrassing him.

"Sorry, Al," she said with total insincerity.

Now, the morning after, they both sat eating breakfast in a small mom and pop diner a couple of blocks from the motel.

"What's the plan for today, Al?" Erika said as she chewed on a big bite of biscuit.

"Didn't anyone ever tell you not to speak with your mouth full?"

"I'm hungry, and I like American breakfasts."

"You're always hungry. By rights you ought to weigh about 250 pounds."

Erika put the rest of the biscuit in her mouth and mumbled, "You didn't answer my question."

"The plan for today is for you to keep your ass out of trouble. I'm going to Lowry and collect my things and tell them that if Singleton calls they should tell him I left Denver. I don't want him to know I'm still around."

◊ ◊ ◊

[same time]

Chris Singleton just got off the phone with his boss, J. Edgar Hoover. Hoover was a man with a long memory and an aversion to any other government agency horning in on anything he considered the FBI's area of jurisdiction. Senators, congressmen, and even presidents knew to treat Hoover with care. He had files on everyone and was willing to use any negative or embarrassing bit of information he possessed if he felt the need.

Hoover told Singleton to stay on the case in Denver until the fugitive was caught or until he had positive proof that the woman was no longer in the area. Singleton was ordered to do anything he could to locate her and use any means necessary to spirit her away from the CIA. She was to be brought back to Washington where she would be tried for her crimes. Hoover told Singleton he would put an end to the CIA's interference when the FBI got their hands on the former German spy.

Hoover had said, "I'll tell Macelhenny (the agent in charge of the Denver field office) to give you whatever help you need. I told you the other day to assemble a task force. If you need more men I'll send them from Washington. Find her, Singleton, and bring her back here."

Hoover's orders suited Chris Singleton fine. When the war ended, the case was moved to the cold case files. The thinking among the higher ups at the Bureau being she was dead or long gone out of the country. Singleton had been trying to find her during his down time ever since then. Even if she didn't pull the trigger, his partner, Charlie Pulaski, would still be alive if she hadn't come to the United States on an espionage mission for Germany in '43. Now it was once again a hot case, and he would have a task force.

Singleton picked up his phone and dialed the phone number the CIA man, Al Hodge, had given him. Hodge had told him he was staying at Lowry. If Hodge was still in town it would tell him so was Erika.

[two hours later]

Erika was in the motel room when Al Hodge got back from Lowry Air Force base.

"Pack your things, Lehmann," Hodge said. "I'm getting you out of town."

"Why?" Erika asked.

"Singleton called the base this morning before I could get to the WAF switchboard operators. He knows I'm still in Denver which has to mean he thinks I'm still here looking for you."

"Where are we going?"

"*You're* going out of state to Cheyenne, Wyoming. It's the closest town outside of Colorado. It's only about a two-hour drive. I'll take you there and then I'll come back to Lowry. I should be able to be back here by late afternoon then I'll go see Singleton and act like nothing's happened. Now grab your stuff and let's get going."

Hodge walked out with his suitcase and loaded it into the truck of the '46 Chevy he requisitioned from Lowry. The motel had no parking lot to speak of, but guests could park their cars in a gravel lot across the street. He had to wait for a chance to make his way across a busy Alameda Avenue. When he finally got back to the room, Erika and her small bag were gone and the bedroom window facing an alley behind the motel was open.

A quickly scribbled note lying on Hodge's bed read: *I'll call you tonight at Lowry, Al. It might be very late.*

[10:30 p.m. that evening]

The Brown Palace Hotel in downtown Denver where Singleton stayed was just across the street from where a street vendor set up his hot cart each day. The Mexican emigrant was a hard-working man, wheeling his heavy cart many blocks to this spot before lunch time and staying sometimes until very late, depending on when his wife's burritos sold out.

Chris Singleton had worked very late and he was hungry. This morning, he left the hotel for his office without having breakfast, and lunch was only half of an egg salad sandwich offered to him by a pretty secretary who obviously had her sights set on the dashing FBI agent. Not leaving his office until a half-hour ago, and too tired to sit around in the hotel restaurant for dinner, Singleton bought burritos from the street vendor. The G-man had bought food from this man before. The burritos were only fifty cents each and Singleton bought three.

"Ah, Señor, I see you again. You must like my wife's cooking," said the vendor happily.

"Yes, Luis, they're very good. My compliments to your wife." Singleton handed the man two dollars and told him to keep the change.

"Gracias, Señor."

Singleton took the bag of burritos up the elevator to his small suite on the sixth floor. He turned the key to his room, and before he had a chance to turn on the light he felt a gun to his neck.

Chapter 10

Denver
Same night—Thursday, 08 April 1948

"Slowly take your gun out and hold it by the barrel," she said from behind him.

"Forget it. I'm not giving you my gun."

She had to give him credit; the young FBI man had iron nerves. She finally switched on the light. "Then go sit on the sofa."

Singleton didn't have any reason to refuse this, so with her holding her gun on him, he walked the few feet and sat down. She sat down on an upholstered chair opposite him. A small coffee table separated them.

"Take your gun and lay it on the table," she said.

"Why should I?"

His attitude surprised and impressed her.

"Because you want to learn more about me, and that's not going to happen until I see your gun on that table."

This was the second time she had gotten to him in his hotel. Needless to say, he had never had a fugitive he pursued show up at his home or hotel looking for him. Her offer was irresistible.

"You're telling me if I lay my weapon on the table, you'll answer my questions truthfully?"

"Yes, as much as I can."

"How will I know you're telling the truth?"

"You won't, unless you decide to believe me."

He looked at her for a long moment then slowly took his gun from its holster under his suit jacket. He laid it on the table and sat back. He didn't trust her, but he wanted to hear what she had to say.

She smiled. "Turn the barrel around so it faces you, not me."

He shrugged and did so.

To his surprise, she also laid her pistol on the coffee table, although she left her gun pointing at him.

"Why don't you point your barrel away from me like you told me to do?"

"I haven't lived this long by underestimating my enemies," she said.

"Why are you here? Why do you care what I think?" Singleton was referring to the meeting when she showed up unexpectedly at the bar so she could stress to him that she didn't kill his partner back in '43.

"I want the FBI to drop its charges against me so I can become a citizen of the United States."

Singleton laughed out loud.

"You think this is funny?"

"Very funny," he said.

"Your charges against me are unfounded. Yes, I worked for Germany, my country, just as you work for yours. I've never killed anyone who was not trying to kill me or someone else. They deserved to die. Since 1944, when I found out Heinrich Himmler had my father killed at the same time I found out about the exterminations happening at the concentration camps, I have worked faithfully for your country. You can ask Al Hodge. Hopefully he won't lie to you, though I can't guarantee that he won't."

"Why would he lie?"

"The CIA wants me to remain deep undercover."

"So why come to me?"

"I did not come to you. I did not break my allegiance to the CIA. You found out about me from my arrest here in Denver. I have a daughter. I want to have a life with her. The only way that will happen is if I'm not constantly hidden away by the CIA. That can only happen if your charges are dropped. Then I can apply for citizenship."

"Since you are supposedly being honest, what is your real name?"

"Erika Marie Lehmann. I was born in Oberschopfheim, Germany. My father was Karl Lehmann, a German. My mother was British. Her name was Louise Minton. My mother is also dead."

"Where is this daughter you mentioned?"

"I'm not going to tell you that for her safety."

"So I'm supposed to trust you, but you think I would bring some harm to your daughter."

"I don't think you or the FBI would harm her, Agent Singleton, but I want her left out of this. I told you about her only to explain my reasons for wanting charges against me dropped so I can apply for citizenship."

"Why does the CIA have you in Denver?"

"You know I could not tell you that, even if I knew. As I said, I work for the CIA and will not betray them. I owe a debt to Leroy Carr, Al Hodge's boss. Mr. Carr has so far protected me from imprisonment. But the truth is, I don't know why I'm in Denver. I was sent here a month ago with no other instructions other than to acquaint myself with the city.

"So what is your answer, Agent Singleton? Will you help me?"

Without hesitation, Singleton said, "Absolutely not." He went for his gun, but she was much faster, hers being pointed to his heart before he had his off the table.

"Sit back." The look in her eyes was hard and wolf-like.

She took his gun, stood up, and put it under her blouse behind her back. She kept her gun pointed at him and walked out the door.

Singleton had a spare weapon in the suite's bedroom, but by the time he retrieved it and rushed out into the hallway she was long gone.

[two hours later]

It was past one o'clock in the morning when Al Hodge finally got the phone call from Erika.

"Al, it's me."

"Goddammit Lehmann, where in hell are you?"

"I'm still here, in Denver."

"This is the same old shit from you, Erika. You almost got your ass canned after the South American mission last year. You disobeyed your orders and went rogue. The only thing that saved you was the objective was accomplished despite you disobeying orders."

"That's the best argument I have for not being canned."

"Bull shit! Now you're rogue again. I'm telling you Lehmann, as far as I'm concerned, this is the last straw. I'm ordering you to come in immediately."

"Al, you said Leroy will be here Saturday. I'll contact you then."

"Lehmann, come in now or . . ."

Hodge heard the phone hang up on the other end.

Chapter 11

Denver, Colorado
Saturday, 10 April 1948

Leroy Carr's Lockheed A-29 Hudson sat down at Stapleton Airport in the late-afternoon. Used frequently during the war by U.S. military generals and admirals, the Hudson was both fast and had a relatively long range. Only a quick refueling stop in Kansas City was required on Carr's journey to Colorado.

Al Hodge was waiting in the bright high-altitude sunlight. It was a beautiful spring day—light jacket or sweater time at the base of the Rocky Mountains (at least for today; tomorrow could be another story).

Hodge had been surprised when Major Reid called and told him Leroy would land at the public airport and not at Lowry Air Force Base.

Carr cut to the chase as his first foot stepped onto the tarmac. "Have you heard from her since you called Sheila yesterday, Al?"

Hodge had relayed a message to Carr through Sheila Reid about Erika disappearing again and all the details about the FBI agent, Chris Singleton, and his involvement. Or at least the facts that Hodge knew. Leroy Carr's top lieutenant knew nothing about Erika's two visits with the FBI Special Agent.

"Nope," Hodge grunted.

An Air Force private followed Carr out of the plane with the CIA Deputy Director's luggage. Carr did so much traveling he had learned to travel light. The private held just one medium-sized suitcase and a garment bag containing a great coat and an extra suit.

Hodge asked about Carr's wife. "How's Kay doing?"

"She's fine. We got to spend only a couple of hours together before I had to hop on the plane to come here."

"I'm sorry about all this Leroy. I know you and Kay haven't seen much of each other in a while."

"Al, I know how Erika is. She has disappeared on me, too. More than once, I might add. If I get stuck out here for more than a day or two, I'll get Kay a flight here. Did you get in to see the FBI guy yesterday?"

"No, his secretary told me he was out for the day. I left a message but he never called."

"Sounds like he's avoiding us." Carr looked at his wristwatch. "It's Saturday and I doubt Singleton is at the Federal Building. Where is he staying?"

"The Brown Palace."

"Then that's where we'll stay. Both of us. Sheila said Erika told you she would call you tonight at your room at Lowry, is that right?"

"That's what Lehmann told me."

"Contact the Lowry switchboard WAF sergeant-in-charge. Ask her to make sure any calls to you get redirected to the hotel. We'll ask General Curry's aide to have someone deliver your stuff to the hotel."

Hodge nodded, then said, "Leroy, we can use Kathryn Fischer for this assignment. Please don't tell me you're still considering Lehmann for this mission."

"No. I'm not saying that at all. We might end up bringing in Fischer. The mission must go forward with or without Erika. First things first; we have to get to Singleton this weekend."

[9:15 this evening]

The Brown Palace Hotel had very few single, run-of-the mill accommodations. The vast number of guest rooms in the posh hotel were suites of various sizes; from small, single bedroom suites with a separate sitting area, to two-bedroom or even three-bedroom suites with a living room area and dining room. Carr and Hodge took the cheapest rooms available; each ended up with a one-bedroom suite— one across the hall from the other.

Al Hodge was forced to register under his real name so he would receive Erika's promised phone call patched through from Lowry. Leroy Carr registered under a false name.

Since checking in four hours ago, both men had sat in Hodge's room waiting for the phone call. Dinner had been ordered from room service.

Finally, the room telephone rang. Hodge picked up. It was the hotel switchboard operator.

"Mr. Hodge?"

"Yes, this is Hodge, operator."

"I have a phone call from a woman who identifies herself as Lorelei. She gave no last name but she claims you know her. Do you accept the call?"

"Yes, put her through." Hodge turned to Carr, pointed at the receiver, and nodded. *Lorelei* was Erika's code name.

Hodge heard a couple of clicks and then the voice.

"Al?"

"Yes, Erika."

"Has Leroy arrived?"

"He's sitting right here."

"What name is he using?"

"David Jones."

"Meet me at Gaetano's in two hours. You know it. You and I had dinner there last Wednesday. The bartender tonight is named William. Tell Leroy to identify himself by his alias and tell William you're there to see 'Erika.' No last name is needed; that's the only name they know me by. They don't know my last name. And Al, don't come early."

Hodge heard the phone click and the immediate empty dial tone.

"She wants to meet at a restaurant, Leroy. I had dinner with her there Wednesday night. Erika told me about it, but the next day I checked out the place with the Denver cops just to verify her story. It's owned and run by a crime family called the Smaldones. They're local thugs who control the organized crime in Denver. The Denver cops have been after them since Prohibition when they bootlegged liquor into Denver from Canada. Now they control gambling, bookmaking, and loan-sharking. A couple of their enforcers have been charged with murder, yet the DA hasn't succeeded in getting anywhere with those indictments. The cops have arrested several of the Smaldones or their goons multiple times for various crimes but so far witnesses suddenly develop bad memories when they're called to the stand. The hooligans walk out of court the same day the trial starts. Erika seemed pretty chummy with them during our dinner."

Leroy Carr knew what all this meant. Erika had set herself up with backup so he and Al couldn't take her into custody—at least not tonight.

[Two hours later]

Even though it was past eleven o'clock in the evening, every table in the Gaetano's dining area was occupied this Saturday night and every bar stool taken. Several couples, either waiting for a table for a late night meal, or just a drink at the bar, stood just inside the door.

Leroy Carr and Al Hodge entered and told the receptionist, a very Mediterranean-looking teenage girl with jet hair, olive skin, and wearing a black dress, that they were there to see the bartender.

Unlike the young girl at the door, the bartender didn't look Italian at all. He had sandy-blonde hair and freckles.

"Are you William?" Carr asked him.

"Yes, I'm William, and who are you, might I ask?" His Scottish brogue was evident.

"I'm David Jones. We're here to see Erika. She told me she would inform you that we were coming."

"Just a minute," the bartender said. He stepped away, mixed a couple of drinks and returned, handing a gin and tonic to Carr and a Scotch on the rocks to Hodge. "Erika told me this is what you normally drink. The drinks are on the house. Just go up the stairs." He pointed to the stairs at the back of the dining area. "Erika's up there."

As Carr and Hodge stepped away from the bar, Hodge said, "Well, at least Erika is sending us a clear message with the free drinks, Leroy. We're fucked."

Chapter 12

Denver
Same night—Saturday, 10 April 1948

When Leroy Carr and Al Hodge got to the top of the stairs at Gaetano's restaurant, a burly man stood on the large landing outside the second storey door. It quickly became apparent that he had been notified ahead of time of their arrival.

"Are you the two fucks Erika said would be coming?"

"Yeah, we're the two fucks," Carr answered. *Al was right,* Carr thought. *Erika has played it smart. We'll never be able to get her out of here against her will.*

The man frisked them and took their handguns. He opened the door and waved them in, then closed it behind them. Inside the large, smoke-filled room, seven people sat around a poker table—six men and Erika. Everyone was smoking something—either a cigarette or a cigar. Carr had seen Erika smoking cigars in the past, but this time a cigarette hung from her lips. A skinny young man sat off from the table. Apparently, his job was to keep the players glasses of Bourbon full because he immediately jumped up and topped off the glass of one of the players.

Erika looked up and said, "Fellas, here are my friends I told you were coming."

Everyone looked at Carr and Hodge but most said nothing. One man grunted to indicate he wasn't impressed. Another man threw a couple of chips onto the pot and said, "I call."

Erika said, "I fold," and threw her cards down. "Checkers, you said we can use your office. May we do that now?"

Checkers was one of the players. Hodge remembered him from before when Erika introduced him downstairs. The Smaldone boss was behind for the night and was obviously in a less than gracious mood.

"Go ahead. Just don't let either of those two cocksuckers bother any of my shit."

Erika smashed out her cigarette in the table ashtray, rose, and led Carr and Hodge into another room. The office had the obligatory desk and a few file cabinets. Outside the lone window was a fire escape that dropped into an alley behind the restaurant. Floors, walls, and ceiling were dark-stained wood. Several chairs were lined up against a wall. Erika moved one so they could sit in a triangle.

For a moment, nothing was said. Carr and Hodge stared at Erika and she looked back and forth to their faces, expressionless.

Finally, Leroy Carr started. "I assume our weapons will be returned to us when we're allowed to leave."

Erika nodded.

"But, of course that won't happen until after you're long gone. How long will we have to stay here?"

"Just for ten minutes after I leave," she answered.

Hodge said, "Lehmann, I'd have thought you would have had your fill of mobsters after the mission in Cuba with Luciano, Siegel, Albert Anastasia and that lot."

"You know I like to gamble, Al. In this town all that is controlled by the Smaldone family."

Hodge countered, "Except at the dive bar where you got your ass arrested and put all of us in this pickle. Meaning that the FBI now knows you're still alive."

"Even that bar has to give the Smaldones their cut, Al."

Carr now took over. "Erika. You disappearing on Al until I arrived here tells me that you want something. What is it? Is it about the mission?"

"You haven't told me what the mission is, Leroy. How could it be about that?"

"Then what is it?"

"First of all, Leroy, I have never broken my agreement with you and the CIA. Let's agree on that. Yes, I will admit that there have been times where I've deviated from orders during missions, but my actions have always worked out. The mission objectives have always been accomplished. You have to admit that. Yet, outside of winging it on a few assignments I have never betrayed our agreement to remain underground, even though it has kept me from making a life with my daughter."

She continued. "But now the cat is out of the bag, as you Americans say. The FBI knows I'm still around."

Hodge interrupted. "That's your fault, Lehmann. You got yourself arrested over a damn dart game in a sleezy saloon."

"The undercover policemen in there overreacted," Erika countered. "I could have easily gotten out of there. The police saw a woman, thought she was in trouble, and jumped on their white horses. It was ridiculous and totally unnecessary."

"You clubbed one of the cops with a pool cue," Hodge grumbled heatedly.

"I didn't know he was a cop. He was dressed undercover."

Carr held up his hand. "Okay, okay! What's done is done. Let's get back to the subject. You've made sure we can't take you out of here against your will. What do you want, Erika?"

"I want you to get the charges against me dropped so I can become a citizen of this country and bring Ada to the States and be her mother instead of a stranger who shows up in London once in a blue moon (her daughter Adelaide, Ada for short, lived with Erika's maternal grandparents in London). My grandparents won't be around forever. What is to become of Ada after that?"

"Hoover will never agree to dropping charges in a million years," Carr stated.

"Then go over his head to the State Department or the Department of Justice, Leroy."

Hodge interrupted and spurted out, "Lehmann, you're as crazy as a drunken coot."

"Maybe you're right, Al." Then she looked at Carr. "What's your answer, Leroy? If you will do this for me you can trust me to go ahead with the mission, whatever it is, and I will be forever grateful."

Carr shook his head. "I see no way the mission can go forward with you now, Erika. You've got this Singleton guy on your tail here in Denver. Al tells me he's smart and he's a bloodhound."

Erika didn't mention that she had talked to Singleton and he had already refused her request. And it was now clear that the FBI man had not told Al Hodge about her visits. As long as Singleton kept it from them, it was to her advantage to do the same.

45

"Singleton will have to abandon all that if the FBI is called off by higher ups, Leroy. I don't need to tell you that."

Carr looked at her and paused for a long moment. "I'll try, Erika."

Al Hodge was flabbergasted. "You've got to be joking, Leroy."

Erika ignored Hodge. "If you're giving me your word, Leroy, you can count on me to do everything I can to fulfill the mission. Are you giving me your word?"

"I'm giving you my promise that I will try to get charges against you dropped. I don't know if we can proceed with the mission, however. That's going to be even trickier now with this FBI guy on our butts."

"I accept that, but I'm still willing to try," she said.

"I'll have to think about all of this, Erika. You know the CIA can't ask for help from the FBI or the local police, and bringing in our own backup from Washington would take a couple of days. Let's be honest, you've got us exactly where you want us. Can we meet tomorrow morning? Where are you staying? We know it hasn't been at the apartment we got you in Golden."

Now it was Erika's turn to study Carr. After a pause, she said, "I trust you, Leroy. I will meet you tomorrow morning at seven o'clock at a diner in Golden called 'Dixie's Kitchen.'"

Chapter 13

Golden, Colorado
Sunday, 11 April 1948

Golden, Colorado, lay at the base of the Rocky Mountain foothills about a forty-minute drive west from downtown Denver and the Brown Palace Hotel.

Although in the same hotel as the FBI's Chris Singleton, last night was Carr and Hodge's first night there and they had gotten in late, after the rendezvous with Erika at Gaetano's. The two CIA men had not had a chance to visit with Singleton and truth be told, Carr had changed his mind and didn't want to call on Singleton until he had the situation with Erika straightened out.

Carr and Hodge left the hotel shortly after six. A spring breeze brought cold morning air down from the Rockies, but the sun shone bright. As he drove the Chevy, Al asked his old friend casually, "What are your thoughts about this morning, Leroy?"

"I'd like to get Erika out of here, Al, but we might as well forget about trying to arrest her. She's not going to allow that to happen, and you know how much mayhem Erika can create if someone gives her the slightest reason—at least a reason in *her* mind. I'm going to have to cut her a deal; that's the only thing that's worked with her in the past."

"What kind of deal?"

"I wish I knew. I'll have to wing it."

"You do know that's she's crazy, right Leroy?"

"I don't know that I would call her crazy. She's different, that's for sure."

"She's as crazy as a road lizard, Leroy. Let's face it. Not only that—besides being nuts, she's a gangster in a woman's body. That's why she gets along so good with mobsters. Are you going to give her any real facts about the mission?"

"No. I'll try to reason with her and see how that goes. She knows how things work in the spy game. And Al, I know you two don't get along, but let's keep feelings out of this. That's important. Just go along with what I say and take my lead this morning."

47

◊ ◊ ◊

The men arrived ten minutes early to find Erika already seated at a booth with a cup of coffee in front of her. She smiled at them as they took their seats in the opposite side of the booth. Outside the dinner, just one block away, loomed the vast Adolf Coors Brewery. *Dixie's Kitchen* stayed in business offering 24-hour breakfast and a lunch/dinner menu to the shift workers from the nearby brewery that operated around the clock.

"It's good we're meeting here this early," Erika said. "This place always has good business because of the brewery workers, but it's always packed later in the morning on Sundays after churches let out. A couple of hours from now there will be a line of people waiting outside."

"Since you're familiar with this place, I take it you have been staying in the apartment we got you here in Golden," said Carr. A waitress showed up, dropped off menus, and took Carr's and Hodge's orders for coffee.

"Of course. Why wouldn't I? I only left the place after the latest trouble."

Hodge chuckled as he lit a Pall Mall. He had the inclination to say something about her being the cause of it all, but he had already told her as much, so he avoided being redundant.

Carr said, "Erika, we first have to talk about this FBI agent—Singleton. Al's been to see him and he's filled me in on the guy. The FBI man killed by Ryker in Evansville was his partner, and it looks like Singleton is not going away."

"Like you said, Ryker killed his partner, not me" Erika responded. "Singleton saw the whole thing, but he thinks Ryker and I were working together. I told him Ryker was there trying to kill me, but he doesn't believe me."

The waitress, a middle-aged lady holding a coffee pot and wearing a white apron with embroidered yellow daisies, returned to get their breakfast orders. Carr and Hodge had not yet opened their menus. As she had done with Al at Gaetano's, Erika didn't wait and ordered for all of them. "We'll all have the Buffalo Bill Special, Irene."

"Thanks, Erika," Irene said. "That makes it easy." The waitress topped off their coffee before walking away.

"What's the 'Buffalo Bill Special'?" Hodge asked.

"It's a lot of food. You'll like it, Al. Did you know Buffalo Bill Cody is buried not far from here? His grave is on one of the mountains nearby."

"Let's get back to Agent Singleton," said Carr. "I can't yet think of a way to call him off, and the mission will be difficult enough without you having him on your tail here in Denver."

"Since you brought it up," Erika said, "why don't we start with you telling me what exactly is the mission? I've been here over a month now. You told me to get to know my way around the area and I've done that."

Breakfast was delivered quickly. Irene, followed by a teenage girl, showed up with a platter holding one breakfast, which she sat in front of Erika. It took up two plates. The teenage girl carried a larger platter with the two breakfasts for the men. Irene saw that their coffee cups were still full, so she said, "Enjoy," and walked away with the girl. Each breakfast had scrambled eggs, a large piece of ham, hash browns, and biscuits and gravy.

Carr commented, "This looks good, Erika, if you're a four-hundred-pound gorilla." Then he got back to the conversation. "The assignment specifics don't matter much now. It can't go forward as long as Singleton is in town. What I propose is we take you back to Camp Peary and you can resume your job as a trainer at the Farm (the Farm at Camp Peary, Virginia, is where the CIA trained plebe agents. Erika worked there as a trainer between missions)."

"Leroy, you promised me at Gaetano's that you would work to get the charges against me dropped."

"Yes, and I'm trying to come to an agreement with you that will allow me to do that."

"What about the mission?" she asked as she began shoveling food into her mouth like a starved jackal.

"We'll readdress that when this situation with the FBI is resolved."

"Kathryn and I can work together."

Carr shook his head. "Not going to happen, Erika. I broke up the Shield Maidens after the last mission to South America. You know that."

Hodge said, "You eat like a slob, Lehmann."

Instead of replying, she reached across the table and stole one of the biscuits off his plate.

"I have a plan, Leroy," she mumbled with her mouth full.

"I'm all ears," said Carr.

"Singleton thinks Ryker is dead. I say we turn him over to Singleton and let that bastard Ryker reap what he sowed."

A henchman for Heinrich Himmler during the war, Axel Ryker was currently at Fort Huachuca, Arizona, undergoing classes to improve his English. Ryker was yet another one of the numerous ex-Nazis the United States had brought into its fold after the war, many of whom had war crimes charges pending against them back in Germany. The list was long, including dozens of former SS and Gestapo members and over 200 Nazi rocket scientists including names like Werner von Braun. If the State Department considered these people might be of help to them in the new and increasingly competitive Cold War with the Soviets, they were considered for employment by the various American agencies that could possibly be aided by their skill set. Ryker, who was smart, ruthless, and could speak both German and Russian like a native speaker, was currently being kept hidden by Leroy Carr and the CIA.

Erika continued, "Turning over Ryker should satisfy the FBI and allow you to get charges against me dropped. Then I can bring Ada to this country and make a life with her. I will become a U.S. citizen. This would also be to your advantage. You would no longer have to play the cat and mouse game of protecting me from the Justice Department and the FBI."

Erika's case was different from the aforementioned Nazis. Unlike the others, she had charges against her for crimes committed in the United States, so the Department of Justice was involved. Consequently, J. Edgar Hoover and the FBI had entered the picture. This made Carr's job much more difficult to protect her. Hoover was a very large monkey wrench thrown into the mix. Until now they had lied to the FBI about knowing anything about Erika's whereabouts. All that went out the window because of a dart game at the Loro Rojo.

Carr had to think quickly.

"Here's what I'm willing do, Erika," Carr said. "Ryker is ready to continue his CIA training and that next step is at the Farm. We can afford to delay the mission for a certain time. You return to Camp Peary, and I'll make sure Ryker is placed in your charge."

Erika stopped eating and dropped her fork and knife on the table. She looked at Carr. He could see the glint in her eyes.

"That sounds like a fine plan, Leroy."

Carr had a strong feeling that Erika Lehmann had no intention of letting Axel Ryker leave Camp Peary alive.

"I have a reason for this, Erika. You and Ryker have to refrain from trying to kill each other on sight. You're going to have to work with him. When you return to Denver for your assignment, Ryker will be with you. He will be critical to the operation. That's why I haven't told you anything about the mission. I felt it best to delay informing you that Ryker will be on your team until the last minute."

Erika's face grew dark. "Why is Ryker necessary? Send me Kathryn."

"I told you I split up the Shield Maidens. Besides, you'll see why Ryker is needed when the time comes for your detailed briefing. This is the deal I'll offer you: return to the Farm and finish supervising Ryker's training. That will give Al and me some time to do damage control with the FBI. If Hoover thinks you are no longer in Denver, he'll recall Singleton to Washington and we'll have him out of Denver before you return. If you'll walk a straight line and do what I ask with Ryker at the Farm and later, on the mission, I give you my word that I'll do everything in my power to get charges against you dropped so you can become an American citizen and bring Ada over from London. Do we have a deal?"

Erika studied Carr for a moment. "You're a clever man, Leroy. You know I'll do anything to bring my daughter and me together." Then she said rather ominously, "I agree, and I trust you won't betray me."

She was willing to do anything to have a life with her daughter, even if that meant a mission alongside the ghastly Axel Ryker.

A New Valhalla

Part 2

Lorelei \ lõr-ê-lī *n* [German] : a siren of Germanic legend whose singing lures Rhine River boatmen to destruction on a reef

—*Merriam Webster's Collegiate Dictionary: Tenth Edition*

Chapter 14

In the air over the Midwest
Monday, 12 April 1948

During the Lockheed Hudson's flight from Denver, Erika and Leroy Carr had a long time to talk. Other than the crew, they were the only ones onboard. Al Hodge was on an Air Force C-47 out of Lowry on his way to Arizona. His job was to pick up Axel Ryker at Fort Huachuca and deliver him to Camp Peary.

Even on the flight, Carr still refused to give her any specifics about the Colorado assignment or why Axel Ryker had to be involved.

At one point during the flight, Erika asked about her fellow Shield Maidens. "How are they, Leroy?"

"I can't tell you much about Zhanna. I promised you I'd leave her alone if she stayed out of trouble and remained at the convent in Honduras. Honestly, Erika, all I know from the last report is that she is still at the convent. As far as Kathryn, she's doing her job as an instructor at the Naval War College in Rhode Island."

"Has Kathryn gone on any missions since our last one together in South America?" Erika asked.

"No."

"Well, at least I'll get to see Sheila," the German said.

"Maybe. If for some reason I want you in Washington then you can catch up on old times with Major Reid."

As for the other two Shield Maidens besides Erika and Sheila Reid, Kathryn Fischer was a Gestapo officer during the war, and Zhanna Rogova had served during the war as a sniper and assassin for her Mother Russia.

On a mission to South America that ended last September, Erika had taken Kathryn and Zhanna rogue, disobeying Carr's orders. Making matters worse, Carr's wife Kay was with them, going along as their Spanish interpreter. One the other hand, Carr had tricked Erika into finding Axel Ryker with the pretense they were going to Argentina to investigate the rumors that Adolf Hitler had survived the bunker and had fled to that South American country. That extenuating circumstance and the fact the mission was a success as far as the CIA was concerned led Carr to not imprison the women. Nevertheless, he subsequently broke up the Shield Maiden team.

Erika considered it unfair but there was nothing she could do about it. In the end, she trusted Carr. Even though he had withheld information from her on several occasions—information she thought she should have known about when going into a mission—and he had tricked her on the South American assignment, he had never broken his word to her once he had given it.

As for Al Hodge, she knew he wasn't a clever as Leroy Carr, yet she respected Hodge. She and Hodge had their clashes, but she gave him credit for being a loyal lieutenant to Carr, and she had seen Hodge respond with courage in dangerous situations in the past. Plus, she enjoyed teasing him.

So, she left the café in Golden with the men yesterday. She now had a chance to get her daughter back and would do anything Carr asked of her to accomplish that goal—even collaborate with the monstrous Axel Ryker . . . at least collaborate on the surface.

Chapter 15

Fort Huachuca, Arizona
Same day—Monday, 12 April 1948

Al Hodge flew directly to Fort Huachuca, an Army base located in southernmost Arizona skirting the Mexican border. Fort Huachuca served as a training center for military intelligence and was used by not only the military but also government agencies that had the need to educate certain people in intelligence techniques. Normally, the CIA first sent prospective operatives and analysts to Fort Huachuca. After completing initial training there, the analysts were sent to places such as the Naval War College in Newport, Rhode Island to complete their training. When field agent prospects left Arizona, they were sent to the Farm at Camp Peary.

The flight from Denver to Arizona took much less time for Hodge than the time it would take Carr and Erika to reach Virginia. Being that the distance for Hodge was much less and a refueling stop wasn't necessary, by three o'clock this afternoon Hodge had already seen the base commandant and was now waiting in a small conference room for Ryker to be brought in. His wait wasn't long.

Axel Ryker walked in and without speaking, sat down in the chair across the table from Hodge.

After the war, with his name on numerous war crimes tribunal lists, Ryker fled to South America. Knowing he was living on borrowed time in Argentina, Ryker accepted within minutes Leroy Carr's offer to work for the Americans. The Americans were now the world's only super power—no one else had the atomic bomb. Ryker considered it his good fortune, and perhaps the Americans would let him return to his favorite pastimes—killing and cruelty.

Al Hodge laid his CIA identification on the table so Ryker could see it, a move that should not be unnecessary but Hodge did it anyway. "Mr. Ryker, I assume you remember me from when Mr. Carr and I picked you up in Argentina last fall. I'm Al Hodge."

Ryker did not look at the I.D, only at Hodge and said, "I remember."

Hodge pushed a piece of paper across the table. "Here is a paragraph written in Russian. Read it and translate it into English for me."

It was a paragraph about the history of the Wright Brothers. One of the main reasons Ryker had been at Fort Huachuca for the past seven months was to improve his English language skills.

Ryker read it and translated it into English. He misplaced a couple of English verbs, putting them into the position they would be in within a Russian sentence, but his translation was understandable, although his mixed accent was thick.

"Your English has improved quite a bit since last September," Hodge said.

Ryker said nothing and tossed the paper back on the table.

Hodge handed him another piece of paper, this one blank, along with a pencil. "Now, from memory, write in German what was in the paragraph."

"I have done before all these tests at here your Indian fort," Ryker said, again slightly misarranging his English syntax.

"'Indian fort?' Is that Gestapo humor? Just do what I tell you to do, Ryker."

Ryker gave Hodge a sinister grin and scrawled on the paper. When he finished, he tossed it nonchalantly back toward Hodge. Al didn't read German, but he would find out later that, unlike his English, Ryker's German was perfect.

"Ryker, I'm taking you to a CIA facility in Virginia. There you will receive general advanced training along with training for a specific mission which you won't get any specifics about until Mr. Carr and I feel you are ready. Your immediate supervisor at this facility will be Erika Lehmann; she will give us frequent updates on your progress."

Ryker looked at Hodge with his lifeless eyes. "I have conducted many missions. This is why you offered me a position. Why do I need this endless training, and why am I made to answer to the whore?"

"You need training because the United States doesn't conduct itself like Nazi Germany. Listen to me carefully, Ryker. Lehmann holds your ass in her hands. You will do everything she asks of you. If you don't, you forfeit our agreement. You know what that means; it's off to

Nuremberg for you. Is that clear? Is there anything about this you don't understand?"

"What does the whore say about working with me?"

"First of all, quit referring to a fellow agent as a 'whore'. Secondly, it doesn't matter what she thinks. She'll do her job just as you will do yours if you want your relationship with the United States to continue. We fly out at dawn tomorrow morning. Have your shit packed and be ready. Don't make me wait, Ryker."

Chapter 16

Washington, D.C.
Tuesday, 13 April 1948

The plane carrying Leroy Carr and Erika Lehmann landed at Camp Peary in the early morning hours. It was before dawn when Carr dropped Erika off at the camp before continued his short flight to Washington, landing at Andrews Air Force Base.

Hodge didn't return to the East Coast until much later in the day, delivering Ryker to Camp Peary around dinnertime before returning to D.C.

Now, at 9 p.m., Carr and Hodge sat at a tavern booth with a drink in front of them. Carr lived in Annapolis and Jocko's Pub was a favorite place where he and Hodge often met for a drink. The two old friends and comrades hadn't seen each other since leaving Denver.

"How did it go with Lehmann, Leroy?"

"Fine. We had a long time to talk on the plane and I told her what I expected of her with Ryker at the Farm. How did it go with Ryker?"

Hodge smirked and shook his head. "I thought Lehmann was bad, Leroy, but at least she has a personality. Ryker . . . well, that son-of-a-bitch is a fucking walking nightmare."

"Does he understand where he stands?"

"I read the riot act to him. Whether he goes along, I can't tell you. I don't know about that guy, Leroy. I hope putting him together with Lehmann doesn't become something we regret."

"I can't argue with you, Al. That same feeling haunts me, but the die is cast. First thing on our agenda now is we have to get Singleton out of Denver."

Chapter 17

The CIA 'Farm' at Camp Peary, Virginia
Wednesday, 14 April 1948

Last night, his first night at the Farm, Ryker was given a billet in an Army style barracks where ten bunkbeds were lined up, five on each side of the room. Ten other men filled up five of the bunkbeds. Ryker took the bottom bunk of one of the empty ones as far away from the others as possible. He wasn't interested in the useless chit chat and horseplay that these Americans seemed so proficient at. It surprised him that he was allowed to choose his bunk. *The Amis are certainly not as disciplined as we Germans,* Ryker thought.

He had not yet seen Erika, but at 0530 reveille an Army sergeant walked in and told Ryker to get dressed and come with him. The sergeant led Ryker to another barracks, this one divided into small rooms. This was the barracks used by the training supervisors who each had their own small room about the size of a prison cell. The sergeant knocked on one of the doors and in a moment Erika Lehmann opened the door.

She and Ryker stared at each other, then she said, "Thank you, Sergeant. That will be all."

She waved Ryker into the room that was only big enough to house an Army cot, a small writing table with a reading lamp, and two chairs.

She pointed to one of the chairs and said, "Sit there." Ryker took his time but sat down without comment. She took the other chair.

"Ryker, we both know what we think of each other and it's nothing good. Before we start training today I want to make a few things clear. First of all, I was informed that your English has improved but still needs work. We speak only English here unless a plebe is in a foreign language class. You won't be in any of those classes, so I want to hear only English from you. Consider this to be part of your training.

"The ten men in your barracks are in my battery. That's why I put you there. Last night I read the report from the instructor who has been training them in my absence and he thinks about half of the men won't make it as field agents but thinks four or five have potential. I also have two women assigned to me. They stay in another barracks, of course. I won't match you against any of them, although they compete with some of the other men. As far as the men, they might be tough and strong but I know they stand no chance against you in some of the drills such as hand-to-hand combat or knife fighting. It's my job to keep them in one piece. I don't want you going overboard when you train with any of them. If they get bumps and bruises, that's part of the game. I want you to apply yourself, but do not seriously injure anyone. Is that clear? Look at me when I speak to you!" Ryker had been looking around the room.

Ryker leered. "I always follow my orders, Sonderführer. You of all people should know that."

"Don't ever call me that around here, or anywhere for that matter," she said sternly. Sonderführer was Erika's rank with the German Abwehr. "You will also not speak of your background to anyone other than me while we are here, and that's only if I ask you a question in private."

"I'm not going to talk to anyone that I don't have to unless in the line of . . . what is the word? . . . *business.* All these Amis want to do is talk and chew their gum." (As the slang term 'Kraut' had been used by American forces during the war referring to Germans, 'Amis' was used by the Germans to refer to Americans.)

◊ ◊ ◊

A typical day at the Farm for CIA field hopefuls was a two-mile run before breakfast, a meal they were given fifteen minutes to eat. The rest of the morning was taken up by various classroom work. Some subjects were mandatory for everyone, including classes as diversified as international relations and lock picking. Other classes were postulated for certain plebe agents depending on the area the powers-that-be at the Farm felt were best suited to that trainee's strengths or potential.

For Ryker, besides the mandatory international studies, a subject he couldn't care less about, lockpicking and invisible ink instruction where other subjects that bored him. He considered himself a policeman—more specifically an investigator and interrogator—not a spy. Ryker wondered why he had to learn to pick a door lock, a task that might take several minutes, when he could smash the door down in a second or two. However, Ryker did pay attention in his English classes. He felt that was to his advantage.

For Erika's morning, she led her flock on the early morning run and was then basically free until the physical training began after lunch.

Trainees learned quickly to eat lightly at the noon meal. Those who didn't usually regretted it, losing their lunch during the course of the grueling afternoon of physical training.

Since it was her first day with this group of recruits, Erika introduced herself, something she had not done at the run early that morning. Everyone was dressed in dark gray fatigues, including Erika. The only difference was her trainers patch sewn on her shirt above her left breast. Thirteen people were lined up in front of her on the Farm obstacle course—eleven men, including Ryker, and two women.

"My name is Lorelei," Erika said loudly so all could hear. "I'm taking over for Solomon who trained you in my absence. Most of you have been in the military and our goal is not to repeat basic training. Your time here at Camp Peary is an evaluation, pure and simple. If you prove yourself to be someone who shows promise as a CIA field agent, you will continue on after this initial session is complete. If you don't, you'll be discharged or reassigned to a position that might better serve your talents.

"I don't know how Solomon conducted things and I don't care. I do know that he did not include swim training in the camp lake because of the time of year, but we will do that starting today. Each day we will start out with calisthenics then negotiate the obstacle course. After that we will do hand-to-hand combat, knife training and target practice with handguns. Swimming will be the last exercise of the day then you'll return to the mess hall for dinner. Your training on tailing someone or eluding a tail, both while walking and while in a car, will continue in the evenings four days each week.

"Sunday is your personal day for attending church services in the morning and catching up on your classroom homework in the afternoon. As I'm sure was the case while Solomon trained you in my absence, you will not leave the base or receive any visitors until this training is over."

Erika didn't ask if there were any questions but immediately lined up everyone for stretching and calisthenics. Ryker kept his mouth shut during calisthenics but again seemed bored. The obstacle course was a different matter. Erika demonstrated, finishing the course in a time that would prove to be better than any of the men in the group. The 270-pound musclebound Ryker was one of the slowest, but pure strength got him over walls, fences, and through the other obstacles.

The tactical training was a much different story. Ryker made short work of anyone pitted against him in hand-to-hand combat and knife fighting which was done using dull wooden blades. Everyone facing Ryker came away with injuries of some sort, but to Erika's surprise, Ryker obeyed her orders to not seriously injure anyone. Handgun marksmanship was another area where Ryker excelled.

The most enjoyable part of the day for Erika was the last event because she knew Ryker was a terrible swimmer. The Farm's lake was small, perhaps fifty yards from bank to bank. She ordered the plebes to swim across the lake, stand on the opposite shore and swim back to the small dock from where they entered the freezing water. This was done while wearing their fatigues. "In the field, it's unlikely the enemy will give you time to change into a swimsuit," Erika had told them. As she suspected would happen, Ryker started floundering before he was halfway across the first lap. She grabbed a lifesaver and jumped in. Reaching him quickly, he tried to push her away, seemingly more content to drown than accept her help. Erika slapped him hard across the face—a blow he barely reacted to. She said, "Drown if you want to, you bastard," and swam away. Ryker finally used the lifesaver and clumsily splashed his way back to the dock.

When the time allotted at the lake was over, Erika told everyone to report back to their billets and be ready for dinner at 1800 hours. The shivering men and women needed no encouragement to double-time it back to the barracks where they could change out of their wet clothes.

Ryker on the other hand delayed returning; instead, he stood on the dock and lit a cigarette from a pack he had left on the shore before he jumped in the water. This fiend of a man seemed oblivious to the cold.

Erika dressed him down. "Ryker, you're not supposed to have cigarettes on you during training."

"No one gave me those instructions." He took another drag.

"No more cigarettes during training, Ryker."

"As you wish, Sonderführer." It was the Abwehr rank she had ordered him to never call her. He smiled at her, dropped the cigarette at her feet, and began walking back to the barracks.

Chapter 18

Detroit, Michigan
Two days later—Friday, 16 April 1948

It happened in the late afternoon.

When the Detroit police entered the Corktown Tavern near the Detroit River the bartender was sitting on a stool looking exhausted. The inside of the bar looked as if it had been struck by an Oklahoma twister. Most customers had hurriedly left before the police arrived; a few of the curious who had not been involved in the melee stood outside on the curb smoking cigarettes.

Detroit was one of the few cities in America that allowed black men to apply for a position with the police force. One of the black officers who had frequented the tavern in the past knew the bartender by name.

"What in the hell happened, Otis?"

Otis was a pudgy, baldheaded black man in his late 50s.

Otis looked up and shook his head. "Hell if I know, Roy. Some white woman walks in, sits down at the bar. I was afraid right away that there would be trouble. All was fine for a while until two Negro men approached her. After a few minutes the woman and the men start arguing then the woman broke her beer bottle over one of the guy's head, pulls a knife and stabs the other one. Then others got involved and you see what I have left here."

"Where is the guy who was stabbed?"

"Gone. His buddy helped him limp out of here. The woman is gone, too."

"Give us a description of the woman."

"White gal, like I said—a blonde," Otis said, "Maybe 5'8' or a little taller. Looked to be . . . I don't know, maybe late 20s."

"How about the men?"

Otis shrugged. "Negros I've never seen before. Normal-looking, I guess, average height. They had on T-shirts that I see a lot of Chrysler workers wear."

"Anything else you can tell us, Otis?"

"When the gal was sitting alone, before the trouble started, she was friendly and told me her name was Erika." Otis pointed to a table. "The knife she used is laying on the floor under that table. I'm afraid Mr. Henry (the bar owner) will fire me."

[late that night—Denver]

Chris Singleton was in bed when the call to his room at the Brown Palace came through.

"Mr. Singleton," the hotel switchboard operator said. *"I know it's late, but you asked that the switchboard put calls through regardless of the hour."*

"Yes, operator," Singleton said. "Where is the call from?"

"Washington, sir."

"Put it through, please." Singleton heard the call click through. "Hello."

"Agent Singleton, this is Director Hoover."

Singleton sat up on the edge of his bed. "Yes, Director."

"Agent Singleton, we know you've run into a wall there in Denver. It's little wonder. We know now that the fugitive has fled from that city. Her prints were found earlier today on a knife in Detroit. Apparently, the woman can't stay out of trouble in bars. Get a flight out to Detroit as early as possible tomorrow morning. I'll contact the Special Agent in Charge of our Detroit office tomorrow morning and give him the details of what we know. He'll be ready to fill you in when you get there."

Chapter 19

Arlington, Virginia
Sunday, 18 April 1948

Did it work, Leroy?" Al Hodge asked.

Leroy Carr and Al Hodge sat in a booth at Hamilton's Restaurant in Arlington, just across the Potomac River from Washington, D.C. Both men had already ordered breakfast and were waiting for it to be delivered to their table. Hamilton's was a popular place that served good food. Instead of meeting in Carr's office (if a meeting was necessary on a Sunday morning), both men preferred meeting over breakfast at Hamilton's. They had had several Sunday morning meetings here, going back to the early years of the war when they teamed up in the OSS. As they waited on their food, they drank coffee and smoked.

"It looks like it did, Al. Our man I sent to Detroit to watch for Singleton called me at home last night to tell me he had arrived."

"So, Singleton is gone from Denver," Hodge said. "Good work, Leroy."

"Kathryn went a bit overboard. We have a wrecked bar in Detroit, but the owner's insurance should hopefully take care of that. Regardless, Kathryn was the right choice for this job. No one knows Erika better than Kathryn, and she told me the outcome was what she thought it would be if Erika was really involved."

Last Thursday, Carr sent an agent to Camp Peary with a knife; Erika was instructed to touch it in several places, leaving her fingerprints. Kathryn Fischer, one member of the now-disbanded Shield Maiden team, was the woman in the bar posing as Erika. Kathryn was close to Erika's height, and the blonde wig over Fischer's brunette hair seemed to have done the trick.

"Was anyone injured?" Hodge asked.

"Nothing serious. The PFCs Jackson and Monroe did a good job. Kathryn broke a beer bottle over Jackson's head and he came away with a bump and small cut on his scalp. She used the other knife skillfully, penetrating only Monroe's jacket close to his stomach area. Monroe, who everyone in the place thought was stabbed, actually came out of it better than Jackson."

The entire tussle at the Corktown Tavern had been a CIA setup. Besides Kathryn Fischer posing as Erika, the two men she skirmished with were black Army privates stationed at Fort Dix, New Jersey. Kathryn used an identical knife to the one with Erika's fingerprints. Before running out of the bar, she acted like she accidentally dropped it as she bolted to get away, but Kathryn had switched knives and the one she left behind was the knife with Erika's fingerprints.

It was now Carr's turn to ask questions.

"How are things at the Farm between Erika and Ryker," Carr asked. Among other duties, Al Hodge oversaw the monitoring all CIA training at the Farm.

"Lots of friction between those two, Leroy. So far, they haven't killed each other. That's the only positive report I can give you."

Talk paused when breakfast was delivered; the waitress returned a moment later to top off their coffee cups.

"Anything new about the Denver mission?" Hodge asked as he smashed out his cigarette before diving into his meal.

"Not yet, Al, but I'm expecting an update to arrive at E Street by noon tomorrow."

Chapter 20

Washington, D.C.
CIA Headquarters on E Street
Monday, 19 April 1948

When lunchtime came around, instead of leaving the building for lunch, a busy Al Hodge walked down the corridor outside his office at E Street and dropped coins into a vending machine. A ham and cheese on rye sandwich fell to the slot. He returned to his office with the sandwich, but before he had a chance to take the tape off the wax paper, his secretary intercepted him.

"Mr. Hodge, Mr. Carr would like to see you in his office right away."

Hodge gave the sandwich to the secretary. "Here's lunch, Donna."

When Hodge entered Carr's office, just a short walk down the hallway, Carr was standing and gazing out his window onto E Street.

"I assume this is about the update you told me you'd get concerning Denver," Hodge said before sitting down. "Let me have it."

"Not good news, Al. It looks like the Denver problem is coming to a head before we expected. Erika will have to return to Denver next week with Ryker as her partner. Go to Camp Peary tomorrow morning and bring them both here to D.C. for an initial briefing. Take the Hudson and fly them in; I don't want Erika and Ryker in the same car for a four-hour drive."

"I agree, Leroy, but that begs the question: 'How are they going to work together on an assignment when we don't trust them to be together in a car for four hours?'"

"I'll explain to them again how much they both have at stake," Carr said. "Erika wants charges against her dropped so she can bring her daughter Stateside. That's plenty of motivation for her. Ryker is no dummy. He knows if he doesn't follow orders to the letter we'll ship him off to the war crimes tribunal courts."

"I hope you're right, Leroy."

"So do I, but I'm not leaving it to pure chance. Besides their briefings over the course of the rest of the week, we'll put them to the test in both social situations and a practice mission."

"By the way, Leroy, Lehmann asked me if she would be allowed to go to Williamsburg and see that guy she has dated on occasion. I told her 'no.'" Williamsburg, Virginia, was a short drive from Camp Peary.

"That's the guy named Nick who works at a tavern in that town, right?" Carr asked.

"That's right."

"Good call, Al. No, she's not getting off the base until she leaves there to come here to D.C. Then it's back to Denver."

Chapter 21

**E Street Complex
Washington, D.C.
Tuesday, 20 April 1948**

Erika and Ryker sat in wooden chairs across the desk from Leroy Carr. Al Hodge preferred to stand, leaning against a narrow piece of wall that divided two windows on the left side from Carr. On the wall to Carr's right the Stars & Stripes hung from a pole—a photo of Harry Truman on the wall beside it.

Erika had gotten to see Sheila Reid briefly in her office. As fellow Shield Maidens they were close. They had been through dangerous missions together. Now they were disbanded and worked independently, something Erika considered a mistake on Leroy Carr's part. Even much worse, Carr was now teaming her with Axel Ryker on an assignment.

Carr addressed Ryker. "I know you've been at the Farm only one week, Ryker. I have the reports here from your classroom instructors. The general evaluation is you seem uninterested in any class except English."

"The English will benefit me and the CIA. I fail to see how studying international politics is something I need to concern myself with. That's not why a job you offered me."

Ryker was right, but Carr didn't comment. He turned to Erika. "I know he's only been with you for a week, Erika. How's Ryker doing with the field training?"

"Slow on the obstacle course; exceptional in the fighting skills and with handguns. A terrible swimmer."

"Unfortunately, we're running out of time," Carr said. "The mission has to begin next week. You'll stay here in Washington until then for your briefings."

"What is the mission, Leroy?" Erika asked. "I presume it's in Denver since you sent me there for a month to learn my way around."

"Yes, it's in Denver but that's all I'm going to say about it today. You and Ryker must prove to me that you two can work together. I'm sending you on a brief practice mission on Thursday. On Saturday evening you two will pose as a couple and attended a formal cocktail party that will be held here in the Washington area."

The thought of taking Ryker's arm at a party almost made Erika nauseous. "Do we have to go as a couple?"

"Yes, you have to go as a couple," Carr said. "But first up is the practice mission. You'll be briefed about that tomorrow and it will take place Thursday night," Carr said. "That will give you one day to prepare. You won't have to travel. Like the reception, it will also take place nearby."

"Where will I be staying while I'm here?" Erika asked.

"You and Ryker will stay at the Mayflower posing as husband and wife. You'll be in the same hotel room, of course." Carr handed them both a gold wedding band.

"Leroy, please!"

Carr shook his head, refusing her. "We'll get a suite with two bedrooms. You won't have to sleep in the same room, but I want you to be seen together: eating meals together in the hotel restaurant like a normal couple, having a drink in the bar, etc. Since Ryker's accent would never let him pass as an American, you'll be Mr. and Mrs. Divak. Erika, use your British accent. For this week you're from London. Ryker, you're a Polish refugee who met your wife in London shortly after the war ended. With your mixed bag accent no one at that hotel will be able to tell it's not an authentic Polish accent.

"Any questions?"

Erika asked, "Why can't you give us at least an initial briefing about Denver?"

"I told you why. Al and I have to feel confident you and Ryker can function together. That's what the rest of this week will be about." Carr turned to Ryker. "Ryker, this is your one and only chance to prove you can be of service to the United States. If you screw this up, all you'll get out of our deal is a one-way ticket to a cell in Nuremberg."

Ryker looked at Hodge and then Carr. "I think I understand what 'screw this up' means; it means make a mistake, yes? I follow my orders. I can work with the Abwehr slut."

Hodge spoke up. "I told him not to use offensive names toward any colleague, Leroy. The sonuvabitch doesn't listen. I say we ship his ass to Nuremberg as soon as possible and let him pay the piper."

"I agree with Al," Erika added quickly.

"Ryker," said Carr firmly, "you have this week to prove to us that you're not a liability. That's something that you *should* listen to. If not, you're on a plane back to Germany this weekend. Do I make myself perfectly clear?"

Ryker stared at Carr for a moment. "I told you before that I obey my orders."

Erika butted in. "Why is it important that this animal be involved in the mission, Leroy? If it takes a man/woman team, I know we have several male agents that would be better suited?"

"You'll find out why Ryker is needed when it comes time for your briefings. Prove to me this week that you can work together. And don't think it's just Ryker we worry about, Erika. After South America and then forcing us to deal with the FBI because you got arrested in Denver for a stupid altercation in a dive bar, I have plenty of concerns about you, as well. You and Ryker are both on a short leash; don't forget that."

Chapter 22

Mayflower Hotel, Washington, D.C.
Next day—Wednesday, 21 April 1948

Last night in the hotel room the two mortal enemies said nothing to one another. One of Al Hodge's men knocked on the door around nine o'clock with some extra clothes and toiletries for them both. Ryker shaved and took his shower first, emerged from the bathroom in a hotel robe then went to his bedroom. That was the last Erika saw of him until this morning.

Now, at eight o'clock, they sat at a small table in one of the Mayflower Hotel restaurants. This one, the *Senator,* served breakfast.

"What should I call you?" Ryker asked.

"Just call me 'Erika.' We're married, remember? What a sickening thought that is, don't you agree? It surely is for me."

Ryker didn't respond to her comment, saying only, "I'll let you order for me. I want pancakes." He was familiar with American menus, having been in Evansville for several months in 1943 while pursuing her.

"Order for yourself, ass-hole. If you don't know what that means you'll have to figure it out."

Ryker smirked. "I know what it means. It's English for 'arseloch' yes? Very well, *Erika.* I will order."

The waitress showed up with a coffee pot and filled their cups. Erika wanted to get this over with as quickly as possible and ordered breakfast right away. Ryker ordered his pancakes. When the waitress walked away, Erika said, "Ryker, I don't know how we're going to do it, but we have to work together for both of our sakes. You understand that, don't you?"

"I am a professional. If you are one as well, things can work."

And that was the end of the table conversation at the *Senator.*

◊ ◊ ◊

[10:00 a.m.]

"How did it go between you two last night?" Leroy Carr asked. The four people in Carr's office the previous day: Carr, Al Hodge, Erika, and Axel Ryker, were once again together.

"Fine," answered Erika emotionless. She knew asking Carr again to free her from working with Ryker was a waste of time.

Carr was in a no-nonsense mood. "That's what I expect—it to be *fine.*"

"Here is your practice mission," Carr continued. "Erika is mission leader. Do you understand that, Ryker?"

Ryker nodded.

"This will be done tomorrow night. Erika, you and Ryker will break into the FBI headquarters and steal the FBI file from its archives on their investigation during the time they were chasing you in Evansville in '43. You'll also take anything else with your name on it. You'll deliver everything here on Friday morning before noon. Al has blueprints of the FBI building you can go over in his office. You have no backup. You will be responsible for your transportation to and from the FBI building. If you're caught, forget about claiming you were on a mission for the CIA. We'll deny everything and let the Justice Department have both of you. If certain security personnel need to be dealt with you can do that, but no one is to be killed or permanently maimed." He looked specifically at Ryker. "Is that clear?"

"I obey orders. I have said this many times."

Carr looked at Erika.

"I understand," she said. "Thank you, Leroy." She thanked him because she realized that before she could make a case for citizenship, evidence of her past had to disappear. She knew Carr was forcing her to work for her request to be a citizen of the United States, and that was fine by her. Before the war, Germany had been her Heaven on earth. Now she would have to earn her new Valhalla—the United States.

"Now go with Al; besides the blueprints, he'll have his people get you any equipment or clothes you need for the assignment. What that is will be up to you. You're totally on your own here.

"I expect to see you back here with the dossiers Friday morning. I'm having lunch that day with CIA Director Hillenkoetter and two congressmen who don't know their ass from buttermilk but who like sticking their noses in our business. The director and I will mention nothing about you two, but if I don't have the files by the time I leave for lunch, you're both relieved from duty. Surely you realize what that means."

[that evening]

Back in their hotel room, Erika and Ryker had been discussing the mission for almost three hours. Ryker wasn't as experienced in clandestine operations as Erika. Ryker was an enforcer—a bone breaker. Yet, he was wily and made several valid suggestions.

Erika considered some of his ideas and threw out others she thought unworkable.

Finally, she said, "This is what we'll do."

Chapter 23

Washington, D.C.
Next day—Thursday, 22 April 1948

An elderly black man mopped the corridor outside the archives room in the bowels of the FBI headquarters. Pete had been a janitor at this building since the early thirties, back when Hoover's men hunted John Dillinger. He preferred the graveyard shift—not as many people walking around marking up his still wet floors. Also, all the females were gone for the day so he didn't have to be concerned that he would walk in on a lady when it came time to clean the women's restrooms. If he accidentally walked in on a white woman he felt he would surely be fired. There were male agents around this time of night, however, and he would see them during the graveyard shift several times each night when they came down to access the archives or fingerprint files.

When it came time to clean the women's bathroom he pushed his cleaning cart through the door. He was shocked to see a woman standing in front of one of the stalls. The brunette looked at the nametag sewn to his shirt, smiled and said, "Hello, Pete." Pete never saw the large man standing behind the door.

Twenty minutes later, two FBI agents stepped off the elevator to the subterranean floor. They needed fingerprints of a man who had kidnapped a woman in Atlanta and had driven her across the Georgia state line into South Carolina. The man had previous felony convictions, so the agents knew his fingerprints would be on file.

When the two agents turned a corner, they saw at the far end of the hall, just outside the archives door, a huge man mopping the floor. When they reached him, one of the agents asked, "Where's Pete?"

"Off tonight," the man replied in a strange accent. He was dressed in janitor clothes that were much too small for him and had no nametag.

The two FBI men looked at each other. The same one looked back at Axel Ryker and said, "Pete hasn't missed a day in years. Where's your nametag?" The men were starting to grow suspicious.

"I'm new, no name tag."

"Why are you wearing gloves?"

"Detergent hurts my hands." (Ryker pronounced it 'debtor-gent')

Both men looked at the door to the archives room. It was shut, but some damage around the lock was evident from where Ryker kicked open the heavy steel door so Erika could enter. Both agents started to draw their guns from under their suit jackets.

Erika had been inside the archives room since Ryker put an end to Pete's night of work. The old man was securely tied up and gagged in one of the stalls in the ladies' restroom. Erika had been picking the locks on huge, five-foot-wide file cabinet drawers for twenty minutes. The locks weren't difficult to pick; there were just so many of them—long aisle after long aisle. There were maybe a dozen file cabinets tagged with the letter 'L'. That's where she looked first, searching for a file that might be labeled 'Lehmann' or 'Lorelei.' She found nothing there.

Next she looked in the 'K's. Maybe the FBI used her alias 'Sarah Klein' for a file—the name she used in Evansville. Again, she came up blank.

Fifteen more minutes passed. She was trying to hurry. She checked three drawers under 'E'. Nothing with Evansville on it.

As a last resort, Erika tried the 'A' files. In the first drawer she checked—the 'AB' cabinet—there it was. The tag read:

ABWEHR – Evansville, Indiana, 1943

Chapter 24

FBI Headquarters
Washington, D.C.
Next day—Friday, 23 April 1948

J. Edgar Hoover had been called at his home shortly after 7:00 a.m. Twenty minutes later he was in his office looking a bit disheveled from quickly throwing on his suit and skipping his morning shave.

Waiting for him when he arrived was his longtime assistant, Clyde Tolson, whose title was now Associate Director of the FBI; along with the agent in charge of headquarters security, Howard Ward. The two men followed Hoover into his office.

"What in the hell happened last night?" Hoover bellowed as he sat down heavily in the chair behind his massive desk. "Clyde said on the telephone that there was a breach last night. What kind of breach?"

Tolson looked at Ward whose duty it was to explain.

"At around 2 a.m. a man and woman entered the building through a second-floor window. Special Agent Straus was in his office working late. He was taken by surprise and drugged with the use of a syringe. That's the last thing he remembers, Director Hoover."

Hoover waved his hand in a circular motion. "Keep going!"

"We know their target was the archives room. Two agents received multiple injuries on the archives floor. Agent Oliver suffered a broken wrist and cracked ribs. Agent Hronek's jaw was fractured and he has a dislocated shoulder; both were taken to Walter Reed. The door to the room had been busted open. Also, a Negro janitor on that floor was tied up and gagged. The agents were also tied up. All three were found this morning in the ladies' restroom on that floor by a secretary who works in the print room. Every agent available is scouring the archives room for fingerprints as we speak."

Hoover steamed. This was unbelievable that someone had burglarized FBI headquarters. It was sure to be a major embarrassment if it became known to Congress and the public. "Was anything taken?"

A nervous Ward cleared his throat. "We don't know, Director. It will take some time to go through all the files. And it's possible nothing was taken. Perhaps the intruders simply photographed what they were looking for, if they found it at all."

J. Edgar Hoover had a special glare for any of his agents who disappointed him. Ward now suffered that look and knew he would have a price to pay.

"Put a team together immediately to search the files, Ward," Hoover said with menace. "I want to know if anything was removed."

"Of course, Director," Ward said tensely, "but you realize it will take time to hand search all the files."

"I didn't ask you how long it would take, goddammit! Get to work! I want answers, Ward, not excuses! And nothing about this is to leak out!"

[two hours later—9:00 a.m.]

Erika handed the FBI dossier to Leroy Carr. Ryker was also in Carr's office. This time Al Hodge was not present. Hodge was in a meeting with other agents focused on a different mission he was supervising.

Carr quickly thumbed through the dossier then laid in on his desk.

"I'll go over it thoroughly this afternoon. I'm sure you read it," Carr said to Erika. "What's in it?"

"Just what the FBI knows about my Abwehr mission in Evansville. It's sketchy. Big gaps are missing. Most of the information in it comes from debriefings of Agent Singleton."

"How did you get into the FBI building?" Carr asked.

The athletic Erika Lehmann could scale a wall like a spider. All she needed was a little indentation in the mortar between bricks.

"I saw an open window on the second floor. There was a light on so I assumed someone was working late. I put a rope over my shoulder and climbed up to the window. The agent sat at his desk with his back to the window. It was an easy matter. I drugged him with a syringe of Nembutal. He never heard me enter and I stuck the needle in his neck before he knew I was even there. The syringe was among the equipment requests I gave Al. I dropped the rope to Ryker and we were in. We escaped through the same window."

"I assume you wore the brown wig."

"Yes," Erika confirmed, "and Ryker and I both wore gloves, of course."

Carr looked at Ryker. "Was anyone hurt?"

"Yes, two of the FBI men started to pull weapons on me as I stood guard outside the archives (Ryker pronounced it 'our-kifes') room as backup to Fräulein Lehmann, but their injuries are not permanent," Ryker answered. "They will heal. My orders were that no permanent injuries would be inflicted. I obeyed those orders."

Carr stared at Ryker for a moment then continued. "I will accept that until I find out differently. For both of your sakes, let's hope I don't."

"Now," Carr continued, "the second part of your assessment is to attend a reception at Director Hillenkoetter's home this Saturday night. Some members of the president's cabinet will be in attendance along with a few elected officials. It's a formal affair and you both will need formal attire. When you leave my office see Sheila; she'll have someone get you set up with all that. I will be there with Kay. Sheila will be there, as well. This time I can personally watch you. Your assignment this time is simple. Convince everyone you rub shoulders with that you are a happy couple."

"I don't understand this 'rub shoulders'," Ryker stated.

"It means 'people who you talk to,'" Carr responded. "Now, there should be no questions about this simple assignment. Go see Sheila. She will give you your invitations and other details."

Chapter 25

Annapolis, Maryland
Saturday, 24 April 1948

Like Leroy Carr, CIA Director Roscoe H. Hillenkoetter lived in Annapolis, a one-hour drive from Washington. Despite the daily commute, the retired U.S. Navy Rear Admiral felt this town that was the home of the United States Naval Academy was where his heart lie and where he felt he belonged.

After the war, his plans had been to retire peacefully—maybe teach a class or two at the academy and spend a lot time fishing the Chesapeake Bay. But when President Truman called him to the White House and asked him to take over as director of the new intelligence agency he felt it his duty to accept.

Unlike Leroy Carr and his wife Kay who lived in a nice, but not flashy house in the Loretta Heights area of Annapolis, Hillenkoetter and his wife resided in the upscale and expensive Eastport area in a mansion overlooking the Bay.

Guests invited to tonight's eight o'clock reception began arriving fashionably late about fifteen minutes after the hour with most arriving by nine. The room for the reception was to the right of the atrium. The reception room wasn't huge, but it was spacious enough for a small band and dance floor, and the approximately thirty guests and eight attendants, who were senior Midshipman from the Academy. The three-piece band was just beginning to set up in a far corner. When Erika arrived with Axel Ryker (wearing their wedding rings), noticeably not yet present was Leroy and Kay Carr.

Nevertheless, Sheila Reid and her husband Ricky were there. As soon as Erika spotted her she told Ryker to get lost for a while and then she walked toward Sheila. Erika's friend and fellow Shield Maiden and her husband were engaged with another couple. When Sheila spotted Erika coming she excused herself and walked to meet her friend. The two women embraced. Sheila Reid, the Army major, wore a pale orange gown that underscored her red hair. The two former comrades had seen each other only briefly and solely for the sake of the business at

83

hand during the course of the past week. Tonight was the first time they could talk privately.

"Where's your loving bridegroom?" Sheila said with a grin.

"You're a real riot, Sheila." Erika looked around and spotted Ryker. "He's over there at the food table stuffing his ugly face. Look at him. Putting a tuxedo on Ryker is like dressing a gorilla in a zoot suit."

Sheila laughed.

"Is there anything about the Denver mission you can tell me, Sheila?"

"I honestly know nothing, Erika. This Denver worry has been the most tight-lipped thing I've seen with Leroy. He normally briefs me, but he hasn't told me anything."

Just then the two women saw Leroy and Kay Carr walk in.

"I'm sure Leroy will want to talk to you and I need to get back to Ricky. We were in a conversation with Senator Groves and his wife. It will look rude if I'm gone too long. I'll talk to you later, Erika." The two women again embraced then Sheila walked away.

One of the Midshipmen carrying trays of flutes filled with champagne approached Erika. Etiquette demanded no staring at guests, but the young man found himself admiring the beautiful woman. She wore a glittering pale-yellow evening gown that bared her shoulders. In the front, the dress dipped down between her breasts revealing an appealing amount of cleavage. In the back, the V-slit dipped to the base of her spine. A diamond-studded hair comb entrapped the blonde hair piled high on her head. An elegant, but not gaudy, diamond pendant rested just above her breasts, suspended there by a thin gold chain. Gloves that matched the color of her gown covered her hands and extended up past her elbows.

Despite the young waiter's efforts to avoid being caught ogling, Erika noticed him glancing at her breasts and decided to flirt. She looked at his name tag.

"Good evening, Midshipman Knappe," she said to him, smiled, then unnecessarily moved a little closer to take the glass of champagne.

"Good evening," the young man replied tactfully.

"What are you doing after the party?"

He looked shocked and didn't reply. Erika said no more but continued to look him in the eyes and smile over her drink. The stockpiling of hormonal urges within the young man forced him to look away and quickly move on. He had invested much in blood and sweat getting to this point at the Academy and was six weeks away from graduation. He thought walking away promptly from the siren was the prudent thing to do for his future.

Erika wasn't serious about meeting him after the reception and regretted that she probably went too far with her enticing, but she succumbed to the urge to have a bit of fun. *That's a good man who will make a fine Naval officer,* she thought after he walked away. She walked over to Leroy and Kay Carr. She hadn't seen Kay in seven months, not since the mission in South America ended that had gotten her in Leroy Carr's doghouse.

At 44-years-old, Kay Carr was several years younger than her husband. She wore a purple, full-length, form fitting gown that actuated both her smart figure and brunette hair. A choker of pearls encircled her neck. As did all the men, Leroy wore a tuxedo.

"Kay, you look lovely," Erika said.

To put it lightly, Kay Carr had never been a fan of the former Nazi spy who had kidnapped her husband during the war; nevertheless, she knew the reason Erika Lehmann was here tonight—an assignment from her husband. She replied with diplomacy, "Thank you, Erika. You look stunning."

Leroy Carr wasn't in the mood for pleasantries and cut to the chase. "Why aren't you with Ryker?"

"I spoke to Sheila for a moment. I'll rejoin Ryker, Leroy. I know that's what you want."

"Good idea," said Carr. "The only reason you and Ryker are here is to be evaluated. Don't forget that."

Erika took her time but eventually returned to Ryker's side. He was still eating.

"Quit stuffing your face, Ryker. We have to mingle."

Erika gritted her teeth and took Ryker's arm. She saw Leroy and Kay talking to a small group of people on the other side of the room and steered Ryker that way. Besides the Carr's, Erika recognized only one person in the group—CIA Director Hillenkoetter. She had met him briefly once; after the South America mission when she got into hot water with Leroy. Hillenkoetter used the occasion to bring her to his office and read her the riot act.

When Erika and Ryker reached the group, Leroy turned and said, "Everyone, this is Mr. and Mrs. Divak, friends of mine." Besides the Carrs and Hilllenkoetter, no one else in the small group new who the couple really was.

Carr made the introductions. "Mr. and Mrs. Divak, this is Admiral Hillenkoetter and his wife, Debra." Hillenkoetter acted like he didn't know Erika and shook her and Ryker's hand. Carr motioned to another couple. "This is Secretary of Defense Louis Johnson and his wife Amanda, and the Senator from Florida, Jeremiah Brantz." Apparently, the senator was not married as Erika saw no wedding ring. They all shook hands, but instead of admiring the beautiful women just introduced to them, the Secretary of Defense, his wife, and the Senator couldn't take their eyes off the woman's massive and grizzly-looking husband. The Senator silently thought, *these two must have inspired the recent Broadway play 'The Beauty and the Beast.'*

A few words were exchanged, then the three-piece band struck up a rendition of Artie Shaw's *Begin the Beguine.*

Leroy Carr said to Erika and Ryker. "I'm sure you two newlywed love birds will want to dance."

Erika looked at him. She wanted to tell him he was an asshole, but, of course, did not.

Erika Lehmann and Axel Ryker took to the dance floor. Ryker was certainly not a seasoned dancer, but he got by. Erika had to put her hand on Ryker's shoulder while he placed his hand on the side of her back. She didn't know if she could bare it, and during the dance they stared malignantly at each other. Somehow, they managed to complete the slow dance.

Chapter 26

Washington, D.C.
CIA Headquarters on E Street
Monday, 26 April 1948

Finally, the day for the Denver briefing arrived. Erika couldn't endure much more of sharing a hotel room with Axel Ryker. Leroy Carr was certainly keeping his word after she went rogue in South America. He told her there would be a price to pay, and she felt inflicting Ryker on her was Carr's payback.

Ryker had not bothered her when they retired for the night in their suite at the Mayflower; still, sharing meals with him, dancing at Saturday night's cocktail party, and just knowing the creature was in the next room at night was a tough penalty Leroy was extracting.

One of Al Hodge's men picked them up at the Mayflower at 8:00 a.m. They were taken to Carr's office. Waiting were Carr, Hodge, and another man Erika didn't recognize. A large map of the Denver area hung on the wall to the right of Carr's desk.

"Have a seat." Carr said. Erika and Ryker sat down in two chairs already pulled up for them. Carr looked at the man Erika didn't recognize. "Mr. Beckman, this is Erika Lehmann and Axel Ryker." Then Carr looked at Erika and Ryker. "As you just heard, this is Mr. Beckman. My work with him dates back to the war when we both worked for the OSS. Mr. Beckman is one of our top analysts. He will begin the briefing." Carr looked at the man. "Mr. Beckman."

Beckman was a thin, almost to the point of being gaunt, man who looked to be in his late 40s. His receding hairline and eyeglasses gave him the look of the archetypal college professor. Instead of a suit, he wore a white shirt and brown pants held up by orange suspenders.

Beckman rose and walked over to the map. Using a yardstick, he pointed to an area just northeast of Denver.

"This area of 20,000 acres is the Rocky Mountain Arsenal," Beckman said. "This top-secret site was completed in December of 1942 to enable the United States to offer our own deterrents to the possible threat of the Germans or the Japanese use of chemical weapons, either against our country or our allies. Our national stockpile of chemical weapons is manufactured and stored there at the arsenal. Some of the chemical agents include mustard gas, lewisite, chlorine gas, and Sarin gas." Beckman looked at Leroy. "Should I continue, Deputy Director Carr?"

Carr nodded.

Beckman continued, "Our team of analysts have received intelligence that convinces us a group of saboteurs intend to gain entrance to the arsenal and set explosive charges. If this were to happen the consequences would be devastating. The entire Denver area and a radius of up to 100 miles of Colorado would be under a cloud of various poison gases. Tens of thousands of people would die, and many more thousands would be permanently injured as far as their breathing and eye sight were concerned. As of yet, we have no evidence that these saboteurs are being sent by the Soviets. I repeat, we have no evidence that the Soviets are behind this." Beckman was finished and lowered his ruler.

"Thank you, Mr. Beckman," Carr said. "I'll speak again with you later."

Beckman nodded and without speaking left the room.

"Beckman is very good at what he does," Carr said. "Ryker, he's the one who found out you were still alive and living somewhere in Argentina."

"So, you've known about this sabotage attack for some time, Leroy," Erika said. "Now I know why you sent me to Denver."

"That's right. Beckman came to me with this about two months ago. We've had some time to set up our plans because Beckman uncovered one name, an Irishman who spent time in a Belfast prison for his IRA activities just before the war. This man is now a mercenary and hires other mercenaries. They do jobs around the world for anyone who has the money to pay them. His name is Cyril O'Grady. He's been in Istanbul for the past several months apparently planning this attack. We found out last week that he left Istanbul for Greece. The trail ends there, but by leaving Istanbul we must assume he might be on his way to the States. O'Grady is too smart to fly here or come by ocean liner; that would be too easy to trace. My guess is he and his men boarded a freighter in Greece. Our problem is we don't know the name of the freighter or where it will dock once it arrives. That's why we have no alternative but to have a team waiting in Denver."

"Do you have any idea when he will get here?" Erika asked.

"Unless the freighter has several stops or other delays, it could arrive here from the Mediterranean as early as Thursday. If he and his team take a flight to Denver, they could be there by Saturday. Al already has some of his men in Denver monitoring the airport, train, and bus stations, but, as I said, it's unlikely that O'Grady and his men could arrive before Saturday."

Erika asked, "Do you know how many men he will bring?"

"No idea," said Carr. "Here's your mission. Thwart the sabotage at any cost and capture O'Grady so Ryker can interrogate him. We must find out who is behind all of this. O'Grady will be a tough nut to crack, Ryker. He has undergone intense grilling many times by the British for his activities as an IRA leader and gave up nothing."

Ryker grinned. "I'm sure I can convince him to give us what we want."

Erika finally knew why Carr included Ryker in the assignment. It was because of his brutal Gestapo interrogation techniques—torture that wouldn't be done by any American CIA interrogator, or condoned if it came to light in the Congress. Erika realized Carr was pulling out all stops because of the enormous threat on American soil.

The CIA deputy director picked up two mugshots taken of O'Grady by the British and handed one to Erika and one to Ryker.

"These mugshots are nine years old, but they will give you an idea of what O'Grady looks like. When we find out that he has arrived in Denver, Al will fly out there. His team will aid you when necessary. Of course, we have to be concerned that he won't take a plane, train, or bus to Denver once he enters this country, but gets there by other means. Perhaps his team will purchase cars and drive in. O'Grady is clever. He seldom leaves a trail. Your job is to find O'Grady in Denver, simple as that. Al and his team will help with the capture of the group, then O'Grady will be interrogated by Ryker.

"Return here tomorrow for updates and further briefing," Carr told Erika and Ryker. "You'll leave for Denver from Andrews later in the week."

Part 3

We stand upon the brink of a precipice. We peer into the abyss—we grow sick and dizzy. Our first impulse is to shrink from the danger, and yet, unaccountably, we remain.

—*Edgar Allan Poe, 1845*

Chapter 27

Denver, Colorado
Friday, 30 April 1948

The dubious pair of Erika Lehmann and Axel Ryker flew out late yesterday afternoon from Andrews Air Force base on the Hudson aircraft Leroy Carr normally used for trips within the United States. After a refueling stop and aircraft maintenance check, this time at Fort Leonard Wood in Missouri, they arrived in Denver just as the sun rose in the east.

They were now at the Oxford Hotel. This downtown Denver hotel was the Brown Palace's main competitor for upscale amenities. The hotel dated back to Denver's Wild West days and had been updated into a luxury art deco hotel in the 1920s. Erika was very thankful that Leroy Carr did not force them to share the same suite as he had done at the Mayflower in Washington. In fact, she and Ryker were not even on the same floor. Her room was on the fourth floor, Ryker's on the third. Erika breathed a sigh of relief when they reported to the hotel registration desk where she found out about the accommodations. At least she would have some privacy from the human horror at night.

Two hours after they checked into the hotel, Al Hodge's men showed up at her door. Knowing ahead of time when Erika and Ryker would arrive, and their room numbers, one of Hodge's men had gone to Ryker's room to bring him along. Hodge had six men in Denver, so it was crowded in Erika's one-bedroom suite.

"I'm Agent Houchen," said one of the CIA men. "I'm in charge of Agent Hodge's task force in this city until he arrives." He introduced the other five CIA agents. "Agent Lehmann, I've been told you know the severity of this assignment."

"Yes. Are there any updates you can give me, Agent Houchen?"

"Only that we have been monitoring the airport, the train station, and the Greyhound bus depot. Unfortunately, that's about the only thing we can do at the present. There has been no sign of O'Grady, but as Mr. Carr has briefed you, it is unlikely that he nor any members of a team he has probably assembled could arrive here before tomorrow."

There wasn't much more to discuss, yet the conversation continued for about twenty more minutes. Ryker had basically been left out of the discussion, brought there only to listen. Finally, Houchen told Erika that he and his team were billeting at Lowry Air Force Base and handed her a small piece of paper with a phone number.

Everyone eventually departed and about a half hour later, Erika called the front desk to summon a taxi. It was time for dinner. She told the cabbie to take her to Gaetano's. She looked forward to a good Italian meal and a spirited poker game.

[much later that night; in the wee hours of Saturday morning]
Its voyage from the Mediterranean Sea had taken longer than expected. Foul weather and high seas in the Mid-Atlantic had slowed down the Greek freighter, *Athenia,* but, finally, at around two o'clock in the morning, the rusty freighter pulled into a fog-cloaked Galveston Bay.

Chapter 28

Detroit, Michigan
Sunday, 02 May 1948

Chris Singleton had now been in Detroit for two weeks searching for any clues on the whereabouts of Erika Lehmann. Every alley of the investigation he and his men walked down turned into a dead-end.

Singleton had interviewed Otis several times—the bartender at the wrecked tavern. Otis had feared he would be fired by the tavern's owner but luckily for him that didn't happen. Most of the damage had been limited to tables and chairs (only one window had been smashed out) and it took only a few days for the bar to re-open.

Otis was an intelligent man and over the course of several questionings gave Singleton a detailed account of what happened and a viable description of the white woman who all the trouble surrounded.

Singleton knew from the interrogation of her mark in Evansville in 1943 that Erika had what looked to be a noticeable knife scar on the inside of her upper right arm, but that information was useless. Otis told him she wore a light jacket.

Also, Otis told him the woman spoke with what he thought was some type of accent (unknown to Singleton, Kathryn Fischer who posed as Erika, spoke perfect English, but just a tiny hint of a German accent lingered to an attentive ear). Singleton had questioned Erika Lehmann in Denver and knew she had a perfect American Midwestern accent.

He had asked Otis about her eye color and the bartender had said he thought they were brown. Again, Singleton had questioned her in Denver and knew that her eyes were hazel—and the light shade of hazel where the green was very evident.

To the adroit young FBI agent, even though Erika's fingerprints had been found on the knife, things weren't adding up.

Chapter 29

Washington, D.C.
Monday, 03 May 1948

This time it was Leroy Carr who walked into Al Hodge's office on E Street, instead of the other way around.

As his boss sat down, Hodge asked, "Anything from Denver yet from the pain-in-my-ass Lehmann or her partner, Agent Frankenstein?"

"Nothing yet."

"My men are still monitoring the airport, train, and bus stations twenty-four hours a day," Hodge reported. "Nothing yet from them, either."

"Al, I've got a list here of places that will probably have some type of files on Erika."

"How many can there be, Leroy? The Nazis did a good job of burning up records as the Allies moved in during '45. There's no records on her left in Germany as far as we know. We just had Lehmann steal her FBI files, and in early '46 we burned down the administration building that contained all files at the Evansville Shipyard."

"I know there are some records concerning her at the State Department."

"But if they don't have FBI files to substantiate them, what good are they?" Hodge asked.

"The validity of the State Department's dossiers is definitely weakened, but still they are out there."

Hodge said, "So what I gather from all this is you are going to keep your promise to Lehmann to stump for her citizenship if she thwarts this threat from O'Grady."

"Yes."

"Well, that doesn't surprise me, Leroy. You've always been a man of your word. Still, fulfilling that promise won't be easy."

"I'm aware of that, Al."

◊ ◊ ◊

[same morning—FBI Headquarters]

"Yes, Clyde. What is it?" J. Edgar Hoover said impatiently.

Clyde Tolson had just entered Hoover's office. The Director had been especially irascible and out-of-sorts since the break-in last week.

"We finally found something that is missing from the archive files."

"Well, what the hell is it?" Hoover said intolerantly, almost shouting.

"The file on the investigation in Evansville, Indiana, in 1943 is missing. It contained all of our findings on the woman Agent Singleton found was the Abwehr spy during the war—the one who infiltrated the Naval Shipyard in Indiana."

Hoover stared at Tolson.

Tolson finally said, "Do you think Hillenkoetter is behind this?"

Hoover took his time, but finally answered, "No, Hillenkoetter is just Truman's figurehead. He'd rather be on a golf course or fishing off his boat than sitting behind a desk at the CIA. He would never risk something like a break-in of FBI Headquarters. That fucking OSS jerk Leroy Carr has to be behind this!"

Chapter 30

Denver, Colorado
Wednesday, 05 May 1948

Erika Lehmann and Axel Ryker entered Gaetano's restaurant at just past seven o'clock in the evening. She had received no updates from Al Hodge's men who were covering the public transportation venues in Denver. Erika was handcuffed in a waiting game. There was nothing she could do until Hodge's men gave her a lead, or perhaps even arrest O'Grady on sight if the situation presented itself.

Instead of eating downstairs in the restaurant, she took Ryker directly upstairs. She had more-or-less avoided Ryker since they arrived in Denver last week. She wasn't sure quite why she brought him along to Gaetano's tonight, other than she knew she had to work with him and thought Ryker would fit in with the severe men at the mob restaurant.

The seven-man poker table was full, so they sat down in chairs to wait. Erika doubted Ryker knew anything about poker, but she didn't care. He could lose his money as far as she was concerned.

As usual, Checkers Smaldone was at the table along with other regulars.

One of the players, a large, fierce-looking man who was a Smaldone enforcer called 'Fat Paulie' looked at Ryker. Ryker was wearing his ever-present black porkpie hat that he always kept cocked to one side over his shaven head. It did nothing to hide his hideous facial scars and Ryker didn't care. "Erika," said Fat Paulie, "if that guy is your date, you can do better than that ugly fuck."

Before Erika could stop him, Ryker went over to the man and offered his hand to Paulie as if in friendship.

"Hey, maybe this fuck is okay," Paulie said to the others at the table. He offered his hand to Ryker. It took only seconds for Ryker to squeeze the man's hand until several bones broke and he fell off his chair in agony onto the floor.

Instead of pulling guns, as Erika expected, Checkers and the others at the table broke out in riotous laughter.

[same evening—Albuquerque, New Mexico]

After arriving in Galveston Bay early Saturday morning, Cyril O'Grady and his five men waited in Houston until Monday to buy cars for their drive to Denver. Although the team consisted of only six men, it required four cars for the men and their equipment.

They had taken back roads across Texas and were now only to New Mexico. They would spend the night in Albuquerque and finish their journey to Denver tomorrow.

Chapter 31

[Three days later]
Washington, D.C.
Saturday, 08 May 1948

It was common for both J. Edgar Hoover and Leroy Carr to work on Saturdays, so it was no surprise when they met on a private veranda of the Mayflower Hotel this morning. This was a neutral site since neither were inclined to visit the other man's office. This meeting was at Hoover's request.

Even though it was slightly before noon, both men carried a drink out onto the veranda: Carr a gin and tonic, Hoover a Manhattan.

For a moment they both sat silently, watching the traffic on Connecticut Avenue five stories below. Finally, Hoover spoke.

"Mr. Carr, is there anything you'd feel inclined to tell me about an event that happened at my headquarters last week?"

Carr lit a cigarette. "I don't know anything about what goes on at the FBI, Mr. Hoover."

[same day]

It had taken a few days after the break-in at FBI Headquarters, but eventually J. Edgar Hoover had summoned Agent Singleton back from Detroit to Washington. That happened this past Wednesday.

After Hoover told Singleton about the break-in last week and what was missing—the Abwehr file from Evansville—Singleton was convinced the CIA had tricked the FBI into drawing Singleton away from Denver. Singleton had been suspicious of the fracas at the Detroit tavern for several days. Things weren't adding up. "For some reason," Singleton had said to Hoover two days ago, "they wanted me out of Denver, Director Hoover."

Hoover now agreed.

The tires of Chris Singleton's airplane splashed down on a wet runway at the Denver airport shortly after noon today. Besides

Singleton's airplane, also descending from the clouds was a very cold rain mixed with sleet.

[that evening, the Gaeilge Maighden Pub in Denver, Colorado]

Denver sported a rich history with the Irish. In the 19th century, countless Irish men and their families teemed across the ocean during the potato famine. Many eventually came west, finding jobs working on the Transcontinental Railroad.

In present day Denver, several popular Irish pubs enjoyed brisk business.

The information Erika had been briefed on by Leroy Carr concerning what they knew about Cyril O'Grady wasn't a lot. Besides his prison record in Ireland, upon his release in 1944 he was brought in by the British and warned about his pro-Germany speeches in Dublin. Since Dublin was not in the area of Ireland that the British controlled, all they could do was issue him a warning. O'Grady supported any country or organization that opposed England, and the chastisement from the British fell on deaf ears. O'Grady knew the Brits couldn't arrest him for speeches in that area of Ireland that had declared war neutrality.

Carr also told Erika that reports were that O'Grady had a fondness for Irish Pubs.

With still nothing to go on from Al Hodge's men, that last bit of information about O'Grady led her to frequent some of the more popular Irish pubs in Denver. She got a list of pub names from the Oxford Hotel concierge. On previous nights, she had stopped in and dawdled for a while at O'Leary's, The Scrum, and the Red Fox. She had left Ryker behind. The last thing she wanted was to deal with him on a scouting mission.

Tonight, her taxi dropped her off at the Gaeilge Maighden. The words were Gaelic for 'Irish Maiden.' Regular customers usually referred to it in the English translation.

Erika ran into the pub through the still vigorous sleet, walked to the bar and sat down. Two men sat four stools away, at the end of the bar, talking over drams of whiskey. One looked older than his mugshot, but Erika immediately recognized Cyril O'Grady.

She ordered a Guinness with her German accent.

Chapter 32

The Irish Maiden Pub, Denver
Same night—Saturday, 08 1948

Erika avoided looking at O'Grady. After about fifteen minutes, when she was almost finished with her first Guinness, she ordered another, again with a German accent. Finally, she nonchalantly glanced to the right, and then to the left and caught O'Grady looking at her. The man next to him continued talking but O'Grady seemed to be ignoring him. Erika smiled very briefly at O'Grady then turned away.

She ignored him from then on. When she finished her second Guinness she summoned the bartender. "I'm finished. I'll pay for my drinks now," she said. As she began getting out her money, O'Grady interrupted.

"Her drinks are on me, bartender." His Irish accent was strong.

Erika looked at him and said, "I will pay for my own drinks."

O'Grady rose from his barstool, walked over and stood beside her. "May I sit down?"

Erika acted like she had to think about it for a moment, then finally said, "You can sit were you want to sit."

"You're from Germany?" O'Grady asked as he deposited himself on the empty stool next to her.

"Yes, and you are from Ireland. Now we both have figured out each other's accents. I will gather that you do not hate Germans like so many others, blaming us for the war. If you did, you wouldn't offer to buy my drinks." She added the phrase 'blaming us for the war' for a reason. This would hint to O'Grady that she was not apologetic; something she thought would work to her favor with the IRA fanatic.

"I like the Germans," O'Grady said. He didn't elaborate and tell her why. It didn't matter because Erika knew why. Leroy Carr had told her O'Grady had been a vocal supporter of Germany during the war.

"Since you won't let me buy your beers, may I treat you to dinner?"

"I've already eaten dinner," she said.

"They have very good bangers and mash here. I had some last night. We could split a serving if you're less than hungry."

She looked at him and smiled. "You Irish are persistent, aren't you?"

"With a beautiful lass, yes."

Erika figured she had played hard-to-get long enough to keep his interest and better stop now. "I might like that."

O'Grady smiled and waved over the bartender. He ordered a serving of bangers and mash and told the man they were moving to a table. O'Grady looked at the man he had been sitting with, lifted his hand, and with his thumb pointed to the door. The man got up and walked out of the pub. Erika knew then that the man was one of O'Grady's team. She placed in her memory a detailed description of his accomplice.

All tables were occupied, but O'Grady noticed an empty booth. After they slid in across from one another, he said, "By the way, my name is Cyril O'Grady."

Erika was shocked he used his real name but didn't show it. He was bold; there could be no denying that. O'Grady was a very common Irish name; he probably felt safe in that regard. Nevertheless, it also told her he had no concern that anyone knew anything about his presence in America. *Leroy Carr's Mr. Beckman is very good at what he does*, she thought.

From her standpoint, it would be counterproductive for her to use an alias. She would eventually reveal to him parts of her back ground at Abwehr in hopes he would allow her into his circle. There was no way he would find out about her activities with the Americans since the war. Leroy Carr had taken good care of that, even as far as withholding knowledge of her when it came to the U.S. Congressional Committee on Intelligence.

"My name is Erika Lehmann."

They shook hands. Neither had a drink.

"I noticed you were drinking Guinness," he said. "Do you drink whiskey?"

"Occasionally."

O'Grady looked around, got the attention of one of the pub's two waitresses, and flagged her over.

"Maureen, we've already ordered a plate of bangers and mash from the bar. While we wait, we'll have two Jamesons with just one ice cube in a separate glass and a spoon."

When the waitress walked away, Erika said, "You know the name of the waitress. You must come here often."

"Just for the past couple of days," O'Grady said. "I arrived here just a few days ago. I'm here visiting a cousin I was close to when we were growing up in Ireland. And you? What brings you here?"

Erika shrugged. "After I arrived in America a year ago, I've been living in Cincinnati. There is a large German heritage community there. But I came here just over a month ago. I grew up in Bavaria and spent much of my childhood in the Alps."

"What do you do . . . here in Denver, that is?"

"In Cincinnati I worked in a Woolworth's department store selling perfumes and cosmetics, but I've yet to find a job here."

O'Grady was a handsome, fit man in his mid-30s. His hair was brown. Erika had not been able to distinguish his eye color from the black and white mug shot Carr had given her. She now knew his eyes were green. Greener than her light-hazel eyes. She did notice a small scar, probably about an inch long, on the left side of his chin. She had a knife wound on the inside of one her arms and thought his looked similar.

The waitress delivered the drinks.

"I'll show you how an Irishman from County Cork drinks whiskey." O'Grady took the spoon, scooped up the ice cube and dropped it into one of the drams of whiskey. "You let it set for ten or fifteen seconds then take it out." That's what O'Grady did, then he handed it to Erika before he prepared his. She waited for him to take the cube out of his glass.

"Erin go Bragh and Deutschland ober Alles," was his toast.

Erika smiled agreeably at his toast of 'Ireland be Free' and 'Germany over All.' She clinked her glass with his just before Maureen delivered the plate of bangers and mash.

Chit chat followed as they both ate from the same plate that sat midway between them. When they finished, O'Grady ordered them another whiskey.

"This is my last one," Erika said. "Then I'll say goodnight."

"May I see you again, Erika?" O'Grady asked with an aggressive look in his eyes.

"You can call me tomorrow if you wish. I'm staying at the Oxford Hotel, room 460."

"The Oxford Hotel?" O'Grady seemed surprised. "Isn't that expensive? Especially for someone out of work?" He had done his research on Denver. He wondered how an out-of-work store clerk could afford such a hotel.

"I inherited some money from my father. He was a top official at Joseph Goebbels' Propaganda Ministry during the war."

This was true; although, her money was in a Zurich bank. That she had some money hidden might be the only thing Leroy Carr didn't know about her.

O'Grady looked resolutely at her. "I will call you tomorrow. Thank you, Erika. You've given me a wonderful evening." The waitress came by and O'Grady went about his ritual with the ice cube preparing their last drink.

Chapter 33

Annapolis, Maryland
Sunday, 09 May 1948

As he had done in the past (too many times to count), Al Hodge woke Leroy Carr at home with a very early morning telephone call. It was not yet two o'clock.

"Yes," Carr said into the receiver as he sat up on the edge of the bed.

"Leroy, it's me."

"What a surprise," Carr quipped. "I thought it might be the Chinese food delivery man. What's up, Al?"

"Lehmann found O'Grady."

Carr stood up. "Keep going."

"You know I can't stand that broad, but I have to give her credit. She called me around midnight. Beckman said in his briefing that O'Grady has a penchant for Irish pubs, so Lehmann spent the past week or so visiting them around Denver. This evening she spotted him sitting at a bar with another guy Erika has reason to believe is a member of his team. The sonuvabitch didn't arrive here by plane, train, or bus. My guys have been covering those places like a polar bear skin on an Eskimo. They must have driven in."

"So what's the current status?" Carr asked.

"Lehmann flirted with him a bit and they ended up having a couple of drinks together. He told her he'd call her later today. The guy told her his real name. Figure that one out."

"Did she tell him the name of her hotel?"

"Yep. She's going to try and get O'Grady to let her into his inner circle."

"Was Ryker with her at the pub?"

"No, she left his ass back at the hotel."

"Okay, it looks like you're heading to the Mile High City, Al."

"One more thing, Leroy. Lehmann requested that Marienne Schenk be flown out to Denver immediately."

Marienne Schenk worked for the OSS during the war and made herself a reputation for being the agency's best shadow. It seemed

Marienne could follow anyone without them ever knowing it even if they were wary of being followed.

"Who does Erika want tailed?" Carr asked.

"She wasn't sure. She told me she had to find out more but is confident she'll need Marienne sooner or later. She knows Ryker can't tail anyone."

"Ryker's good at tailing someone in a car if he's in a following car, but she's right about him if the mark is walking. Ryker can't shadow anyone on foot. He sticks out like a rhino in a group of house cats. I'll contact Marienne and find out if she'll do it. If so, she can fly out with you."

Marienne Schenk did not work for the CIA, at least not regularly. She and her husband now ran a successful river barge tugboat business in Pittsburgh and had started a family. The wartime OSS's best shadow had agreed to a job or two after the war when Carr requested, but not always. She had turned him down on a couple of occasions.

"What's next on the agenda, Al? You mentioned O'Grady is supposed to call Erika, right?"

"That's what she told me."

"Okay, call me with another report as soon as you get one," Carr instructed. "Contact Erika and tell her you're coming and that I'll get Marienne for her. When I brief Marienne about what is at stake, she'll agree. Remind Erika that she has help available from your men out there right now if she needs it. She knows that but remind her anyway."

"Yeah, my men in Denver know how to tail someone. I told her that, but she kept insisting on Marienne. Typical Lehmann—anything to be a pain in the ass."

"Al, you can't blame Erika for wanting Marienne. You know the gravity of this mission."

"I know. You're right, Leroy. It's just that when it comes to Lehmann, nothing ever comes easy."

[Same day—10:00 a.m., Pittsburgh, Pennsylvania]

Leroy Carr entered an office in a building on the banks of the Allegheny River near where that river and the Monongahela fed into each other to form the mighty Ohio River. Carr had called ahead before he boarded the airplane for the short, ninety-minute flight from Washington.

When he entered, Marienne Schenk rose from the chair behind her desk and circled around to give Carr a hug.

"Leroy, what a treat to get your call this morning, and of course to have you here. I don't think you've ever been here to our company before."

"No, I haven't," said Carr. "It looks like you and Harold have quite the operation here." Harold was her husband.

Marienne poured Carr a cup of coffee from a pot resting on a Bunsen Burner that sat on a small table by the window.

"There's cream and sugar there, but I remember you take your coffee black."

Carr smiled. "Thanks."

"Have a seat, Leroy." They both sat down.

"So how have you been, Marienne?"

"We're doing well. God has been kind to us. Our daughter turned one-year-old last month." Marienne was in her mid-thirties.

"That's wonderful."

A brief lull in the conversation followed. Finally, the former OSS super shadow said, "Leroy, you didn't tell me anything on the phone this morning but I'm assuming you didn't fly here from Washington to take me to lunch."

"That's right, Marienne."

"It must be important. You've never come here before. Since I resigned the OSS and moved here, when you wanted my help you've always asked me to come to Washington for a briefing."

"Marienne, we need your help now more than ever. I cannot overstate how much. We have a situation that could cost many thousands of Americans their lives or health. It's an attack on American soil. Something that hasn't happened since Pearl Harbor and this time we're not talking about an attack on an American territory far away like Hawaii. This is an attack here in the continental United States."

Carr had made sure Marienne had retained her security clearance since she had served occasionally after the war. He briefed her about

Denver, O'Grady, and the chemical weapons at the Rocky Mountain Arsenal.

Carr ended with, "Erika has asked for you specifically and I agree. Your country is at risk. The United States needs your help, Marienne."

[four o'clock that afternoon]

Erika had been back in her hotel room no more than fifteen minutes when the phone rang.

"Yes," she said after she picked up.

"Madam, this is Sofia at the switchboard. I have a phone call for you from a Mr. O'Grady. He's called several times this afternoon."

"I'll take the call, Sofia. Thank you."

Erika heard a series of clicks.

"Hello," she said.

"Erika, this is Cyril."

"Oh, hello, Cyril."

"I've called several times. I'm glad I finally reached you."

"I went out for lunch then did a bit of shopping."

"I hope you'll agree to let me take you to dinner."

"That sounds fine, Cyril. I would like that."

"The place I'd like to take you is about an hour drive from Denver. It's in the mountains. You told me you came out here from Cincinnati because you grew up near the Alps and enjoyed the mountains. I thought you might like this place."

"That's sweet of you."

"I haven't eaten at this place, but I understand it has a reputation for the finest steaks. If I pick you up at six, we can be there by seven."

"What are the dress requirements?"

"I'm told it's not formal. I plan on wearing a suit jacket but not a tie."

"I think I have an appropriate dress. I'll be ready. If you'll wait in my hotel lobby, I'll come down at six and see you then." O'Grady seemed pleased and the conversation ended.

Erika had told Axel Ryker nothing about finding O'Grady yesterday. She picked up the phone and asked the switchboard operator to connect her to his room.

When he picked up, she said, "Ryker, I'm going out tonight. Do what you want to do tonight, just don't put anyone in the hospital, and do not be anywhere near the hotel lobby at six o'clock. I'll brief you sometime tomorrow."

"Whatever you say, Sonderführer." He again used her Abwehr rank that she had ordered him not to use when referring to her.

She slammed down the phone.

Chapter 34

Denver
Same day—Sunday, 09 May 1948

Cyril O'Grady told the man behind the wheel to pull up in front of the hotel and wait. The time was 5:45 p.m. When the Oxford Hotel valet appeared, O'Grady was already out of the car.

"I'll park that for you, sir," the teenage valet said. Apparently, the kid hadn't noticed the driver.

"The car will stay where it is," O'Grady said as he handed the boy a $10 bill. The teenager's eyes spread open. His average parking tip was a quarter, maybe a quarter and a dime from the generous.

"Yes, sir!"

The doorman held the door for O'Grady as he entered the lobby. He quickly looked around. She was not there (he knew he was early) so he found a seat on an upholstered chair in a circle of chairs and sofas not far from the registration desk.

O'Grady had found himself bewitched by the German woman. Not only was she beautiful and intelligent, during their brief meeting at the Gaeilge Maighden Pub last night he got the impression she shared his hatred for the British.

Six o'clock came and went. At last, he saw her descending the stairs at fifteen minutes past the hour. He rose and walked to joined her. She smiled.

"I know I'm a few minutes late, Cyril. I apologize. Women have so much to do. I envy you men. All you have to do is shave and throw on your clothes."

She looked lovely. Her yellow dress nearly matched her bright blonde hair. The dress revealed just enough cleavage to be charming but not overly tantalizing. A pale blue belt forced the dress to hug her figure. It was still cool in Denver, so over the top of the dress she wore a pale blue cardigan that matched her belt, open in the front, and dropping only to her waist. (Knowing O'Grady would call, these were the clothes Erika had shopped for earlier in the day.) Her makeup was understated. Unlike the bright red lipstick that was popular among women of that day, hers was light pink. Her nails matched the lipstick and she wore some frugal mascara but no eye shadow or fake eyelashes.

He wore dark gray pants, white shirt, and a lighter gray blazer.

"You certainly look enchanting, Erika."

"Thank you, Cyril."

"Our car is waiting."

She took his arm as they walked out onto the street. O'Grady opened the back door for her. She ducked in and he slid in beside her. Erika immediately looked at the driver. He was not the man she had seen O'Grady with at the Irish Maiden last night. This man was much younger and looked like he might be a Turk or a Greek. O'Grady didn't introduce them, but when O'Grady said his name, she assumed the man was Greek.

"We can go now, Petros."

"You have a car and driver?" Erika asked, acting astonished. "Am I being treated to dinner by a rich man?"

O'Grady chuckled. "No, Petros is a friend who agreed to drive, that's all. I hope that doesn't disappoint you."

She touched his arm and smiled. "Don't be silly." Erika sat directly behind Petros so a good view of his face couldn't be had, but she'd get a better look at him when they arrived at the restaurant. Surely the young Greek must be another member of O'Grady's team.

◊ ◊ ◊

Axel Ryker walked two blocks from the Oxford to a striptease club on Market Street called the *Thirsty Tiger Gentlemen's Club.* With the luxury Oxford Hotel close by, this area of Market Street was a perfect location for a club with scantily-clad women on stage. Out of town men who could afford to stay at the Oxford had money in their pockets.

It was an easy matter for Ryker to stay out of trouble in such places. Only the extremely foolish would bother Axel Ryker once they got a look at him.

Most of the men sat at tables near the stage watching a voluptuous redheaded belly dancer twirling tassels attached to her pasties. From her waist down she wore a green harem girl skirt. Ryker picked a seat at the bar where only one other man sat near the other end. The man was too far away to bore Ryker with conversation, something he always preferred.

The bartender approached and asked Ryker what he was having. "Vodka."

"On the rocks?" the man asked.

"Just Vodka and a glass," Ryker growled, "and set the bottle in front of me."

◊ ◊ ◊

The *El Dorado* restaurant sat high on a mountain of that name west and out of sight of Denver. The El Dorado mountain wasn't one of the Rocky Mountains' tallest peaks. Those were still farther west; still, the elevation was nearly 9000 feet, making the air even thinner than the air of the Mile High City, the city that earned its nickname because the 13th step of the capitol building was 5,280 feet above sea level.

Petros pulled the car to a stop in front of the restaurant's door. He stayed behind the wheel. O'Grady got out and held the car door for Erika as she slid over and emerged.

As she exited, she got a good look at the driver. "Isn't Petros joining us?" Erika asked O'Grady.

"No, he'll wait in the car." He offered his arm, Erika took it, and they walked into the restaurant.

The El Dorado sported a rustic, mountain cabin look with exposed, heavy timber rafters and stained, wood plank walls. The floor matched the walls and even the tables looked like they had been roughly hewn by a mountain man. In true Wild West style, the El Dorado did not bother with a hostess. The place was busy, but not packed. O'Grady spotted a table and escorted Erika to it.

Despite its rough-and-tumble Wild West setting, the El Dorado was a place worthy of its high regard among those who had previously dined there. A waitress appeared at their table almost immediately. She wore a cowgirl outfit complete with cowboy boots and cowboy hat. She handed Erika and O'Grady a menu.

"What can I bring you to drink?" she asked.

O'Grady looked at Erika. "I'll have what you're having," he said to her.

"Do you have Asbach brandy?" Erika asked the waitress.

"No, I'm sorry, we have no brandy."

"Then I'll have wine," Erika said.

"I'll have the same," O'Grady interjected. "Bring us a bottle of one of your finest reds. I'll put my trust in your decision."

"Yes, sir," the waitress said then walked away.

Instead of idle chat, Erika opened her menu folder right away. Watching her, O'Grady did the same. He scanned the list of entrées for a moment, then asked, "It says here 'Buffalo Steaks'. Do you know what that means?"

Erika answered, "'Buffalo' is what the Americans call bison."

◊ ◊ ◊

Ryker had downed only one Vodka at the Thirsty Tiger when the woman came over and sat down on the bar stool next to him. She was a brunette who looked to be in her mid-20s and wore a low-cut, shimmering red dress that revealed a lot of leg and cleavage.

"Hello," she said to Ryker. "My name is Roxanne. Would you like some company?" She was thin and not what most would consider a classic beauty, but her hair and makeup were done nicely, not gaudy like many of the other women in the club.

Ryker ignored her as he downed his shooter of Vodka. Roxanne stood up with the intention of walking away when Ryker grabbed her arm. "Remain seated," he said rather gruffly, then he softened his tone. "Please. What will be your drink?"

"Champagne."

The bartender was near, and Ryker ordered her drink. The man brought over a bottle and a glass. "That's $15, bub," he said to Ryker as he poured. All Ryker had to do was look at the man. "I mean, $15, sir," the bartender stuttered out.

"You are cheating me," Ryker told him, "but I will pay your price if that is real champagne."

The bartender thought it in his best interest to quickly take away the glass of carbonated white grape juice. He brought over and poured Roxanne a glass of real champagne. Roxanne was in on the swindle, of course. Her job at the Thirsty Tiger demanded she soak the male clients for expensive drinks. The grape juice was passed off as champagne in the drinks given to the girls; tea became whiskey.

Roxanne couldn't keep herself from smiling. She always considered the bartender an ass who scammed part of her tips. Even though none of this would help her financially to support her young son—any tips given her from the scary man beside her would be divided up by the bartender who took his cut first. Nevertheless, she enjoyed seeing the fear in the bartender's eyes. "Thank you," she said to Ryker.

◊ ◊ ◊

The buffalo steaks at the El Dorado were huge and over an inch thick. So big that a steak had to be served on a plate by itself. The rest of the meal: sweet potato, a biscuit, a cob of corn, and a generous helping of steamed pea pods, was served on a second plate. Both Erika and Cyril O'Grady had ordered their steaks medium rare.

Erika took a sip of wine before she began eating.

O'Grady spoke. "You didn't tell me much about yourself last night at the pub. I want to know more about Erika Lehmann."

"I don't like to speak of my past, Cyril. I hope you'll understand."

"Why not?"

"I'm afraid you'd be shocked."

O'Grady looked at her as he cut into his steak.

Chapter 35

Denver, Colorado
Next day—Monday, 10 May 1948

Cyril O'Grady and his men were laying low in two cabins a few miles south of Evergreen, Colorado. Evergreen was a small mountain town in the Rocky Mountain foothills west of Denver. Only one of the cabins had phone service—the cabin where O'Grady and two of his men slept. O'Grady had made a telephone call three hours earlier to Juárez, Mexico. Stationed there temporarily was the top lieutenant of the man who had hired O'Grady and his team of mercenaries. The phone rang in O'Grady's cabin and he answered.

"Here is the information on Erika Lehmann, the subject on whom you requested information," the man on the other end said in perfect English. *"She was an Abwehr spy during the war, a committed Nazi who is now being hunted by Allied war crimes tribunals and the new State of Israel."*

There was a pause before O'Grady said, "Very well." Then he promptly hung up the telephone.

A few minutes later, O'Grady called the Oxford Hotel. The switchboard patched him through to Erika's room.

O'Grady recognized her voice when she said, *"Hello."*

"Erika, this is Cyril."

"Hello, Cyril."

"I very much enjoyed our dinner last night."

"So did I," she said.

"May I see you again? How about tonight for a movie? Your choice."

There was a pause. *"I guess that's fine, Cyril."*

"I'll pick you up at your hotel at eight." The current time was three in the afternoon.

"That will be nice."

Two hours later a large bouquet of flowers was delivered to Erika's room. The small card confirmed it was from O'Grady.

◊ ◊ ◊

Erika checked the movie listings in the Denver Post. Then, instead of summoning Axel Ryker to her room, she descended one floor of the Oxford Hotel to his room. Until now, she had told Ryker nothing about finding Cyril O'Grady.

When Ryker answered his door, she walked in and looked around, curious as to how Ryker kept up a hotel room. She rather expected a mess, with clothes scattered helter-skelter, but the room was relatively neat. A smell of cheap perfume lingered in the air.

"What did you do, Ryker? Did you have a woman in here last night?"

"I hired one, yes." Roxanne had charged him $20.

"Tell me you didn't hurt her, Ryker! We can't afford police getting involved."

"Don't worry, Sonderführer."

"I do worry when it comes to you."

"We made an agreement and she left satisfied with the money I paid her."

Erika tried to imagine what kind of woman would have the nerve, or the stomach, to bed Axel Ryker. She put the thought out of her mind. "Sit down and I'll brief you.

"I found Cyril O'Grady Saturday night at an Irish pub here in Denver."

"You only now tell me?"

"It wasn't necessary that I tell you until now. Capturing and interrogating O'Grady before we can identify his team could work against us. If they're as professional as we've been told, they'll have alternative plans in place if anyone is captured, even if it's O'Grady himself."

"How are we proceeding?" Ryker asked.

"I'm going to a movie tonight with O'Grady. I'm attempting to gain his confidence and perhaps learn more about his plans or his team."

"What reason would he have to allow you to get that close? That would be the opposite of professional."

"He supported Germany during the war. I'm going to tell him about my past." (Erika didn't know that O'Grady had already found out.) "You get to go to work tonight, Ryker. You'll need a woman with you. I hope you know how to get in touch with your prostitute?"

Chapter 36

Denver, Colorado
That evening—Monday, 10 May 1948

Built in 1930, the Mayan Theatre was located on Broadway. Showing first run or very popular newer releases, the Mayan was Denver's most fashionable movie theater. Tonight, the feature film was *The Lady from Shanghai* starring Rita Hayworth and Orson Welles.

O'Grady had picked up Erika in a taxi. After the Irishman bought their tickets, Erika said as they passed the concession stand, "Americans always eat their popcorn at film theatres."

O'Grady bought two sacks of popcorn and two Coca-Cola's. A teenage usher with a flashlight found them two seats near the middle of the theatre, four rows from the front.

"What is your favorite American movie, Erika?" O'Grady asked as they settled in their seats.

"That's a tough question, Cyril. One of my favorites is the *The Blue Angel* with Marlene Dietrich but that's a German film. *Ecstasy* with Hedy Lamarr is also a favorite but that's also not a Hollywood film. I guess I'm not answering your question, am I? As far as American films I enjoy just about anything with Greta Garbo in it. And you?"

O'Grady shrugged. "I haven't seen many films over the past several years, but I like Maureen O'Hara."

The theater darkened, and the introductory credits of *The Lady of Shanghai* began rolling. In the back of the theater, on a dark balcony over the main floor, Roxanne sat eating popcorn next to Axel Ryker. The prostitute reflected on her good luck. She had never been paid to watch a movie until now.

Two hours later, when the movie ended, Erika asked O'Grady if they could stay through the intermission before the beginning of the second movie of the double feature.

"I love the *Three Stooges,*" she said. The Stooges short began and O'Grady watched the insane antics of Curly, Larry, and Moe. Erika had a reason for requesting the delay in walking out of the theater.

[same time]

The sun had set an hour earlier as Marienne Schenk and her husband waited on the tarmac when Al Hodge's plane set down at the Pittsburgh airport. Harold carried her suitcase to the airplane as the props still whirled dangerously. The pilot never cut the engines. The side door opened, and Al Hodge stood at the top of the small set of five metal stairs that the ground crew had rolled up. Marienne hugged her husband, took her bag, and climbed the stairs into the airplane.

Fifteen minutes later the wheels of Hodge's Hudson left the ground and the plane banked sharply in the night sky over the lights of Pittsburgh on its journey west.

◊ ◊ ◊

When the taxi pulled up in front of Erika's hotel, she asked O'Grady if he'd like to join her for a cup of coffee. This they had in the Oxford Hotel's coffee shop that stayed open until midnight. Apparently, many hotel guests felt 11:00 p.m. was not too late for coffee; the small café was at least half full.

When they finished the coffee, Erika took a last sip and asked, "Cyril, would you like to go up to my room?"

During her days at Abwehr, Erika used any means necessary to extract information from her mark. She had gone to bed with diplomats, and sometimes enemy spies. She told Leroy Carr she was not going to engage in any more 'siren' work after her husband died. She was willing to break her own rule if it would help accomplish the mission: keep thousands from dying and allow her to gain citizenship and bring her daughter to America.

Chapter 37

Denver, Colorado
Tuesday, 11 May 1948

Cyril O'Grady left Erika's room at just before seven o'clock this morning. It was in bed when she told him about her past, and she told him a great deal: her father's friendship with Adolf Hitler, her friendship with Eva Braun, and some details about her various missions for German Military Intelligence during the war. Everything she told him was true.

"I took the blood oath to Hitler and conducted missions against both the British and the Americans. I'm a wanted woman, Cyril," she had said. "That's why I have to move around often. You'd be wise to forget about me. We had a nice night. Let's leave it there."

O'Grady hadn't seemed surprised or put off. Instead telling her he wanted to see her again. "I'll call you, Erika."

Fifteen minutes after O'Grady left, she called Ryker's room.

"Is that woman there?" Erika asked him.

"No."

"Are you dressed?"

"Nearly," Ryker answered.

"Finish dressing and report to my room."

[same time]
The weather had cooperated during the entire flight from Pittsburgh, and the refueling stop at Fort Leonard Wood had been completed quickly.

The Lockheed Hudson carrying Al Hodge and Marienne Schenk touched down at Lowry Air Force Base on a cool but beautiful Colorado spring morning.

◊ ◊ ◊

"Did anyone follow us out of the theatre?" Erika asked Ryker. His simple assignment last night was to watch as she and O'Grady left. That was her reason for telling O'Grady she wanted to watch the *Three Stooges* short—to allow the crowd to thin out. Erika ordered Ryker not to follow them outside as Ryker was too conspicuous to be an effective tail on foot. It would ruin everything if O'Grady spotted a shadow.

"No one followed you out who might be considered suspicious," Ryker answered.

"And you had the woman with you?" A single man, especially a man like Ryker, sitting alone in a theater would draw more attention than a couple.

"Yes."

"Having no one follow us out makes it apparent that O'Grady doesn't think he needs body guards following him around. He's bold, that's clear. And that's good for us."

"What is next?" Ryker asked.

"O'Grady told me he'd call me today. Also, Al Hodge and a woman you've never met are scheduled to arrive here in Denver today. We'll meet with them."

"Who is this woman?"

"You'll find out when you meet her."

[three hours later]

The CIA still had the apartment in Golden under rent, under a pseudonym, of course. This is where Hodge, Marienne, Erika and Ryker met after Hodge and Marienne picked them up at a bus stop outside a department store several blocks from the Oxford. The Oxford was avoided in case O'Grady was having the hotel watched. Both Hodge and Marienne drove separate cars. Erika rode with Marienne; Ryker with Hodge.

When they reached the apartment in Golden they huddled around the kitchen table. Marienne had never met Ryker and couldn't help but stare at him. He simply glowered back at her and asked Hodge, "Who is this woman?"

"Her name is Marienne Schenk," Hodge answered. "She's our best shadow. Now let's get to business." Hodge redirected his attention to Erika. "Give me an update."

"I think I'm gaining O'Grady's confidence. How much? I'm not sure."

"Do you have any idea where he and his team are holed up?" Hodge asked.

"No, not yet. I have to be careful of the questions I ask him."

"What's your take on O'Grady?"

"He can be charming and funny. That makes him even more intimidating when you know what he is here to do."

"What's our next step in your opinion?"

She looked at Marienne. "I might have to ask Marienne to do something very dangerous."

Hodge asked, "What is that?"

"I'm not sure yet, Al. First, I have to go dark for a while."

Hodge instantly objected. "You're not going off the radar, Erika! You can forget that idea right now! Leroy and I are both tired of the chaos you cause when you go dark." Going 'dark' was a CIA euphemism for a CIA agent going deep undercover with no contact with the agency.

Hodge switched gears and looked at Ryker. "What have you been doing since you got to Denver?"

"I have obeyed my orders from Fräulein Lehmann. That is what Herr Carr and you instructed me to do. You know I am a professional. If you did not believe this I would not be here, yes?"

Hodge looked at Erika and reiterated. "None of this going dark, Erika. You could end up dead and we wouldn't know it. Then we'd have to start all over and in the meantime O'Grady could complete his mission. Marienne will stay here at this apartment. I'll be at Lowry. I want you to contact me or Marienne daily with an update. We brought two cars. You can have one. Marienne will take me back to Lowry then return here and keep the second car for her use. My men have cars so that takes care of me.

"But I repeat, you are not authorized to go dark, Erika. Is that understood?"

"Yes."

Eventually, Erika and Ryker took one of the cars and headed back into downtown Denver and the Oxford Hotel so Erika would be in her room for O'Grady's phone call.

As Marienne drove Hodge back to Lowry, she started to speak and Hodge held up his hand. "You don't have to say it, Marienne. I know Lehmann's going to go dark regardless of what I said. She has a reason for wanting you here. That's the only cards we hold. We'll have to wait until she contacts you. In the meantime, I want you to start hanging out at a restaurant called Gaetano's in the evenings. It's a mob hangout and Lehmann has an affinity for the place and she knows I know that. Lehmann will realize that my only move is to send you there to look for her after she goes dark, so I figure she'll show up to talk to you."

[that night]

Erika had stayed in her hotel room all afternoon and well into the evening waiting on Cyril O'Grady to call. She had even ordered room service for dinner so she would be in her room. Hour after hour passed until she began to think he wouldn't call at all. It was after eleven o'clock as she began preparing for bed when her phone rang. She told the hotel switchboard operator to put the call through.

"Erika, this is Cyril. I apologize for calling so late. It's been a busy day. May I take you to lunch tomorrow?"

Chapter 38

Denver
Wednesday, 12 May 1948

Al Hodge was on the telephone with Leroy Carr. It was 6:00 a.m. in Denver and 8:00 a.m. in Washington.

"Leroy, Marienne and I met with Lehmann and Ryker yesterday."

"How'd it go?"

"Lehmann said she might have to ask Marienne to do something very dangerous but wouldn't elaborate. When I pressed her, she said she wasn't sure what it would be, which is bullshit. Also, she has apparently built some type of kinship with O'Grady and she wants to go dark."

"What was your answer?"

"I told her no, of course, but you know Lehmann."

"That's okay, Al. If Erika has developed some sort of bond with O'Grady that's a good thing. Has she disappeared yet?

"Not as far as I know, but she will."

"What's your plan when she does?" Carr asked.

"Marienne is going to hang out at the mob restaurant that Lehmann can't seem to keep away from. The one you and I met her at that night when you were here in Denver. Lehmann made sure we knew about that restaurant for a reason. She's setting us up. She knows I'll send Marienne there to look for her, and she's right. That's the only avenue I'll have when she submerges, and Lehmann knows that."

"Sounds like she wants a face-to-face with Marienne without you around."

"Yep."

"Erika is too smart to underestimate you, Al. She knows that you'll figure that out."

"Should I have my men stake out that restaurant and bring her in?"

There was a pause in Washington. *"No, she's expert at spotting anything like that. Leave her alone for now. Marienne will fill us in. What about Ryker? Has he committed any mayhem yet?"*

"So far it looks like he's obeying Lehmann's orders."

"Okay, keep me posted, Al. I can send you more men or we can mobilize the National Guard or send in Army Rangers if needed. We'll do whatever it takes to stop O'Grady and his men. I've used back channels to put the Rocky Mountain Arsenal security troops on high alert."

[noon]

Lunch for Erika and O'Grady was at a café within walking distance of the Oxford Hotel. Instead of picking her up at the hotel, he had asked if they could meet at the café. O'Grady was already seated when Erika arrived. She had spotted a tail during her walk, which she ignored. She now knew why O'Grady requested that they meet at the café, and she also knew that he was having her hotel watched. That was a good sign. The bold O'Grady was now being more cautious, which might mean he was considering taking her into his confidence. It also told her it was time for her to leave the Oxford Hotel and go undercover. She hoped to convince O'Grady that she needed his help.

Erika sat down in the chair beside him and used her considerable acting skills to appear edgy.

"Hello, Erika. Thanks for meeting me here."

"Hello, Cyril." She looked around nervously.

"Is there something wrong?"

"I'm sorry. No, everything is fine."

O'Grady watched her closely as she picked up a menu that already laid on the table. She scanned it for a brief moment then again looked around.

"Something is wrong, Erika. What is it?"

"Let's just order quickly," she said impatiently.

O'Grady grabbed his hat that he had placed on another chair, stood up, and dropped a couple of dollars on the table even though nothing had yet been ordered. "Let's go for a walk."

She rose quickly and they left the café.

As they walked she stopped to adjust her shoe and glanced casually behind her. O'Grady was no fool. She knew that would be enough.

O'Grady said, "You think you're being followed, that's it, isn't it?"

She sighed as they again started walking. "Yes. I received a lot of training before the war on how to spot a shadow at Quenzsee, the German spy school outside Berlin. He's still back there, a block behind us."

Knowing it was his man, and that the man was experienced in tailing people, O'Grady was impressed. "Who do you think it is?"

"It has to be the FBI. Who else could it be? I told you I'm wanted by the Americans and that it would be best for you to forget about me. I have to get out of this town, Cyril. I'm going to duck into one of these stores. If you'll go in with me, you can stay in there. I'll make my way out the back into an alley and you'll be done with me. It's best for you, believe me."

"I don't think that will be necessary, Erika."

"What do you mean?"

"Let's return to your hotel and you can gather your things."

She looked at him curiously. "I can't do that. It's obvious that the FBI knows I'm staying there."

"Let's go back to your hotel; you can pack your bag and checkout. I'll pay for any charges you still owe and have Petros pick us up."

"Don't worry about that man behind us," O'Grady continued. "You don't have to leave town. Actually, there is no real reason you have to leave the Oxford, but I can tell you are uncomfortable, so I'll get you another place to stay to ease your mind."

"I don't understand," Erika said.

"Trust me."

Chapter 39

Denver, Colorado
Thursday, 13 May 1948

"It didn't take long, Leroy. Lehmann's gone. She checked out of her hotel yesterday afternoon. I just found out about it since we're not monitoring the hotel in case one of my men might be spotted by O'Grady. Ryker claims he knows nothing about it; and, knowing Lehmann, he probably doesn't."

"*Alright, Al,*" Carr said from Washington. "*Tell Ryker to stay put at the Oxford. If he leaves the hotel, tell him to let the front desk know where he's going in case you need to get in touch with him quickly. Time to start sending Marienne to Gaetano's.*"

[one hour later]
Chris Singleton walked up to the front desk, placed his suitcase on the floor, and checked into the Brown Palace Hotel. He had convinced Hoover that luring him to Detroit was a set up. There had to be a reason the CIA wanted him out of Denver, and he knew it had to be something to do with Erika Lehmann.

◊ ◊ ◊

Erika had hoped that O'Grady might take her to his lair, but that didn't happen. In fact, he had not even offered an explanation for his willingness to help her. Obviously, he was still wary. After she checked out of the Oxford, O'Grady had Petros drive them to a small bed and breakfast in Lakewood, a small community—a suburb—just west of Denver. There he had deposited her and left, telling her only that he would be in touch soon.

The car Al Hodge had given her and Ryker was still back at the Oxford. When she checked out, she felt it unwise to tell O'Grady she had a car since he assumed she didn't own one, evident by his offer to have Petros pick them up.

129

Luckily, she had plenty of money hidden in a panel of her CIA issued luggage, a common model of Samsonite suitcase that would not draw suspicion, but that had been altered with two secret compartments that would never be discovered unless by trained inspectors specifically looking for them. Adding to the benefits of the Samsonite brand being the most popular in the States among travelers, Denver was in fact the company's headquarters and the location of its manufacturing facility. Although it was a bit pricier than some other brands, no one in Denver would give a second thought to seeing a Samsonite suitcase.

At six o'clock, Erika retrieved some money from the panel, opened the telephone book, and called a taxi cab company.

Leroy should know by now that she has gone dark, meaning Marienne should be at Gaetano's sometime tonight.

◊ ◊ ◊

Erika had the cab driver drop her off three blocks from Gaetano's. She spent time walking the streets and alleys that might supply a line of vision to the restaurant looking for men sitting in cars, on benches reading newspapers, or just loitering around. She didn't see anyone who might raise a red flag. The only minor incident concerned a group of four teenage boys in one of the alleys who stood around smoking and drinking beer. They whistled and hooted at her as she passed but none bothered her. Erika didn't have to pull her switchblade from her pocket, or the gun tucked into the back of her pants under her loose-fitting blouse. *Boys will be boys as the Americans say*, she thought to herself.

She knew Hodge was too wise to have any of his men inside the restaurant. They would stick out like a sore thumb (she had met them all). When she felt comfortable the restaurant was not being watched by Hodge's men from outside, she walked through the front door and quickly spotted Marienne sitting in a booth near the back, facing the door. Their eyes met.

Erika walked back, sat down opposite her, and said, "Hello, Marienne."

"Hello, Erika."

A glass of white wine already set on the table for Erika. She smiled. "Thanks for the drink, and for coming alone."

"You knew I would be alone. You know Al realizes you'd spot a stakeout." Marienne added, "The bartender told me the wine is from Italy."

"Thanks. I hope you're hungry. They have very good pasta dinners here, also some great fish and shellfish dishes."

"Al told me about this place. He said it's run by mobsters. Is that true?"

"Yes, that's right."

The bartender showed up at their table. "Erika, we haven't seen you for some time."

"I was out of town for about a month, Mirko, but here I am. I'm glad to be back."

"Are you and your friend dining with us tonight?"

"Yes," Erika said without consulting Marienne. Each of them took a menu from him.

The bartender announced, "We have mussels that arrived from New York just this morning. They came in frozen, of course, but I'm told they came out of the sea just two days ago."

"Sounds wonderful, Mirko," Erika said. "I'll have the mussels and fettucine. Can I get that with your pesto sauce?"

"Of course."

Marienne took another second to scan the menu and finally ordered clams and linguine in a white wine sauce.

"Wise choices," Mirko said then walked away.

Marienne cut to the chase. "What's going on, Erika?"

There wasn't much chance of them being overheard in their high-back booths by their fellow, boisterous diners, but both leaned forward so they could talk softly.

"Marienne, I might have to ask you to do something dangerous for both you and me. It's something you'll not be able to tell Leroy or Al about until it's all over. You'll have to trust me, Marienne. Do you trust me?"

Marienne looked at her. "I have to report to Leroy, Erika. You know that."

131

"Not on this. Not if you want to help me stop the attack on your country that I know Leroy has briefed you about. I know the decision will be a hard one, Marienne. But you'll have to make that decision."

"What is it, Erika?"

Erika Lehmann got out of her side of the booth and sat down beside Marienne Schenk. The German whispered into the American's ear.

◊ ◊ ◊

After dinner, Erika took Marienne upstairs at Gaetano's. They were disarmed at the door, as usual (Marienne also packed a small handgun), and when they entered, the poker game was in full swing in the perpetually smoke-filled room.

Checkers spotted Erika. "Erika, where 'ya been?"

"I had a trip out of town, Checkers."

"Pull up a chair. Who's the broad with you?"

"This is my friend, Marienne."

Checkers told two of the players to cash out in order to free up seats for Erika and the woman with her. This wasn't done just to be hospitable; the Smaldone's were always open to new money.

After Erika had told her the request made of her at dinner, Marienne had one or two many drinks with the meal and was already feeling the alcohol.

Marienne had not played a lot of poker in her life, but enough that she knew the rules and strategy. The women took a seat.

It was Fat Paulie's turn to deal. Still on his right hand was a cast courtesy of Axel Ryker's bone breaking handshake. Paulie had to deal left-handed, which made for a slow and laborious distribution of cards.

One of the other players, Gino, said to Paulie, "Can't you deal faster than that, you fat fuck?"

"I go faster when your sister gives me a blow job," Paulie shot back.

After playing for a couple of hours, and with Erika's request still consuming her thoughts, Marienne had drank more and was now boldly teasing the men because she had won almost a hundred dollars. After dragging yet another pot, Marienne laughed and said, "I figured gangsters would be better at this game."

132

Fat Paulie looked around at the other men and said, "I can't stand a dame who gets mouthy after a couple of snifters."

Erika couldn't hold back a laugh. Still, it was time to go.

"Marienne and I will now cash out, Checkers."

After they collected their weapons and walked down the stairs to the main floor, Erika asked Mirko to call a taxi for Marienne. Erika waited with her until the cab arrived to take the inebriated OSS super shadow back to her apartment in Golden. Then Erika asked Mirko to call another cab, this one to return her to the bed and breakfast in Lakewood.

◊ ◊ ◊

Night had descended while Erika and Marienne were at Gaetano's. When Erika unlocked the door to her room, she dropped her keys on a small lamp table near the door and flipped on the lamp.

Cyril O'Grady sat in a chair in the opposite corner of the room.

"Hello, Erika. I've been here for quite some time. Where have you been, if you don't mind me asking?"

"I went out to dinner and then stopped at a bar for a couple of drinks, Cyril. Why do you ask? Have you appointed yourself my overseer now because you helped me?"

O'Grady didn't answer.

She walked over to his chair, straddled his legs, kissed him, then began unbuttoning his shirt.

Chapter 40

[Flashback]
Washington, D.C.
04 March 1946

Leroy had assigned Marienne Schenk to shadow and protect Erika Lehmann.

On the other side of L Street, Marienne was calmly making her way through shadows when the shots rang out that busted several of the street lights. She immediately dropped her shopping bag stuffed with nothing but newspapers and ran across the busy street. A few drivers who noticed the street lamps go dark slowed, but still traffic continued on, drivers either failing to hear the shots over traffic noise with early March car windows rolled up, or if they did hear something they thought surely it must be engine backfire from another vehicle.

Ambient light from passing headlights allowed Marienne to see Erika fighting with five men. Marienne ducked into a shadow and pulled a semi-auto handgun from her jacket pocket and clicked off the safety. She watched Erika put up quite a fight, injuring two of the men, but the odds finally overcame her. One of the men struck Erika over the head with a nightstick while she fought with another man. Knocked unconscious, Erika was carried into a narrow, four-feet-wide walkway between two tall, red brick buildings.

Marienne ran to the opening and peered around the corner. Because of light coming from a couple of third floor windows over a closed bakery, lighting in the alleyway was better than on the sidewalk with its busted streetlamps. The narrow walkway led to a wider alley behind the buildings where she saw the men starting to load the unconscious Erika into the trunk of one of two cars. In each car, a man sat behind the steering wheel. Zhanna Rogova stood nearby orchestrating the men, the sniper rifle she used to shoot out the street lamps strung over her shoulder. Marienne ran to the end of the walkway and pointed her gun. "Stop! Leave the woman or I'll shoot!"

Most of the men acted as if they didn't understand her orders but began drawing guns, nevertheless. Marienne began firing and caught one of the men in the shoulder, dropping him to the cobblestones. Zhanna pulled two handguns she had tucked behind her belt and began firing with both hands, forcing Marienne to duck into a shallow door recess in the brick wall—a side door to the bakery. Marienne reached around and got off another shot, but when the sharpshooting and rapidly firing Zhanna sent bullet after bullet into the edge of the brick, she was forced to step back. She tried again, but Zhanna again picked up the barrage and this time a jagged piece of brick shrapnel cut through Marienne's right forearm.

Zhanna stopped firing and Marienne heard the man she wounded beg for his life in Spanish. The former OSS shadow had a working knowledge of the language and edged forward enough to peep around the splintered brick wall in time to see Zhanna raise one of her pistols and pump two bullets into the wounded man's head.

Behind her, back on L Street, Marienne heard tires squeal to a stop and looked back to see Leroy Carr, Al Hodge, and another agent running toward her with guns drawn. Carr had the ersatz plumber's van parked two blocks ahead during the stakeout. When an agent watching Marienne saw her drop the bag (Marienne's signal), he radioed Carr but by the time they arrived Zhanna and the men were loaded into the cars and speeding out of the alley.

"Don't shoot!" Marienne yelled to Carr and the others. "Erika is in the trunk of the rear car."

Everyone ran back to the van. With the walkway that lead to the alley too narrow for a vehicle, Hodge was forced to frantically weave his way through traffic to get around the block, but by the time they reached M Street there was no sign of the getaway cars.

As they drove round and round, hoping to spot the fleeing vehicles, Marienne wrapped her bleeding forearm with her scarf and filled the men in on what went down in the alley. Carr radioed the agents still on L Street and ordered them to secure the alley and guard the body. Bystanders might not have noticed the two shots that put out the street lamps, thinking they were automobile backfires, but the multiple shots fired in the alley would certainly not go unnoticed. Carr didn't want bystanders, or the police, to disturb the body until he had a chance to search it.

"One of the cars is a black Oldsmobile," Marienne said as they drove. "That's the one Erika is in. The other is a dark green Pontiac. Both are late '30s models. The license plate number of the Oldsmobile is SW 242. The Pontiac was parked in front of the Olds and a view of that license plate was blocked from where I stood."

"Good work, Marienne," said the distracted Leroy Carr as he scanned the streets and looked down alleys they passed.

After twenty minutes of making various turns, Carr realized the futility. "Shit!" he shouted in frustration. "They won't still be around here after this much time. Al, take us back to the scene."

When they arrived at the mouth of the alley on M Street there was a small crowd of spectators gathered. A D.C. police cruiser sat parked in the alley and a siren in the distance grew louder—verification that more police were on their way.

Chapter 41

[Back to present]
Colorado
Friday, 14 May 1948

Marienne Schenk awoke with a hangover in the apartment in Golden. She hadn't slept well. Dreams haunted her throughout the night about what Erika had asked her to do.

[same morning—Lakewood, Colorado]
Cyril O'Grady had already dressed.

"Would you like some breakfast, Erika?"

"I don't think so, Cyril. I had a big dinner last night and I'm not especially hungry, but thanks for the offer."

"Very well then. I'll be in touch soon."

That's what he always said when they parted; he never gave specifics. Erika kissed him before he walked out the door.

[same morning—Denver]
Chris Singleton leaned back in his office chair at the FBI's Denver field office. He threw his ink pen on the desk, rose, walked to the window and stared down on Colfax Avenue.

He had no leads; nothing to go on concerning Erika Lehmann. It felt as if he chased a blonde ghost.

[an hour later]
From her apartment in Golden, Marienne called Al Hodge at Lowry Air Force base. She heard Hodge pick up.

"*Hello.*"

"Al, it's Marienne."

"*Yes, Marienne.*"

"Erika showed up at Gaetano's last night."

"She didn't waste any time."

"No, she didn't."

"How'd it go down?" Hodge asked.

Marienne paused. Why, she wasn't sure. She had a tangled history with Erika. They have never been friends, but she had helped save Erika's life when she was kidnapped by Zhanna Rogova. Erika had also protected Marienne on more than one occasion. Finally, she said, "I guess it went okay, but all we did was engage in chit chat." Even though it was her job to fully brief Hodge, Marienne wasn't yet ready to tell Hodge what Erika had asked of her.

"Chit-chat?! That's it?"

"Yes."

This time there was a pause from Hodge. *"There has to be a reason she went to all the work to see you, Marienne. I guess we'll have to sit around with our thumbs up our butts until we know what that reason is."*

Marienne already knew, and when the phone call ended she couldn't help but to feel guilty for not telling Hodge the truth; nevertheless, she couldn't bring herself to do it. At least not yet. She wasn't yet sure what she would do. During the war and until two years ago, she was single and had no one to consider other than herself when it came to putting herself in danger's path. Now she had a family: a husband and small child.

[that afternoon—Washington]

"Al's on the line, Leroy."

"Put him through, Sheila."

After he heard the click, Carr said, "Hello, Al."

"Marienne talked to Erika last night, Leroy."

"I take it that Erika showed up at the restaurant?"

"Yeah."

"What's Marienne's report?"

"She said all they did was chit chat. I don't know what's going on here, Leroy, but the fish stink in Denmark," Hodge messed up the famous Hamlet quote. *"There's no way Lehmann would go to all the trouble to get Marienne in Denver and then only chew the fat about the weather or*

how the Pittsburgh Pirates are doing. I think Lehmann is up to her same old bullshit shenanigans again and she's trying to draw Marienne in."

"I don't think Marienne would purposefully keep something from us, Al."

"I don't either, Leroy, but something's not right."

A New Valhalla

Part 4

Eye for eye, tooth for tooth, hand for hand, foot for foot.

– Exodus 21:24

Chapter 42

[Flashback]
Algiers, Algeria, North Africa
Sunday, 08 November 1942

American Army buck sergeant Lionel Akins and his five men huddled behind a barricade that the Vichy French forces had erected on a street near the outskirts of Algiers. That it was November made no difference here, so close to the Sahara Desert. Akins and his men had perspired all day under the blazing African sun.

The barricade, made of overturned horse carts, empty barrels, and anything else the French could hastily find, was placed there just yesterday. That was one day before Akins's unit, the U.S. 168th Regimental Combat Team that was attached to the U.S. 34th Infantry Group, landed on a North African beach just west of Algiers.

The sergeant and his small group of men didn't know what to expect. Like other units of the 168th, Akins and his men had fanned out into streets across a wide area of the northwestern outskirts of the city. The lieutenant had divided Akins' platoon into groups of six and assigned each team a street. They had been told that the level of Vichy French resistance could vary drastically, from little to no resistance to fierce fighting. Apparently, talks were ongoing with the Vichy French commanders, but no one, not even the Allied generals, knew how the French forces would react to this invasion—the first invasion of the war by American troops. The Americans had not come under fire during the landing, and Akins and his men hoped for that same lack of resistance as they began entering the city. This was their first time in combat for all of them. Three of his men were teenagers, two were both only twenty years old. Akins himself was only twenty-three.

Akins was about ready to advance his men when the first shot rang out, striking one of his men in the neck.

"Get down!" Akins shouted. The men hit the ground behind the barricade. One of the other men got to the wounded soldier. "It's looks bad, Sarge."

When the first shot rang out, anyone still outside ran away or ducked into a building.

Just down the narrow street, Ahlan Djebar heard the first shot, grabbed her two small daughters, and rushed them to the root cellar. She could tell the shots were coming from nearby; to her, she thought they might be coming from the flat roof of the home attached to hers. She had planned to take the girls to the market and had already dressed them in traditional Berber attire of colorful haiks, mandeels, and head scarves. Even though the mandeels covering their noses and mouths weren't required for children of their ages, both girls had insisted they wanted to look like their mother when out and about.

Back behind the barricade, Akins rose slightly to see if he could get a take on from where the gunfire was originating. He saw a puff of smoke from a rooftop of one of the colorful stucco houses and heard the bullet whiz by his head, barely missing. He again hit the ground. He knew if he and his men raised up to return fire they would be sitting ducks from the enemy who had the higher vantage point.

The soldier attending the wounded man said, "Sarge, Hutch is gone! He's dead."

PFC Hutchinson had married his high school sweetheart before he shipped out and his wife was expecting. The child would never see its father.

"Williams!" Akins barked. "Attach your grenade launcher!"

During training, PFC Williams had proven himself the most proficient of the group with the M7 grenade launcher that attached to the barrel of his M1 Garand rifle. Williams, only eighteen years old had never fired any weapon in real combat. His hands shook, but he finally succeeded in attaching the launcher.

Akins rose slightly and peered through a small opening in the barricade between two of the oil drums. "The fire is coming from the rooftop of the fourth house on the left! Come over here so you can see!"

Williams bellycrawled over.

"You see it Williams? It's the yellow house."

"I see it."

"Fire when ready."

Williams adjusted his aim several times before finally launching the grenade over the barricade and into the air like a speedy flare. They could hear the whistling as the rocket rose to its apex, then began descending. Williams's aim was slightly off but close enough to collapse the roof of the attached house and send the sniper scurrying. When Akins saw the sniper reach the street, he stood up and began firing, but the distance was too much for accuracy from his bucking Thompson submachine gun. The man quickly ducked down an alley and out of sight.

"Let's go!" Akins yelled.

The men quickly climbed over the barricade and, staying low, ran forward while hugging the edge of the buildings along the deserted street.

When they reached the target building, one half still stood, and the roof was still intact where the sniper had stationed himself. Akins kicked in the door then took cover beside the opening.

"This is the United States Army!" Akins shouted while keeping out of the line of fire from anybody within. "If anyone is in there come out with your hands up immediately or we'll toss in a grenade!" Akins knew his English wouldn't likely be understood, but surely anyone inside had to know they were in danger.

Akins repeated the command with no response. He knew he should probably use the grenade, but instead he gently peered around the corner. It was silent inside and he saw no one.

"Hillbilly, you and I will check this place for any hostiles or weapon caches." PFC Prather, who hailed from the Appalachian region of West Virginia, had been given the nickname 'Private Hillbilly' by his drill instructor during basic training and the moniker had stuck. "The rest of you guys stay out here and keep your eyes peeled. That sonuvabitch shooting at us is probably a half-mile away by now, but there might be others around. Keep a close eye on rooftops and open windows."

Akins and Hillbilly entered quickly with pointed weapons ready to fire on anything that moved. A cat jumped out from behind a chair and darted toward a broken window at the rear of the house. A startled Prather shot at the cat but missed.

Prather's gunfire brought the other four men rushing in.

"Get back outside," Akins ordered. "It was just a damn cat."

Akins was as nervous as any of the men, but he had to hide it. After the four returned to stand guard outside, Akins said, "Hillbilly, keep your wits about you. You'll get us both killed, dumb shit."

It was a small, one-storey home so it took only a few moments to realize no one was inside. They found no weapons. Akins was ready to rejoin his men on the street when one of them called out, "Sarge, there is someone over here!"

Akins ran out, followed by Hillbilly. The man who had shouted stood in front of the other half of the house. The half that the rocket grenade hit. Although the walls were sturdy stucco, the roofs of these houses were put together haphazardly. Since it seldom rained here, the flat roofs were thin planks of wood covered with a coating of tar. Even though the walls still stood, the speed of the descending rocket propelled it through the roof before it exploded. The inside of the home was totally destroyed.

Akins heard the sound his soldier had heard. It sounded like the whimpering of a small child buried somewhere under the ruble.

"Hillbilly, give me a hand. The rest of you stay on guard."

The two soldiers began working frantically, digging through the ruble. When they finally got to a certain point, Akins and Hillbilly looked on in horror. A dead woman still held two small children. One of the children was dead, the other, who looked to be around four years old, was still alive. It was easy to see the child was severely injured. Blood covered her colorful clothes.

"Williams!" Akins screamed. "Bring the med kit!"

Akins took the whimpering child from her dead mother's arms. Before Williams could climb down through the rubble, the child opened her eyes and looked innocently at Akins. She muttered a word in Berber that Akins didn't understand, then died in his arms.

Chapter 43

[Back to present]
Colorado
Monday, 17 May 1948

Cyril O'Grady had spent each night that weekend with Erika in her room in Lakewood. Each morning he had left early and not returned until after dark. On Monday morning he finally deviated from this routine and took her downstairs for an early morning meal at the mom and pop bed and breakfast where Erika stayed.

"Erika, I can't come by tonight," O'Grady said over their meals of fried eggs, bacon, and biscuits.

"Oh?"

"I'm afraid so." He offered no explanation. Not even a phony one.

Erika knew better than to ask questions and raise suspicion. "I'll miss you, Cyril."

Petros waited in a car outside. When O'Grady walked out, he got in the front seat beside his driver.

Just down the street, Marienne Schenk sat behind the wheel of the 1940 Chevy Al Hodge had supplied Erika and Axel Ryker. When O'Grady's car pulled away, Marienne started the engine and put the car in gear.

It was just over an hour later when Marienne returned and knocked on Erika's door.

"I had to drop the tail, Erika," Marienne said after she entered and Erika had shut the door. "He drove up into the mountains. I followed his car as long as I could, but eventually we got to some long stretches of wending mountain roads with no other cars in sight. He would have spotted me before long."

"Then it's apparent O'Grady and his men are holed up somewhere in the mountains," Erika replied. "That's at least something. Thanks. Marienne. You told me you won't tell Al where I'm staying, right?"

"I already told you I won't, not for now."

"What about the other thing I asked of you?"

147

Marienne looked at her for a long moment. "I'm still thinking about it, Erika, but only because of the gravity of this situation."

After Marienne left, Erika called the Oxford Hotel and asked the switchboard operator to connect her to Ryker's room. She had not been in touch with him since she went dark. The phone rang and rang. Ryker didn't pick up. Erika hung up. "Damn!" she said loudly to no one.

[8:30 that evening—Denver]

Roxanne sat at the bar of the *Thirsty Tiger* next to a large, burly man. He had been trying to barter down her price, so when Axel Ryker walked in and sat down at the other end of the bar, she quickly rose from her stool and joined Ryker. He had never tried to talk down her price; and in fact, he paid her normal rate one night to just watch a movie with him. She didn't care about his hard appearance; he had money to spend.

This strange man with an odd accent bought her a drink, and she had just taken her first sip when a blonde woman came out of nowhere and sat down on the bar stool on the other side of Ryker. Failing to reach him on the telephone, Erika had staked out the Oxford and followed Ryker to the club.

Oh, no! Roxane thought. She had been in this situation before when a wife or girlfriend had showed up unexpectedly. When she had first sat down beside Ryker, Roxanne had dropped one of her dress straps off her shoulder. Now she slid the strap back up.

The woman leaned forward on the bar and looked at Roxanne. "Hello," the blonde said to her.

"Hello," Roxanne said timidly.

The blonde then addressed Ryker. "May I speak to you privately for a minute?"

Roxanne heard and didn't need to be asked to leave. The prostitute quickly got up and walked away, returning to the other end of the bar and the man she had been sitting with when Ryker arrived.

"What do you want?" Ryker said gruffly. "You are no longer my superior. Herr Hodge told me you have gone rogue and I now work under his authority."

"I'm sure he told you if I contact you, you are to then contact him immediately."

"Of course, and I follow orders."

"You won't tell Al Hodge."

Ryker looked at Erika with derision. "And why won't I do that."

"The first reason is that you will be a dead man if you betray me."

Ryker laughed loudly. "You're a fool to try to alarm me. Do you want to fight me, Sonderführer?"

"I won't have to. Unless you do what I ask, the mission will not succeed. Remember, both of our orders are to stop O'Grady. You can call Al Hodge, but he will never find me and your betrayal will prove useless. If the mission fails, you can imagine what your future holds. You don't want to fail your first mission for the CIA, Ryker, not with your history. Leroy Carr is already a hair away from turning you over to the tribunals where a rope around your neck already awaits you. If the mission succeeds, you'll be on much better footing. That's the way things work with Leroy. I know from experience."

Suddenly Ryker's attention was drawn to a loud conversation at the other end of the bar. Roxanne attempted to get off her barstool but the big man next to her grabbed her roughly by the hair and dragged her back down onto her seat.

Ryker rose, walked over, grabbed the man up and violently smashed his face into the bar. Blood spurted from a severely broken nose and the man collapsed unconscious to the floor. Ryker then took some money out of his pocket and handed Roxanne a couple of bills. Erika couldn't see the denominations. The prostitute smiled, patted his face in affection, and walked out of the club.

Erika couldn't believe what she had just witnessed. It couldn't be that the beast who in Hungary during the war had shot dead a mother in front of her children had just come to someone's aid. Ryker's reaction must be solely due to him seeing an opportunity for violence.

[middle of the night—3:00 a.m.]

Cyril O'Grady was scheduled to call his contact in Juárez, Mexico, tonight. He preferred to call in the middle of the night because telephone connections out of the country went much quicker at this time of day than in the earlier and busier hours.

"Yes, this is Sedik," the voice on the other end in Juárez announced.

"It's O'Grady checking in."

"Your employer wants to know when the job will be completed. He is becoming impatient."

"The job will be done. Has the agreed upon secondary amount been sent to my account?"

"Yes, but the last amount will not be given until the job is completed."

"We still have preparations and my men are monitoring the target from afar trying to uncover any security weaknesses," O'Grady said. "I would say we're approximately a week away in our preparations, but then we have to wait on the weather."

"Your employer does not suffer dawdlers well."

"Fook you!" O'Grady said the vulgar word with his heavy Irish accent. "Our agreement is that I would take the time necessary. This is no easy job. I was clear about that from the start. We have to rely on the weather, something I can't control. To achieve maximum damage, we need a wind or breeze coming in from the north or northeast to take the toxins into Denver. Most of the prevailing winds here come out of the mountains and head east. That would blow the chemicals out into the sparsely populated plains. We have to wait."

"Very well. I am just a messenger. I will let your employer know this and tell you his reaction when you next check in."

O'Grady slammed down the phone.

"Fooking amateurs!" he exclaimed out loud.

Chapter 44

The Casbah in Algiers, Algeria, North Africa
Tuesday, 18 May 1948

Even though he owned this building and business in the Casbah, Rafik Djebar always entered by the back door. Walking in the front door would expose him to the heavy opium smoke of the customers in the front room. Although he smoked opium himself, he never partook until late at night after the business of the day was finished.

This was Djebar's headquarters, although he owned several other opium dens in the Casbah, along with similar establishments in other cities and towns in Algeria, Morocco, and Libya.

During the war he only dabbled in selling drugs to supplement his day job as a bricklayer. When the war ended, people had more money and the yearning for opium increased exponentially with the economic boon. One night, Djebar put a bullet in the head of the man called the 'Opium Sultan', took over his business and since had been called the 'High Mufti of the Casbah.' With Djebar's willingness to deal swiftly and cruelly with business rivals, he now had in his grasp 90% of the opium trade in the three countries of North Africa. This had made him a millionaire several times over.

Most of the rooms in his opium dens of the Casbah had colorful beads or pieces of shredded cloth dividing room from room, but Djebar's office in the back was behind a steel door. Even though the building had two floors where customers smoked their drugs, Djebar had his office built on the first floor. Opium smoke rises.

Less than a half hour after he arrived, one of his bodyguards entered. "Sedik is on the telephone from Mexico."

"Bring me the telephone," Djebar ordered.

The man left and returned with a telephone attached to a very long cord and placed it in front of his boss. Djebar picked up. "Yes."

"This is Sedik reporting in." 'Sedik' was Djebar's most trusted lieutenant. That was not that man's real name. Djebar decided on the codename because his wife and two young daughters had been killed

by Americans in 1942 in their home where they lived at the time—Rue Si Sedik. The conversation was in Berber.

"Yes, go on."

"The Irishman reports that his preparations are about a week away, but he said he might need more time if necessary because of necessary weather conditions. I told him you were not a patient man."

"On the contrary, I have been forced to learn patience. A few days here or there is a little matter but the next time you speak with him again remind him I deal swiftly with failure. Anything else?"

"No, not at this time."

Djebar hung up. The Americans would pay for the slaughter of his family during the war.

Chapter 45

Denver, Colorado
Wednesday, 19 May 1948

Erika was on the phone with Axel Ryker. She had reached him at his room in the Oxford Hotel, this time on her first try. It was early in the afternoon.

"What is your decision?" Erika asked Ryker.

"Since my initial orders from Herr Carr are for me to assist you, I will do so."

"And what about your orders from Al Hodge to turn me in?"

"Hodge is secondary in command. Until I hear differently from Herr Carr, I will follow Hodge's orders to assist you."

"Very well. Walk to the phone booth that is on the same street as the hotel entrance, but one block east. I will call you there in fifteen minutes. It's near the corner, in front of a shoe store. I'll give you your instructions over that phone."

◊ ◊ ◊

For the past half hour Marienne had been in the Army Surplus store, taking her time looking over the rifles behind the counter. The store owner was growing weary of her drawn out perusing.

Marienne handed him back an M1 Garand and said, "Let me see the M1 that was next to this one on the shelf."

"Lady, it's the same rifle."

"I don't think so. May I see it please."

The man rolled his eyes and Marienne heard him mutter "Women!" as he turned away. He handed her the rifle she asked for.

"How is this different than the one I just showed you?"

"This is an M1C Garand. It has modifications. This one has mountings for a scope. Surely you knew that." The Garands loaded from the breech, so a top-mount scope was not feasible. The scope mountings were off to the left side of the receiver.

The man had never paid any attention. Since the war, the M1s had flown out of his store so quickly with buyers snatching them up for big game hunting rifles. He had a hard time keeping up. (All the .30-06 Garands were very effective for hunting elk, a popular sport in the Colorado mountains.)

"I'll take this one, and that M81 scope you have at the end of the counter."

The man walked down and looked over the scopes. He saw none labeled M81. The only tag on them was a price tag. "Which one are you referring to lady?"

Marienne walked down and pointed. The man picked up the scope, put on his reading glasses and found 'M81' factory engraved on the bottom of the scope. He looked at her quizzically, but she was busy checking the rifle's bolt action and clip tension.

"Anything else?" he said.

"Do you have a Phillips screwdriver that will fit the screws on the scope?"

"Yes, it's in the store's tool kit."

"I'll buy it."

"You can use the screwdriver here, but my tools aren't for sale."

"Yes, they are," Marienne said. "I'll pay you twice what your screwdriver is worth, and I'll take two boxes of cartridges and a cleaning kit for this rifle. I'm paying in cash."

What Marienne purchased was a modified version of the M1 Garand rifle commonly used by American snipers during the war. She hadn't told Erika yet, but to protect thousands of Americans from dying or being permanently disabled, she would agree to her shocking request.

Marienne walked out of the Army Surplus store with the rifle, scope, cartridges, cleaning kit, and screwdriver, all the while thinking about her husband and small daughter and wondering if she would ever see them again.

[that evening]

Hodge had just called Leroy Carr to deliver his daily report.

"Anything progressing, Al?" Carr asked from Washington. It was nine o'clock on the East Coast but Carr was still at his office.

"Nothing of note, Leroy. Lehmann is still rogue; she's never returned to the Oxford Hotel. I spoke with Marienne on the phone less than an hour ago, and she's heard nothing from Lehmann. And more bad news, Leroy. That FBI guy, Singleton, is back in Denver. Today, one of my men checked the Brown Palace hotel registry because Lehmann had stayed there before. No sign of Lehmann or any of her alias's we know about, but he spotted Singleton's name in the registry."

"Erika would never return to a hotel we knew she had stayed at previously, Al. No surprise there. Yet, Singleton being back in Denver is a problem. Obviously, he figured out that entire Detroit thing was a trick to get him out of Denver. We're going to have to tread carefully with Singleton, Al."

"What do you want me to do, Leroy, as far as Singleton, I mean?"

"I don't believe Marienne when she says she has not been in contact with Erika. Erika does nothing without a reason and she requested Marienne for a purpose. Don't let on that we suspect any of this but tell Marienne that Singleton is in town. She'll relay that to Erika. Somehow, Erika has entrapped Marienne in her web."

Chapter 46

Denver, Colorado
Next day—Thursday, 20 May 1948

The telephone awoke Erika at seven o'clock in the morning. She reluctantly rolled over and picked up the receiver beside her bed.

Still groggy from sleep, she said, "Yes."

"Erika, it's Marienne. The FBI agent Chris Singleton is back in town."

"Where is he staying?"

"Same place as before—the Brown Palace."

"I need to know yes or no on your decision, Marienne."

"Yesterday, I bought the rifle. That's your answer."

"Tonight, I'll have Cyril take me to dinner at Gaetano's. We'll arrive about seven. I have no way of knowing how long we'll be inside. You must be patient.

"When we walk out the front door, I'll stop on the curb and ask him to light me a cigarette. That will give you a stationary target."

"Erika, I'm letting you know up front that after I do this, I'm going to Hodge and tell him everything. When I work for the CIA I'm still under oath to the United States, I take that seriously."

"I understand, Marienne, and thanks."

[that evening]

O'Grady had arrived a half hour late to gather Erika, so it was around 7:30 before Petros pulled the car up in front of Gaetano's.

Mirko came to their table and suggested the eggplant lasagna. "Excellent tonight," he said.

O'Grady looked at Erika and she nodded. "We'll both have that," O'Grady said, "but delay placing our order for about fifteen minutes. We'll have a drink first." Erika told him she'd have what he was drinking. O'Grady asked Mirko, "What type of Irish whiskey do you have?"

"I'm sorry," Mirko apologized," we have no Irish whiskey."

O'Grady stared at Mirko expressionless for a moment, then said, "You need to get some. Bring us two double Scotches and an ice cube in a separate glass."

Mirko bowed slightly and walked off.

"What type of joint is this, Erika? No Irish whiskey?"

Erika smiled. "Sorry, Cyril."

O'Grady looked around. "So, this is the place you come to often. Tell me again why?"

"I've gotten to know the owners and the food is very good."

O'Grady nodded.

"Cyril. Why did you have me followed the other day when I left the Oxford to meet you at that café? You never told me why?"

O'Grady shook his head. "It doesn't matter, Erika."

The conversation paused when Mirko delivered the drinks.

"Why are you still having me followed, Cyril? You don't trust me. Is that it?"

O'Grady had started to raise his glass, then sat it back down. "I'm not having you followed, Erika."

"Somebody is following me; I can sense it."

O'Grady's face became ashen. "You told me you come here often."

"A couple of times a week, at least."

"We have to get out of here. If you're being followed it's foolish to visit a place regularly." The tone in his voice was part anger and part impatience. "You should know that."

O'Grady rose, hurriedly threw some money on the table to cover the drinks and led her swiftly out of the door. Petros had parked the car a half block away. O'Grady signaled him, and he started the engine.

"Do you have a cigarette?" Erika asked him as they waited for the car to pull up. O'Grady pulled out a pack and gave her one and brought out his Zippo lighter.

When he lit the Zippo a gunshot rang out. The bullet penetrated Erika's upper left arm and like a volcano, blood spirted up into the air. She fell to the curb.

O'Grady pulled his pistol and fired two shots toward the roof of the building across the street he thought the shot may have come from, but

Marienne had already dropped the rifle, sprinted across the flat roof, and was descending a fire escape to an alley.

Checkers and his henchmen were upstairs when they heard the shots. They ran down the stairs and out the front door with guns drawn. No one was in sight. O'Grady and Petros had already loaded Erika into the car and sped off.

Petros squealed tires around the first corner but when they were out of sight of the restaurant, O'Grady told him to slow down. "Just do the speed limit, Petros. We don't want the coppers pulling us over."

O'Grady took off his shirt and applied pressure to Erika's wound. "It doesn't look too bad. Do you feel like it hit bone?"

"I don't think so," she answered.

"The bullet passed through," said O'Grady. "I heard it ricochet off the walk. That's good, but the wound is deep. It will require some care and stitches."

"I can't go to the hospital, Cyril. You know why."

O'Grady remained silent for a moment, as if conflicted. He finally said, "One of my men was a medic during the war and has a complete medical kit." He turned his head to his driver, "Petros, take us to our location."

Marienne's aim had been true.

"Erika, I'm afraid I must ask you to lean over in the seat and keep your head down," O'Grady said.

She looked at him. "I don't understand, Cyril."

"I'm afraid I must insist. You cannot know where we are going."

Chapter 47

Denver, Colorado
Next day—Friday, 21 May 1948

Al was awake and shaving in the bathroom when his telephone rang in his small room at Lowry Air Force Base. Hodge looked at his wrist watch. It was not yet 7:00 a.m.

Hodge quickly wiped the shaving cream from his face and walked out to the phone.

"Hello."

"Al, this is Marienne. We have to talk. Can you meet me at Sloan's Lake in an hour?"

Hodge knew the location of the large Denver lake and park.

"Yes."

"There are some park benches at the very south edge of the lake. There's a large aspen tree next to one of the benches. Do you know what as aspen tree looks like?

"No. I forgot to work forestry into my curriculum in college, Marienne."

"It has a white bark, the only one like it around the lake. I'll be sitting on that bench waiting for you."

Hodge heard the phone go dead.

[later that morning—Washington]

Leroy Carr picked up his phone. It was Al Hodge from Denver.

"Al," Leroy Carr said. "I didn't hear from you yesterday."

"I had nothing to report yesterday, Leroy. That's changed now. I met with Marienne this morning."

"And?"

"Marienne shot Erika with a sniper rifle outside that mobster restaurant last night."

"What???"

"Just wounded her. Marienne told me it was at Erika's request. Marienne is here now, I'll put her on."

159

"Hello, Leroy," Carr heard Marienne say from Denver.

"We thought Erika had convinced you to go dark with her, Marienne. I expect things like this from Erika, but this surprises me about you. I thought I could rely on you."

"I didn't go dark, Leroy, but I didn't tell Al everything until this morning. I admit that, but I also told Erika I would fill Al in on everything once the job was done."

"I'm waiting to hear, Marienne," Carr said impatiently. "What's going on?"

"I think what's going on is exactly what Erika wanted. She told me she had run into a wall trying to gain O'Grady's confidence and thought she needed to do something drastic. Last night, before I called Al this morning, I surveilled the place O'Grady had gotten her in Lakewood, a suburb. She didn't stay there last night. I think O'Grady might have taken her to wherever he and his team are hiding out."

"Put Al back on the phone."

"Yes, Leroy," Hodge said.

"Al, I'll be on the first flight I can get to Denver."

[that afternoon]

Erika sat in a mountain cabin with Cyril O'Grady. Unfortunately, she hadn't been able to see the route that took her there as O'Grady had made her lie in the backseat and keep her head down.

His other men were either outside or in the second of the team's two cabins. The left arm of her blouse was ripped off, her upper arm heavily bandaged. Last night, one of O'Grady's men, the one he said was a medic during the war, had cleaned her wound, applied iodine, and stitched it up, all without the use of anesthetic. The iodine burned like fire and being sewed up like a ripped jacket was certainly painful. Erika winced during the process but did not cry out.

O'Grady asked her how she felt.

"A bit tired, probably from loss of blood, Cyril, but other than that, fine. Thank you again for helping me." She had to hand it to Marienne. Her shot was perfect, causing an ugly flesh wound but not injuring bone or sinew.

O'Grady again chastised her for being predictable.

"Erika, with your Abwehr training, it surprises me that if you thought you were being followed you would frequent a place on a regular basis."

Of course, the 'mistake' had been intentional on her part. "I know, Cyril. I let my guard down because I felt safe with you and it cost me. But you were not in danger. No one is after you. May I ask you a question?"

"Go ahead."

"Why do you have these other men surrounding you, and why are you staying here in the mountains?"

O'Grady looked at her for a long moment, as if pondering a reply. Without giving her any specifics about why he and his men were in the Denver area, O'Grady spent the next fifteen minutes confiding in Erika about who he really was.

Erika thought it was time to be bold. "Whatever you're here to do, Cyril, let me join you. I'm tired of running. Give me a chance to prove to you I deserve to be part of the team. A dedicated woman can be of great value to a group like yours. You know this is true."

Chapter 48

Denver, Colorado
Next day—Saturday, 22 May 1948

One of the members of Chris Singleton's Denver task force was on the telephone.

"*Special Agent Singleton?*"

"Yes, Agent Kasinger," said Singleton.

"*CIA Deputy Director Carr landed at Lowry about forty-five minutes ago. Al Hodge was there to meet him. You ordered us not to follow so we didn't. What are your instructions?*"

"Nothing until further notice. Thank you, Agent Kasinger. Job well done."

◊ ◊ ◊

This morning, O'Grady told his team members that he was considering bringing Erika in to their clique. This was met with heavy opposition among several of the men, but O'Grady told them of her Nazi background and that she would have to prove to them that she could be a valuable asset to the team and this mission. O'Grady told them, "All of you had to prove yourselves, don't forget that. A woman can add a lot to the team in certain situations. They draw less suspicion than men."

After that, Erika felt as if she was back at Quenzsee in 1938 undergoing Abwehr training. First thing was target practice. She was given a Colt 1911 .45 caliber pistol. The team could target practice freely. They were miles away from any other people and the surrounding mountains blocked the sound of gunshots. Erika emptied the magazine into the round target nailed to a pine tree 25 feet away. Half of the shots were bullseyes, but the rest landed outside the black, two or three inches away. It was outstanding shooting; still, Erika was not happy.

"This pistol is inaccurate," she told O'Grady who was one of the onlookers. She handed the pistol back to him. "The kick is much too hard for rapid-fire. This is not because I'm a woman. The targets of your men prove this, Cyril. I want a Beretta Brevetatta. Get me one of those and I'll place every round in the black."

◊ ◊ ◊

Axel Ryker had been up half the night because Roxanne had been in his hotel room. Around 3:00 a.m., when they finished, Ryker paid her, she left, and he went back to bed. For that reason, he rose rather late—around 10:00 a.m. When he emerged from the suite's bedroom, he saw the $20 bill he had given her laying on the coffee table. Ryker didn't understand. He had never had a woman he didn't have to pay for.

[that afternoon]

Leroy Carr and Al Hodge were in Carr's room in the Lowry barracks discussing the current situation when they heard the knock on the door.

Carr answered.

Standing outside the door was the FBI agent, Chris Singleton.

"Hello, Deputy Director Carr," Singleton said with a smile. "I'm a bit surprised I caught you in."

Carr looked around. Singleton was alone.

"What a pleasant surprise," Carr lied. "Please come in, Special Agent Singleton."

As Singleton entered, Carr looked at Hodge. It was obvious that his longtime comrade-in-arms was also surprised.

Carr motioned to a chair and Singleton sat down.

"What can we do for you, Agent Singleton?" Carr asked.

"Because you and Mr. Hodge are here I must assume Erika Lehmann is back in town, or never left. You went to a great deal of trouble to sidetrack me to Detroit. My questions concern why she's in Denver? and why have you gone to so much trouble to hide things from the FBI?"

"I'm not sure I follow you, Agent Singleton."

"Mr. Carr, the FBI has greater jurisdiction when it comes to investigations on American soil than the CIA."

163

"I understand that," said Carr, "but I'm still not following what you're trying to get at."

"Come on, Mr. Carr. You went to a lot of trouble breaking into our headquarters and taking all the files on Lehmann. Director Hoover is considering going to the president."

Before the war, Carr had been a successful attorney.

"I know Director Hoover well," Carr said. "It would cause him and the Bureau major embarrassment if it got out that FBI headquarters has been compromised, and he was accusing another government agency without a shred of proof."

"The only thing taken was the file on a person who is now a CIA operative," Singleton argued. "That would look suspicious to anyone."

"I know it's odd," said Carr. "I don't know why anyone would do that."

Singleton looked at Al Hodge, who kept a straight face even though he felt like laughing at Carr's last comment. "I don't know what you're talking about, Singleton," Hodge said. "All I know is Leroy brought me out here for the fly fishing."

Chapter 49

Denver, Colorado
Next day—Sunday, 23 May 1948

At nine o'clock this morning, Erika told Cyril O'Grady that she wanted to attend Sunday Mass.

"I'm Catholic, Cyril. I haven't been to Mass in a while."

"That's out of the question, Erika. I'm sorry."

"As an Irishman, and former IRA member, aren't you also Catholic?"

"Yes, but I haven't been to Mass in many years and I'm not interested in going. And to be honest, I'm surprised as a former Nazi that you want to go."

"Nevertheless, I would. Do I have your permission? Petros can drive me and keep a watch on me if that will ease your mind."

"I forbid it, Erika," O'Grady said.

Erika knew the worst thing she could do was come off as weak. "You forbid it? Do you know who you're taking to? I have taken orders from the Führer himself." She was gambling but had little choice.

Petros was one of the two other men besides O'Grady who billeted in that particular cabin. The young Greek sat at the table eating breakfast. Erika turned to him. "Petros, please get the car ready. The late Sunday morning Mass at the Cathedral is at 11:00 so we have to leave in about 45 minutes."

Petros looked at his boss. O'Grady smiled slightly and nodded his head. Then he turned to Erika. "Petros will stay with you at all times."

"I already suggested as much so you won't fret. Thank you, Cyril."

O'Grady was far from being totally convinced, but he was gradually gaining confidence that his decision to take this strong and ostensibly fearless woman on board was the correct choice.

◊ ◊ ◊

The Cathedral of the Immaculate Conception was located in downtown Denver, on Logan Street, not far from Capitol Hill. Because of its downtown location, parking spots were limited in the church's small parking lot. Arriving only fifteen minutes before Mass, all these parking spots were taken, so Petros had to park on the street, three blocks away.

Erika had to walk briskly to get to the church on time. Petros followed closely on her heels.

They arrived just as the procession of priests and altar boys walked forward down the aisle to the altar. Erika dipped her finger in the fount of holy water and crossed herself. She found a place in the very back pew and Petros stood beside her.

"Petros," Erika whispered after they had found their seats, "I have to use the restroom." They were still standing like the rest of the congregation as the procession to the altar continued with a hymn being sung by the choir in the balcony overhead.

Erika didn't wait for a response. She edged her way back out of the pew, apologizing to the worshippers she passed.

Instead of using the restroom located in the vestibule separated from the worship area, Erika found the door unlocked to the empty parish office. She dialed the apartment in Golden and listened to the phone ring.

Come on, Marienne. Be there!

There was no answer. Erika finally punched the cradle and got another dial tone. This time she dialed the Oxford Hotel and asked to be patched through to Axel Ryker's room. After three rings, he picked up.

Erika said, "Ryker, I need you to do two things, but first, I will give you directions to O'Grady's hideout. Get a pencil and paper." Unlike O'Grady had done during her initial trip to the cabins, on the drive to church, Petros had not instructed her keep her head down. This was a key reason she had insisted on attending church, but not the only reason.

"Proceed," Ryker said. Erika gave him the directions.

"You are not to tell Al Hodge about these directions until I tell you to do so, or if you don't hear from me by the day after tomorrow. Do you understand?" (Erika wasn't aware, nor was Ryker, that Leroy Carr was in Denver).

"*What is not to understand, Sonderführer.*"

166

"First, get in touch with Al Hodge at Lowry and tell him that I am with O'Grady and his men. They'll ask you where that is but tell them I didn't tell you. Wait until tomorrow to make the call."

She continued. "Go to the striptease club where we met that one time. Do this on Monday and Tuesday evening. Arrive at seven o'clock and stay until at least ten o'clock. If I'm not there on one of those nights with O'Grady, that will mean I'm probably dead. That's when you'll give Hodge the directions."

"If you arrive there with O'Grady, should I eliminate him?"

"Absolutely not. I will introduce you to him. I will tell O'Grady about your true background but tell him you and I met in Buenos Aires after the war and you are now my bodyguard. Play the part."

"Why should I not immediately tell our superiors the location? We can arrive and eliminate the threat."

"That's exactly why, Ryker. It would be a shootout to the death. A big part of our mission is to not only stop O'Grady but find out who hired him. He might be the only one of his team who knows that information. O'Grady will never surrender. He'll gladly die in the shootout and we'll never find out who his employer is. You have your orders, Ryker. You're quick to tell everyone you follow orders so I expect you to do so. And Ryker, I've told you not to call me Sonderführer, which you ignore, but that's exactly what I want you to call me in the presence of O'Grady."

Erika hung up the phone and quickly returned to the Mass.

◊ ◊ ◊

Erika and Petros were back at the cabins by 1:30 that afternoon.

"Thanks for allowing me to attend Mass, Cyril. I appreciate it."

O'Grady nodded. "You didn't give me much choice, did you, lassie?"

"I'm going to my room to change clothes," she said. "I assume I'll be doing some training today." Erika went into her room but left the door slightly ajar. She stood just out of sight, listening.

O'Grady asked Petros, "Did she ever leave your sight?"

"No, sir," the young man answered. He did not mention her restroom visit.

Erika knew he should have. That Petros didn't reveal that detail to O'Grady could possibly be attributed to his inexperience, or he might be afraid of O'Grady. She had her doubts that Petros knew who hired the team, but she now realized the young Greek was the weak link she could exploit for other reasons if the need presented itself.

Chapter 50

Denver, Colorado
Next day—Monday, 24 May 1948

After breakfast, it was time for O'Grady's team to train in close quarters combat, both with and without knives.

On the first day she arrived at the cabins (four days ago), O'Grady introduced Erika to his five-man team. Besides Petros, there was *Darragh*, another Irishman who was O'Grady's top deputy, the man she recognized who had been sitting with O'Grady at the Irish Maiden Pub on the first day she found him.

Then there was a man called *Dante* who spoke English with an Italian accent. There was another Greek on the squad, *Lukus,* who was introduced as Petros's uncle. Erika speculated it might be Lukus who suggested his nephew to O'Grady as a driver and gopher. The last man was the most interesting to Erika; *Wotan* spoke English with a heavy German accent. Although Wotan was a legitimate German first name for males, it was also the name of a god from Germanic folklore and Erika realized it could be just a codename, as could be the case with all the names other than O'Grady's.

The group treaded about a quarter of a mile from the cabins through a forest floor littered with pine cones and engrained with the sharp but pleasant perfume of blue spruce. When they reached a small clearing, the team first engaged in naked hand-to-hand with no weapons. O'Grady was the only man who did not participate. Petros struggled, but the other men were strong and tough. When it came Erika's time, she was matched with Darragh. A blow from the heavily muscled Irishman broke open her stiches and she began to bleed. Nonetheless, after that she held her own against the skilled mercenary by using her quickness to stay mostly out of his reach, moving in when the opportunity presented itself to deliver a kick or an elbow punch.

When knives were introduced, Erika was especially expert with the weapon, and her quickness over the men allowed her to deliver faux stabs and swipes that would have felled any competitor in real combat. O'Grady was impressed but did not say as much.

◊ ◊ ◊

Ryker had waited until this morning to call Al Hodge per his orders from Erika.

"Hello," Hodge said into his room phone at Lowry.

"Ryker here."

"Yes, Ryker?"

"I was contacted this morning by the Abwehr slut."

"Shit in my hat! Where is she? Is she with you now?" Hodge was too excited to admonish Ryker again for the derogatory reference to Erika.

"No, she called on the telephone."

"Are you calling from your hotel room?" Hodge asked.

"Yes."

"Don't say any more over the phone, Ryker. Deputy Director Carr is now in town. Stay in your room. We'll be there in twenty minutes or as soon as we can get there through the Monday morning traffic."

Hodge hung up and dialed Carr's room.

◊ ◊ ◊

A half-hour later Carr and Hodge sat in Ryker's suite. Carr now did the talking.

"Tell us everything you know, Ryker."

Axel Ryker was prepared to obey Erika's orders when it came to Al Hodge, but now that Leroy Carr was in front of him, Ryker changed his mind. Ryker possessed cunning survival skills, and he knew it was Leroy Carr who called the shots. Carr was the authority in which he had to remain in good stead, not Erika or Hodge. Against Erika's orders, Ryker handed Carr the directions to O'Grady's lair.

"The Abwehr slut ordered me to lie to Herr Hodge. She did not contact me this morning; she called me yesterday. It was at that time that I received her orders and those directions."

Carr looked at the paper then handed it to Hodge to look over.

"Agent Hodge ordered you to refrain from vulgar references to a fellow agent, Ryker. I don't want to hear one again and Agent Hodge will let me know if he hears one out of you."

"Very well," said Ryker dispassionately.

"Did she tell you how many men O'Grady has with him?"

"A six-man team including this O'Grady. Seven now that the Abwehr . . . woman has apparently succeeded in infiltrating the group."

Carr continued the questioning, "Did she say anything about knowledge of who hired O'Grady?"

"No, she said nothing of that."

This told Carr that Erika did not know. Carr knew how Erika operated. Even though she could be a thorn in everyone's side, she was expert in her secret world and would have included that key information.

Hodge chimed in. "Leroy, I have enough men in town we can take out O'Grady and his group tomorrow. If they're in the mountains like these directions indicate, there must be heavy woods near these cabins. We can position snipers and pick them off like carnival targets."

Carr always considered his friend's ideas, so he paused for a moment. He then asked Ryker, "You said Erika issued you *orders*–in the plural. What were her other orders?"

"She instructed me to be at a certain bar tonight from seven until ten o'clock, and tomorrow night the same."

"Which bar?"

"It's called the Thirsty Tiger. It is two blocks from this hotel. Her orders were that if she did not appear there tonight or tomorrow night with O'Grady, I was to assume she was dead and then hand over the enemies' location directions to Herr Hodge at that point."

Carr looked at Hodge, and then at Ryker.

"I want you to follow those orders, Ryker. I understand and appreciate why you gave me a complete briefing. Nevertheless, from now on I want you to follow Erika Lehmann's instructions without question, just inform me or Mr. Hodge of those instructions regardless of if she orders you not to. Are we on the same page?"

"'On the same page' I assume means do we understand each other," Ryker said. Then he reiterated what he always said when answering that question, "I obey my orders."

"You didn't obey your orders from Erika not to hand over the directions."

"You have greater authority than the woman. I obey any and all orders from my highest authority. This I did for Reichsführer Himmler during the war. You have taken his place."

Carr frowned at being compared to Heinrich Himmler. "Don't ever say that to me again, Ryker."

Ryker grinned. "Very well. As I have said many times, I always . . . "

"Yeah, yeah, we know," Carr cut him off. "You always obey your orders."

[that evening]

Ryker arrived at the Thirsty Tiger at 6:30, a half hour before the appointed time. The Monday night crowd was certainly sparser than a weekend crowd; still, the place was half full. At one table sat two men in Air Force sergeant uniforms. It was not unusual to see servicemen from Lowry Air Force Base at the Thirsty Tiger, but these two happened to be Al Hodge's men in disguise. A third man from Hodge's team sat at the bar dressed in casual civilian attire. Neither Carr nor Hodge were present. These three were newly arrived from Washington and were chosen because Erika Lehmann had never met them. Leroy Carr did not want her to recognize anyone. It would tell her that Ryker had betrayed her confidence and she might leave with O'Grady immediately.

The hours passed. Ryker and Hodge's men stayed until almost midnight, two hours after the time window Erika had stipulated. She and O'Grady never showed. Neither did Roxanne, who Ryker had never failed to see in the place every time he had been there.

Chapter 51

Colorado
Next day—Tuesday, 25 May 1948

Yesterday, O'Grady instructed Petros to drive Dante to Denver in search of the handgun Erika had requested. It took stops at three gun shops before they finally found a Beretta Brevettata.

And as she had promised, during target practice this morning she placed every round in the black bullseye at 25 feet using the 7.65 caliber Beretta.

As they walked back to the cabin, Erika said, "Have you given any more thought to our night on the town, Cyril?"

Yesterday he had refused. Today he repeated himself. "I don't want to go into Denver right now, Erika."

"Why not?"

"My reason is not important."

"I thought it could give us some time alone."

"I would enjoy that," O'Grady replied, "but now is not the time."

Erika knew she had to force the issue. "Cyril, I have a confession to make. I'd certainly like some time alone with you, but I have another motive. I want to introduce you to my bodyguard."

O'Grady stopped in his tracks. "What are you talking about?"

"Take me to Denver tonight and you'll understand. You have to trust me."

[that evening]

Erika's revelation that she had a bodyguard was a surprise, and a red flag, to Cyril O'Grady. His instincts could not diminish his suspicion. Nevertheless, the German woman had proved herself to him that she could add quality to his team, and not on just this mission but future missions, as well. This propelled him to return to Denver with her tonight. Yet, he would proceed with caution. In one car, Petros drove as O'Grady and Erika sat in the back seat. Following behind was a second car of the three cars they had bought in Houston. In that car rode three more members of O'Grady's team: Darragh, Lukus, and Wotan. Dante was left behind to safeguard the cabins and the numerous weapons.

During the drive, Erika filled O'Grady in on Ryker's job history with the Gestapo during the war, including his expertise in the fields of murder, torture interrogations, and investigations.

◊ ◊ ◊

As they had done yesterday, Axel Ryker and Al Hodge's disguised men arrived at the Thirsty Tiger before the 7:00 p.m. time prearranged by Erika. Again tonight, Ryker sat alone at the end of the bar, as he always did.

It was about 8:00 when Darragh, Lukus, and Wotan walked into the club. So, anyone surveilling the place would not assume they were with O'Grady, the Irishman told Petros to drive around for about fifteen minutes.

When the three men walked in, Ryker spotted them immediately. He had no way of knowing they were O'Grady's men, but his keen senses told him the fit-looking men were to be watched.

Finally, about twenty minutes later, O'Grady and Erika walked in (Petros stayed in the car). It was then that the cagey Ryker knew he was right about the other three men. Ryker, talented in much more than just cruelty and mayhem, secured detailed descriptions of each man in his mind.

O'Grady found a table. No one was on stage at the moment, so no music played. O'Grady ordered Erika and himself a double Jamison, and, as always, an ice cube in a separate glass.

"Your bodyguard frequents this shit hole?" O'Grady asked.

"Yes, in fact he's here now," Erika replied. "He's the large man at the far end of the bar."

O'Grady looked at Ryker then back at Erika. "You have to be fooking joking, Erika. Where did you find that ollphéist?" (Ollphéist was Gaelic for 'nightmare' or 'monster').

"I don't understand that word, Cyril," Erika said.

"Never mind. How did you two meet?"

"We never knew each other during the war," Erika lied. "After the war, we both fled to Buenos Aires. There are several German beer halls in Buenos Aires because of the large number of Germans who relocated there before, during, and after the war. It was at one of those German beer halls in that city that we met in 1946. Ryker and I had things in common. Both of us were on war crimes tribunal lists which made us hunted fugitives. Mainly for that reason we decided to cooperate with each other for our mutual benefit."

"And he's now your bodyguard?"

"More or less," Erika answered. "A better way to put it is we look out for each other. We have a mutual understanding."

A severe-looking waitress delivered the drinks, took O'Grady's money and tip, and walked away without saying thank you.

"Let's get your friend over here," said O'Grady.

Erika turned and looked at Ryker, who was already looking at them as any good bodyguard would be doing. She signaled Ryker to come to her table.

The menacing, former Heinrich Himmler ghoul got up from his bar stool and walked their way.

Chapter 52

Denver, Colorado
Same evening—Tuesday, 25 May 1948

Axel Ryker sat down at the table with Cyril O'Grady and Erika Lehmann. Ryker made no verbal comment, he instead stared threateningly at O'Grady which might be Ryker's way of making a statement during such a situation. O'Grady was impressed by Ryker, but not intimated. Erika could see in the Irishman's eyes that he was not scared of Ryker. Few men were not concerned when they found themselves being the object of Axel Ryker's attention. She knew she had a tough mark this time in O'Grady.

"Cyril, this is my associate, Axel Ryker," Erika said. She then looked at Ryker. "Axel, this is someone I recently met, Mr. O'Grady."

Ryker still made no comment, instead holding his ominous focus on O'Grady. The Irishman did the same.

Erika sought to break the ice. "Perhaps after we're finished here we can go to the Irish Maiden. I saw shepherd's pie on its menu; I love lamb."

O'Grady caught the attention of the waitress and ordered another round.

"Mr. Ryker," O'Grady said, "Erika told me a wee bit about your past job history. It sounds to me that you were indeed a specialist in your field."

"I enjoyed my work and conducted my assignments with vigor."

"And some of those assignments were, how should I put it, less than savory?"

"I obeyed my orders."

Erika thought to herself that it would be fitting to chisel those words into Ryker's tombstone, and the sooner the better as far as she was concerned.

Ryker sat facing the door and saw Roxanne enter with a limp. She saw Ryker in return and turned her face away as she sat down on a barstool.

Without asking to be excused, Ryker rose and left the table. Erika turned and saw Roxanne.

"Where is he going?" O'Grady asked Erika.

"He knows the woman at the bar. I'm sure he's just saying 'hello'."

"He doesn't seem to be the type to concern himself with polite decorum."

"I agree, but I'm sure that's all it is, Cyril. He'll be back in a moment." She raised her glass and said, "Sláinte!" an Irish toast.

O'Grady raised his glass.

◊ ◊ ◊

The music now started up once more and a new striptease artist took to the stage as Ryker approached Roxanne at the bar.

"Where were you last night?" Ryker asked gruffly. "I wanted to employ you. And why are you limping?"

Roxanne finally turned her face to Ryker. Her jaw was swollen; she had a cut on the bridge of her nose and sported a black eye.

"I was beaten because I didn't pay Billy his ten dollars. The other night, when I gave you a freebie, I didn't have the money to pay him. He gets half of everything I make."

"Who is this 'Billy'?" Ryker asked without emotion.

"He owns this place," Roxanne answered. "I don't want any trouble, Axel. I have to work here."

"Where is he?"

"Please, Axel, don't cause trouble—for my sake."

Ryker flagged over the bartender. When the man stood across from him, Ryker grabbed his shirt and pulled his head down onto the bar. "Where is Billy?" Ryker demanded.

"Fuck you!" the bartender yelled. "Let go of me!"

The Thirsty Tiger employed one bouncer on weekday nights, two on weekends. The burly weeknight bouncer rushed over. Ryker quickly dispatched him. While keeping one hand on the bartender, Ryker blocked a punch from the bouncer with his free hand, hooked his arm into the man's arm and with what seemed like little effort on his part, broke the man's arm at the elbow. The bouncer shouted in pain and dropped to the floor near Ryker's feet. Ryker stomped on the man's chest, breaking several ribs. He then turned his attention back to the bartender.

Ryker grabbed a nearby empty beer bottle, broke it over the edge of the bar, and slowly pushed the jagged glass into the bartender's face until blood appeared.

"Will you answer my question now?" Ryker asked, again his words containing no discernable emotion, just a calm.

"Okay! Okay!" the bartender muttered loudly in pain. "He's in his office. It's the door at the other end of the bar!"

Ryker lifted the bartender's head up from the bar and shoved him so violently the man literally came off the floor and flew back into the liquor shelves, shattering bottles and the bar mirror painted with a Bengal tiger.

Roxanne shrieked and said, "Stop, Axel!"

Of course, everyone in the place was now transfixed on the scene as it unfolded, including Erika, O'Grady and his men, and Al Hodge's undercover men. The woman on stage had taken off only half of her clothes before she saw the trouble and disappeared behind the curtain. The striptease music from the jukebox kept playing in the cigarette smoke-filled room.

Ryker walked to the opposite end of the bar and tried the doorknob. It was locked. With one kick from Ryker, the steel door exploded from both the lock and the door hinges on the opposite side and flew into the office.

A pale man with a thin black moustache and greasy black hair sat behind a desk counting money. Several stacks of bills laid on the desk in front of him. When the door crashed, and Ryker entered, he jumped out of his seat.

"What the fuck!" the man exclaimed.

"Are you, Billy?" Ryker asked.

The man didn't answer; instead, he yanked open a desk drawer and reached for a revolver. It was much too little and too late. Ryker was upon him and easily twisted the man's hand until the gun dropped to the floor. Ryker put an arm around the man's neck and swiftly applied a jerk. The man fell to the floor. Billy's body laid on its stomach, but the head was turned completely around with the eyes staring in death at the ceiling.

A backdoor to the office supplied Billy an access to an alley. Ryker quickly grabbed up the money on the desk, then used the alley door.

The brutal dispatching of Billy took mere seconds. By the time Erika and O'Grady rushed into the office, and then out the open door into the alley (followed by O'Grady's men), Axel Ryker was nowhere to be seen.

Erika was flabbergasted at what just happened, but she collected herself. "Cyril," she said firmly, "have your men take the woman Ryker was talking to at the bar to the cabins. The only way we'll find him is through his prostitute."

Chapter 53

Denver, Colorado
Next day—Wednesday, 26 May 1948

Late last night, a meeting was held at Lowry Air Force Base. In attendance were Leroy Carr, Al Hodge, and Al's three men who staked-out the Thirsty Tiger. Agent Houchen, one of the men and Hodge's top lieutenant among the team, filled in Carr and Hodge about what went down at the gentlemen's club.

Now it was the morning of the next day and Carr and Hodge met alone. Both men were fuming. Al Hodge started his rant first.

"I would never say this in front of anyone else, that's why I didn't mention it in front of my men last night, but you screwed up, Leroy. We should have captured that group last night like I suggested."

"Hold on a minute, Al. None of us knew O'Grady would bring most of his team with him. Your men were outnumbered. You had three guys! On O'Grady's side there were five including him. I know your men are skilled, but so are they. We're talking about ruthless, professional mercenaries. So don't give me that shit. It was supposed to be a simple surveillance assignment and would have been simple if Ryker wouldn't have slaughtered some low life."

"That sonuvabitch doesn't care about that prostitute," Hodge said about Ryker. "He just saw an opportunity to do what he enjoys."

"You're probably right," Carr replied.

"I told you in the beginning that Ryker was a bad idea, Leroy. Then you told me the reason you brought him in on this was for his interrogation skills—if you want to use that name for torture. We can't interrogate anyone until we take someone into custody. Now we don't know where Ryker is, and we don't know what O'Grady will do after last night. If he's spooked he's liable to do anything, including move his operation."

"We're getting nowhere griping at each other," Carr said. "We've tripled the security at the arsenal. It's well protected. To up the ante, take two of your agents and assign one to surveil the cabins. They'll have to hide their car several miles away and one will hike in; the other one will stay at the car. Give them both walkie-talkies. Tell the man who surveils the cabins to stay hidden and not get closer than 500 yards away, preferably farther than that. If he's close enough to watch the cabins without binoculars he's too close and tell him to move farther away. You have enough men now to go in shifts, so you can stakeout the place day and night, right?"

"Yeah," Hodge answered.

"If there is any indication that O'Grady and his men are packing up and leaving their current location, then we'll move in with plenty of fire power. Your men, plus as many MPs from this base as we need. I think experienced MPs would work better than National Guard troops in this case. The MPs are here on the base and we have no time to waste. I'll start that process today and keep the MP unit on high alert. You can take care of insuring teamwork between the MP squad and your men. Do you feel better now, Al?"

"At least we're doing something besides sitting around with our thumbs up our asses, relying on a couple of Nazis."

"Ex-Nazis," Carr reminded. "At least in Erika's case. I'm not sure that applies to Ryker."

"You have too much confidence in Lehmann, old friend," Hodge stated.

"Maybe so, Al."

◊ ◊ ◊

Since they arrived back at the cabins last night, O'Grady had shunned Erika and had spent the morning meeting with this team in the other cabin where Roxanne was being held.

Finally, she saw O'Grady walking out into the woods alone. She quickly followed and caught up to him.

"Why are you avoiding me, Cyril?"

"I'm not avoiding you, Erika. After last night I've had to make some changes. Now I'm going for a bit of target practice. I prefer to be alone when I do that, so if you don't mind, please return to your cabin. You and the men can train this afternoon."

"If I'm a member of the team, why wasn't I included in your meetings this morning?"

O'Grady stopped and turn toward her. "What do you want, Erika?"

"It's not what I want. It's what we as a team need. We have to find my bodyguard."

"Why?"

"He learned last night that I am with you, and I guarantee he spotted your other men in the club. Ryker is very experienced and cunning. Not only that, he is merciless and cruel. You learned that last night. He's devoted to protecting me and he'll be looking for us. It's better if we have him working with us than against you. Believe me, you don't know what that man is capable of. He's done much worse than what he did last night."

"I'm not worried about him, Erika. If he shows his face, he's dead." O'Grady again began walking.

"You need to listen to me, Cyril. If you *were* able to kill him, it wouldn't be before he had already killed half of your men."

O'Grady impatiently stopped again. "Then we'll see, won't we?"

"Have you talked to Roxanne?"

"She knows nothing as far as his whereabouts."

"I believe her but let me talk to her alone—woman to woman. You have nothing to lose, Cyril."

◊ ◊ ◊

Each day, Chris Singleton had one of the men on his taskforce stop by the Denver Police Headquarters and pick up a copy of the police reports from the previous day. Everything was there, from minor traffic accidents to felonies. Singleton spent the time each day to read them all, but he always began with the serious crime reports.

The reports from yesterday included a non-fatal stabbing in an incident between neighbors in an apartment building on 38th Avenue. On the south side, someone had brandished a gun as he robbed a furniture store. There were several more felonies listed, then Singleton came to a report on a murder in a downtown gentlemen's club. The police had questioned the bartender from his bed at Denver General

Hospital. The bartender had responded that the suspect was a large man with a foreign accent. He also stated that after the suspect forced his way into the murder victim's office, five other customers got out of their seats and rushed into the office behind the suspect. The bartender was incapacitated on the floor behind the bar and didn't see anything that happened in the office, but none of the people in question emerged back out into the club area, meaning they all had to have fled out the back door. When asked to give descriptions of the five, the bartender had little to offer except that one was a woman—a blonde woman.

[that afternoon]

When the afternoon training ended, Erika returned to the cabin to find it empty except for Roxanne, who sat at the small picnic bench table used for meals by the men. This surprised Erika, who assumed O'Grady had denied her request to speak with Roxanne alone. Before talking to the obviously terrified woman, Erika quickly checked the other rooms of the cabin to make sure O'Grady didn't have one of his men lurking out of sight listening. Erika knew O'Grady would never again allow her out on her own, so she had no way to get a message to Marienne or Al Hodge. And the telephone in the cabin wasn't an option. It was rendered useless by removing the speaker piece from the receiver. Something O'Grady kept with him. He replaced it only when he chose to use the phone. Erika's only hope was to use Ryker's prostitute.

"Your name is Roxanne, right?" Erika asked as she sat down across from her.

The woman nodded.

"Roxanne, you can trust me. My name is Erika and I'm a friend of Axel Ryker. I think I can help you get out of here if you will in turn help me." Referring to Ryker as a 'friend' nearly forced Erika to laugh at herself. "Will you trust me?"

Roxanne didn't answer. She meekly sat across the table and visibly shook.

"You have to get ahold of yourself, Roxanne, if you want to get out of here alive."

Roxanne's nerves continued to make her shake, but she finally spoke. "What are you talking about? How can you help me—and why am I here?"

"Never mind why you are here; our time is limited." Erika had yet to be allowed in the other cabin, the one Roxanne stayed in last night. "What did you see in the other cabin? Weapons, I'm sure. Anything that looked like explosives, maybe dynamite?"

"I didn't see any dynamite, but I saw an open box that had a bunch of gasmasks in it. What's going on?"

"Again, we don't have time," Erika said. "Just answer my questions. Did you ever tell Ryker where you live? It's important to remember yes or no."

"No, he never came to my apartment."

"I didn't ask you that. Did you ever tell him where your home is located?"

"No . . . wait, I might have mentioned it once."

"Did you mention it or not, Roxanne? Think!"

The prostitute looked flustered. "Yes, I mentioned it once, okay? But he was never there and won't remember what I said."

Erika knew the crafty Ryker had a near photographic memory.

"You're probably wrong about him not remembering. If I get you out of here, which I think I can, hopefully Ryker will show up at your place. He won't show his face again at his hotel or the gentlemen's club, that's certain. He needs a place to lie low. We must hope he seeks you out. If he shows up, you have to give him a message. Can you do that?"

Roxanne was ready to agree to anything if it would help get her out of this place. "Yes."

Erika needed a message that Ryker would understand but Roxanne would not. "You need to memorize something. Repeat the words: 'Zerstör Männer und Hütten.'"

"What?"

"It's the message you have to deliver to Ryker. 'Zerstör Männer und Hütten'. Repeat it out loud."

"Jester manner and hutting."

"No. Listen carefully." Erika repeated the command.

This time, Roxanne was closer, but still off. Erika spoke it and had Roxanne repeat until the German words were such that Erika knew Ryker would understand.

"Repeat that phrase in your head as often as you can from now until you see Ryker."

"Can you write it down?" Roxanne asked.

"No. They'll likely search you before they take you back to Denver."

Then Erika cautioned the courtesan, "If you betray me and tell this to any of the men at these cabins, they will first kill you, then me. Do you understand, Roxanne?"

Chapter 54

Colorado
Next day—Thursday, 27 May 1948

Cyril O'Grady was a harsh man, but not without empathy for people such as himself who were being pursued by authorities because of their extreme reactionary political views (such as the case with Nazis on the run).

Yet, he was confused about Erika Lehmann. In a way he had grown fond of her; they had spent intimate nights together; yet, he was leery.

After breakfast this morning, she had asked him if they could take a walk together.

As they entered the pine forest, Erika started the conversation.

"Cyril, I have to talk to you again about finding my bodyguard. He can be a great addition to your team. I think I know of a way."

O'Grady didn't look at her or stop walking. She continued.

"If we release the prostitute, I think Ryker will seek her out. You can have some of your men surveil her. We need Ryker on this team, Cyril. He is skilled and ruthless, as you have seen, and he is on the run from prosecution by war crimes tribunals. He will gladly join us if I give him the okay."

O'Grady didn't respond and kept walking.

◊ ◊ ◊

Leroy Carr always checked for message with the Lowry Air Force base switchboard WAFs when he returned to the base after being out and about, mainly in case there were any messages from his office staff at CIA headquarters. When he returned to Lowry shortly before noon, after a trip to the Rocky Mountain Arsenal to check on enhanced security measures, he had a message, but it was not from whom he expected. The message was from the FBI agent Chris Singleton asking Carr to call him.

When Carr got back to his barracks room, he called the FBI Denver field office.

"Special Agent Singleton," Carr said into the phone, "this is Leroy Carr. I got your message."

"Thanks for returning my call, Mr. Carr," Singleton replied over the phone. "May I have a meeting with you today? I would consider it a professional courtesy. I'll be glad to come to you if that is convenient."

Carr shook his head in silence. Was he never going to be rid of this guy? He thought going to Singleton's office to be the best option. That way he could leave when he wanted.

"I'll come to your office, Agent Singleton. Will one o'clock work for you?"

"I'll be here, Mr. Carr. Thank you."

◊ ◊ ◊

Early that afternoon, Cyril O'Grady had Roxanne searched, then he ordered Petros to drive her to Denver and release her, but not near her apartment. Lukus sat with her in the back seat and she was let out of the car twenty blocks from her apartment. Having no money for a bus, she would have to walk home from there.

◊ ◊ ◊

Carr arrived at the FBI field headquarters alone. Hodge stayed behind at Lowry to begin the process of forming a working team made up of his men and four Lowry MPs that Carr had requested from Major General Curry.

Singleton greeted Carr at his office door. "Thank you for coming, Mr. Carr," Singleton said as they shook hands. "Please, come in and have a seat. May I get you something, a cup of coffee, perhaps?"

"Nothing, but thank you Special Agent Singleton."

Singleton motioned to a chair. Carr sat down. Instead of circling behind his desk, the FBI man pulled up another chair near Carr. That gesture alone told Carr he faced a worthy adversary, a man who had no interest in placing himself above a man in Carr's position by staring at him across a desk. Singleton knew what he was doing, and so did Leroy Carr.

"What can I do for you this time, Agent Singleton," Carr asked after both men had settled in.

Placed on the edge of his desk where it could be reached without Singleton being forced to stand was a sheet of paper. The young FBI man reached for it and handed it to Carr.

"Mr. Carr, this is a report from the Denver police about a crime that occurred yesterday."

"I assume you want me to read it," Carr replied.

"Yes, please."

Carr took a moment to do so. Singleton was a good detective and had once again impressed Leroy Carr. When Carr finished reading, instead of acting ignorant of the situation as he had done when Singleton appeared at his door at Lowry, Carr changed directions.

"Very well, Agent Singleton. I know why I'm here. The bartender reported to the police that the male suspect spoke with an accent, and one of the people who followed him out the back was a blonde woman. Yes, the CIA is in Denver conducting an operation. The episode at the striptease club Tuesday night has nothing to do with our objective. That was just an unfortunate incident."

"Especially unfortunate for the man whose neck was snapped like a chicken's," Singleton said.

"Yes, that's true. However, so you know, that man extorted large amounts of the money from the women who worked for him and then beat them mercilessly on many occasions."

"Let me get this straight, what you're telling me is he got what he deserved."

"That's not our focus here. The CIA was in no way involved in what happened. I'm being truthful, Agent Singleton, that's all. I assume that's what you want. Shall I continue, or should we stop our conversation now?"

"Please continue, Mr. Carr."

"I will bring you in on our interests here in Denver, but it will be a hard decision on your part. My condition will be that the FBI participation is limited to just yourself—not your men, and certainly not Director Hoover."

"There's no way that's going to happen, Mr. Carr."

"Then our business is completed here." Carr rose from his chair and warned, "Be careful where you tread, Agent Singleton."

"That sounds like a threat, Mr. Carr."

"No, it's advice," Carr replied. "If by some means you are able to piece things together and find the man with the German accent who is the suspect in the striptease club killing, be careful of him, Agent Singleton. I respect you. I think you're a good man and a clever investigator. That's why I was honest with you here today. I wouldn't want to see something tragic befall you, as usually happens when someone is at odds with the man in question. Ask the bartender and the bouncer; they got off easy. You know what happened to the club's owner; he can't verify but the facts speak for themselves."

[late that evening]

By the time Roxanne had made the long walk from where Petros dropped her off on Colfax Avenue, the evening sky was dark when she finally arrived home at her tiny, rundown studio apartment on Larimer Street. The place was certainly nothing to be proud of; nevertheless, Roxanne breathed a sigh of relief when she entered and shut and locked the door behind her.

When she flipped on the light, she saw Axel Ryker sitting on the small sofa holding a glass of vodka, the bottle on the small table next to him.

Chapter 55

Denver, Colorado
Same day—Thursday, 27 May 1948

"Axel!" Roxanne exclaimed in surprise. Even though he simply sat on the sofa, seeing him there when the light came on startled her.

"You told me you had a young son," Ryker said callously. "Where is he?" Everything was suspicious to Axel Ryker.

"He stays with my mother in Colorado Springs. I'm gone from home too much. I don't want to leave him alone."

"Sit down."

"How long have you been here?" Roxanne asked as she lower herself onto the sofa next to him. The worn upholstery had small rips in several places.

"I stayed here last night."

"How did you get in?"

"The locks are simple. You should get better ones. Where were you last night, and the night before?"

"You're not going to believe it, Axel." Roxanne went on to tell him about the men who had kidnapped her at the Thirsty Tiger then taken her to the mountain cabins, and the mysterious woman who called herself 'Erika' who had succeeded in getting her released.

"She gave me a message to give you, Axel."

"What is it?"

"Just a minute. Let me get it straight. I don't understand the words." Roxanne thought for a moment then said, "Zerstör Männer und Hütten."

Ryker grabbed her arm. "Repeat that!"

Now Roxanne was frightened. "Zerstör Männer und Hütten." She tried to pull her arm away but couldn't. Finally, Ryker released her.

"What does it mean, Axel?"

Roxanne carried a too important message. He could kill her now that she had delivered those orders, but he uncharacteristically decided against it.

"It means you are going to this Colorado Springs to stay with your mother. You're not safe here." Ryker knew O'Grady wouldn't let

Roxanne go without assigning some men to follow her. "We'll stay here tonight, but you leave on a bus tomorrow morning. Do you have any money?"

"No."

"Why is it you never have any money?"

"I told you the other night that I've always had to give half of what I earned to Billy. Out of what's left I keep only enough to buy some food and pay my rent. The rest I send to my mother to use for the care of my son."

"Where is your father?"

"I don't know who my father is, where he is, or if he's even alive."

Ryker's pockets were filled with the cash he had taken from Billy's desk. He counted out $1000 and handed it to her.

Roxanne sat dumbfounded. After giving Billy half of everything she earned, that sum was as much as she made in a year.

An ill-omened smile appeared on Ryker's face. He now had some orders he would enjoy.

"Stay here and keep the door locked," Ryker told her. "Wait for my return."

Ryker descended the filthy stairs and exited out the back of the flea bag apartment building.

A half-block down on Larimer Street, Petros and his uncle Lukus both sat in the front seat of a car, watching the entrance of the building they saw the prostitute enter after following her from where they dropped her off. They snacked on sausages and hard bread while they amused each other with funny family anecdotes from years ago in Athens.

Lukus brought up a memory. "Remember when your father tried to help the old lady who had dropped her sack of food, Petros?" Petros' father was Lukus' brother.

"I remember," said the young man. "She thought he was trying to steal her food and she beat him with her handbag."

"Yeah, the old hag put a big knot on his head."

Both men chuckled.

Suddenly, they heard one of the car's back doors open. A large man quickly entered, sat down and closed the door.

Lukus was inside the Thirsty Tiger on the night of the mayhem and immediately recognized Axel Ryker.

"Guten Abend, gentlemen," Ryker said. "Don't let me interrupt your meal."

"We have been sent here to find you," Lukus said. "The woman said you might show up."

"It seems she was correct," Ryker said calmly.

Lukus and Petros never finished their sausages.

Part 5

Often an entire city has suffered because of an evil man.

—*Hesiod, ca. 8th century B.C.*

Chapter 56

Denver, Colorado
Friday, 28 May 1948

CIA agent Ralph Vaughn, one of Al Hodge's men, sat on a heavy layer of pine needles on the forest floor, 700 yards from the mountain cabins he had spent the past three hours watching through binoculars. He had watched men coming and going from the two cabins. Some disappeared into the forest, presumably for training. Some traveled to the outhouse.

Suddenly, Vaughn heard a twig snap behind him. He turned, but it was too late. Cyril O'Grady lifted his shotgun and pulled the trigger. From outside the cabins, O'Grady had seen the sun reflect off the lens of Vaughn's binoculars. O'Grady searched the body but found no identification. He assumed the man to be from the FBI.

O'Grady was now on high alert. Not only was the location of the cabins known to someone or some agency, but Lukus and Petros had failed to report in that morning.

[four hours later]
Axel Ryker appeared out of the forest and walked into the small clearing where the cabins sat. He was armed to the teeth and ready to kill everyone there—his orders from Erika Lehmann. After all, just the other day, Leroy Carr himself had again instructed Ryker to follow her orders. Knowing that he was outnumbered six to one did not deter Ryker.

He was disappointed. No one emerged to confront him, and after searching the cabins he found nothing—no men, not Erika, and no weapons or explosives.

Ryker burned both wood cabins to the ground.

◊ ◊ ◊

[early that evening—Lowry Air Force Base]
Al Hodge stormed into Leroy Carr's barracks room.

195

"Leroy! Ralph Vaughn is dead!"

"What???"

"Ralph was surveilling the cabins and someone killed him. Agent Burke was stationed down below the mountain; when he didn't get a check-in on the walkie-talkie for two hours in a row, he trekked up to the surveillance point and found Ralph dead. Someone had shot him!"

"Jesus God!" Carr replied loudly. "Okay, Al, we move in tonight. Have your men here in two hours. I'll get in touch with Ryker and Marienne and get them here. After we decide on a strategy, I'll meet with the MPs. We'll take out O'Grady and his men before dawn. Waiting for Erika to find out who hired him just dropped off our totem pole."

[midnight]

Now assembled in Leroy Carr's small room at Lowry were, besides Carr, Hodge and his remaining men and Marienne Schenk. There weren't enough chairs to go around, so most of Hodge's men stood. Carr had been unsuccessful in finding Axel Ryker.

They had barely begun to discuss the planned attack on the cabins when Carr's telephone rang.

"Yes," Carr said impatiently into the receiver. He listened to the WAF operator then, as she made the connection, he told the others that it was Ryker calling in.

"Ryker, where in hell are you?" Carr half-shouted when the connection was complete. The CIA Deputy Director listened, then everyone in the room heard him say, "Stay there, we'll come get you." Carr hung up.

"Al, Ryker is calling from the guard shack at the Lowry main entrance. He doesn't have the proper identification, so the MPs won't let him into the base. Take one of your men, go get Ryker and bring him here."

Twenty minutes later, Hodge walked in with Ryker.

"Okay, Ryker, spill the beans," Carr said.

"I received orders from Fräulein Lehmann to eliminate O'Grady's men and destroy the cabins where they hide."

"Wait a minute," Hodge interrupted. "When did you see Lehmann?"

"I did not. My orders were relayed to me by a third party, a woman who O'Grady took hostage. Lehmann obtained her release."

Carr had too many important things to contend with to concern himself with who this other woman was and why O'Grady had held her hostage. He'd come back to that.

Hodge again interjected. "Ryker, O'Grady or one of his men killed one of my men this morning."

"That seems unfortunate for you," said Ryker, "but then again this is part of our game."

"Fuck you, you sonuvabitch!" A couple of Hodge's men had to restrain their boss, luckily for Hodge.

Carr understood Hodge's raw emotions. "Ryker, we're taking out O'Grady and his men. A team of Al's men and some MPs will attack the cabins tonight. You'll be on that team"

"There are no cabins to attack," Ryker said. "I burned them to the ground this afternoon."

"What are you talking about?"

"I already told you I received orders from Fräulein Lehmann to eliminate the men and destroy the cabins. When I arrived at the cabins, they were deserted. I did manage to encounter two of O'Grady's men last night and they are no longer a threat. This is good protocol, yes?" After the murders, Ryker calmly returned to Roxanne's apartment, cleaned off the blood from his hands and changed out of his blood-soaked clothes. He had brought extra shirts and pants with him when he moved into Roxanne's apartment from the Oxford the day before.

Everyone in the room simply stared at Ryker. He continued, "I kept one alive for a short time in the car where I intercepted them. I interrogated the man and I will tell you what he revealed. After that I followed good procedure and canceled this second man." Ryker had slashed Petros' throat immediately but kept Lukus alive until he was certain in his mind it was useless to let him continue living. "I did well for you, yes? I obeyed my orders from your Fräulein, as you instructed, and I am telling you about it—another one of your orders. The enemy team is now down to four men. I know you are happy with my performance."

Chapter 57

Denver, Colorado
Next day—Saturday, 29 May 1948

Leroy Carr instructed Al Hodge to confirm Ryker's story. Hodge had Agent Houchen drive. They took along Ryker to show them where he had killed O'Grady's two men. Obviously, the bodies had been removed by now but two police cars were parked at either end of the car Ryker pointed out and it was roped off. They didn't stop.

They then took the time to drive into the mountains, and in the middle of the night used flashlights to hike through the thick pine forest where they confirmed Ryker's story about burning down the cabins. It was nearly four in the morning before Hodge returned to Lowry. Carr got Ryker a barracks room at the Air Force base. From now on he didn't want Himmler's fiend out of his sight. Carr told Ryker he was changing his orders. No longer would Ryker take orders from anyone but him. This was fine by Ryker. He didn't like taking orders from Erika Lehmann in the first place.

Now it was seven o'clock in the morning, and after only two hours sleep, Carr and Hodge met one-on-one in the base mess hall for coffee.

"While you were verifying Ryker's story," Carr said, "Marienne and I talked. She requested to be released since she had not done anything in a week. I gave the okay but asked her to stay on standby in case we need her again. She's flying home today."

Hodge nodded, then asked, "How are we going to get a clue on where O'Grady has gone? Do you think he could have called off the mission after he found out the cabins were being watched?"

"I doubt it, Al, but I guess it's possible, especially now that he's two men down. The only way we're going to know is if Erika can somehow manage to contact us. That she hasn't surfaced tells us nothing. If O'Grady aborts his mission, he might release her after he's safely out of town, or he might hold her hostage, or worse, if he suspects her of being a plant."

"She's lived a dangerous life, Leroy. The odds have to catch up to her someday."

[later that morning]

After Chris Singleton read the morning police report, he left the FBI offices and drove to the Denver police station. He requested to see the detective who was assigned to a double homicide that occurred on Larimer Street. The crime had happened too late to be included in that morning's Rocky Mountain News (the Denver Post was the afternoon newspaper).

Singleton was escorted to a Detective Bolles.

"What can I do for you, Agent Singleton?" Bolles asked after he looked over Singleton's badge and I.D.

"I understand you're the detective assigned to a double homicide that took place last night."

"That's right. Two John Doe's found butchered in a car."

Singleton had brought along a few notes from the police report. "And this happened on . . . Larimer Street?"

"Yeah, it's a shady, rundown part of town. Lots of hobos, drunks, and trollops. It's our highest crime area here in Denver."

"What can you tell me that isn't in the report, Detective Bolles?"

"I don't mind telling you, Agent Singleton, but may I ask why the FBI is interested? This is most likely an open and closed case of a heroin deal gone bad, or somebody who didn't pay off a gambling debt owed to one of the Smaldones."

Singleton had been briefed about the Smaldones. "I'll be honest with you, Agent Bolles. I have no specific reason why the FBI is interested. I'm solely asking as a courtesy."

Bolles found his notes. "Two men, one approximately early twenties, the other perhaps late thirties. The bodies are down at the coroner's office now. The coroner will give me more details later today such as height and weight, scars or tattoos—the normal stuff that might be helpful in identifying them."

"How did they die?"

"Knife. The younger man was found slumped over the steering wheel. His throat had been slit. The other guy had three fingers and an ear missing. The fingers and ear were found in the floor board. The coroner thinks they were cut off while the man was still alive. The blood had squirted all over the car, indicating the man's heart was still beating when the extremities were cut off. I'm leaning toward a mob hit. It looked like a professional job. Another reason I think it was not a lowlife drug dealer who killed them is the stiffs still had money on them and still wore identical, expensive foreign wristwatches. And the knife was left behind. Amateurs don't do that, as you know, Agent Singleton."

"I don't suppose you found any fingerprints," Singleton said.

"Not on the knife. Our dusting people are still working on the car, but I don't expect to find any."

"May I ask how you're going to pursue the case?"

"We have uniformed officers canvasing the neighborhood looking for any potential witnesses, and I'm waiting for the coroner's final report. After I read that, I'll be paying a visit to the Smaldones."

[late that afternoon]

"I'm sorry I missed your earlier call, Special Agent Singleton, I've been out all day," Leroy Carr said from his room phone at Lowry. "What's this about?"

"Mr. Carr," said Singleton from the other end. *"I've decided to take you up on your offer to join you and agree to your stipulations that I not inform my superiors. When can we meet?"*

Singleton waited for a pause at the other end, then heard Carr say, "I'll call you within an hour. We'll meet at a neutral site."

"Very well, I'll be here in my office expecting your call."

Singleton had made the phone call because he had no other options. For days he had been sitting on his haunches in Denver going nowhere. He expected the CIA was somehow connected to a string of local murders and he would infiltrate to prove or disprove his hunch.

As soon as Leroy Carr dropped the receiver down on the cradle, he picked it back up and got through to Al Hodge's room.

"Al, I just got an interesting phone call from our young Mr. Singleton. He wants to subvert us."

"Huh?"

"He didn't say that, of course, but that's what he has on his mind."

"What are you going to do, Leroy?"

"I'm going to let him. I think we can use this to our advantage."

[that evening]

Carr decided to meet Singleton in the bar at the Brown Palace Hotel where the FBI man stayed. Singleton now sat in a corner booth across from Carr and Hodge. They had ordered drinks and had already been served. Even though it was Saturday night, the bar was not crowded. Most guests of the Brown Palace preferred to get out of the hotel and enjoy other venues in Denver on the weekends. No one sat in the booth next to them or in the one after that; they could talk.

Carr started, "Special Agent Singleton, you told me on the phone that you agree to not inform Director Hoover if I fill you in on why the CIA is here in Denver. I need to hear that from you face-to-face."

"That's right," Singleton answered, "and call me Chris."

"Then feel free to call Al and me by our first names." Carr took a drink of his gin and tonic then filled Singleton in on the basics. He was truthful about the issue of the threat to the Rocky Mountain arsenal and told Singleton about Cyril O'Grady. Hodge was surprised at how much factual information his boss divulged, but then again, he had already been surprised many times when it came to this mission. Hodge took it in stride. He knew Leroy had reasons for doing things.

Singleton asked, "So what's my role, Mr. Carr . . . Leroy?"

"I need a photograph and article published in the local newspapers. The CIA cannot do this because we have to remain covert, but the FBI, our country's top law enforcement agency, can get it done."

"If I get something in the newspapers," Singleton warned, "and the FBI is mentioned, our headquarters in Denver will know about it immediately and inform our headquarters in Washington."

"I realize that, Chris," Leroy replied "but our purpose will have been served by then. Not even the FBI can erase a newspaper article after everyone in the Denver area has read it."

Chapter 58

Boulder, Colorado
Two days later—Monday, 31 May 1948

O'Grady and his team (including Erika) were now lying low in a small, rented warehouse in Boulder. O'Grady had rented this backup location weeks ago, as soon as he arrived in Denver. He always had a backup hideout on all his jobs. Many times they were never used; this time the move paid off.

The spartan warehouse had formerly stocked plumbing supplies, but now everything was gone, leaving behind a stark empty area. Wotan and Dante were sent out yesterday to buy army cots and that's where everyone slept—in the same room. There was a toilet and sink, but not a shower. The men jury-rigged a shower with a canvas draped across a water line for Erika's privacy, but the showers were taken using a garden hose supplying only cold water. Both of their remaining automobiles were parked inside the warehouse (Lukus and Petros had never returned with the third).

Breakfast was hard rolls and beans heated in a pan over a Bunsen Burner.

O'Grady and his men had been ready to undertake their mission for over a week, but the weather had not cooperated. For maximum effect, a wind, or at least a breeze, coming from the north or northeast was needed. Unfortunately for O'Grady, winds over Denver nearly always came down from the Rockies west of town and blew east, out into the plains.

Time had come to make a decision. O'Grady couldn't put it off any longer. Everyone sat on the various cots, Erika among them.

"I don't know what has happened to Lukus and Petros," O'Grady said to the group, "but they haven't asked for relief and have been missing for two days. If they have been captured, we have a problem. Petros knows nothing about the mission, but Lukus does."

Wotan interjected, "Lukus would never sing." The other men agreed.

"We have two choices," O'Grady said. "Scrap the mission, which will force me to return the money I've been given so far and none of you will get paid, or we can proceed regardless of the weather. If the winds aren't right, not as much damage will be done, but then again, we've completed the mission and can collect our money. We will proceed."

"When?" Darragh, the other Irishman, asked.

"Before the weekend," O'Grady answered. "We need at least two or three more nights to surveil the arsenal, especially now that we're down two men."

After the meeting, Dante left for his daily duty of procuring a morning newspaper for O'Grady who used it mainly to check the weather forecast.

When Dante returned with that morning's *Rocky Mountain News*, O'Grady never got to the weather page; instead, the front page froze his attention.

[close to the same time, Denver]
Carr and Hodge had just finished their bacon and French toast in the Lowry mess hall. Both had seen that morning's *Rocky Mountain News.*

"Leroy, you realize this is going to put Lehmann in danger, if she's still alive that is and still with O'Grady," Hodge said, referring to the front-page article.

"I know that, Al, but we have no choice. We have to do something to flush out O'Grady."

On the front page of the newspaper, prominently displayed, was a mug shot of Axel Ryker. The accompanying story read:

An unidentified man is being held in the Denver County Jail in connection with a string of recent murders in Denver. These crimes include the murder of the owner of a club on Market Street, and the murders of two men whose bodies were discovered in a car parked on Larimer Street. The suspect carried no identification and refuses to tell authorities his name. Anyone with information that might lead to this man's identification should call the Denver Police Department.

◊ ◊ ◊

In Boulder, Cyril O'Grady hid the newspaper so Erika wouldn't see it. Her 'bodyguard' had killed two of his men, and he was now certain that she had betrayed him.

Chapter 59

Boulder, Colorado
Next day—Tuesday, 01 June 1948

The first day of June brought with it bright sunshine and a brief rain. The sky remained bright during the shower, a phenomenon more common at higher altitudes because clouds were closer to the ground allowing the sun to ferret out places to find the earth by angling through the rain clouds. In Denver, it was possible to get a suntan during a rain.

Erika told Cyril O'Grady she would like to take a walk in the rain. Not wanting her to suspect he knew of her betrayal, he agreed. Still, he sent Wotan with her. "For your protection, Erika," O'Grady told her.

Of course, now their walk was not in the mountains, but on a city street on the southern edge of Boulder.

As they left the warehouse, Erika smelled the crisp and clean rain-scrubbed air, one of her favorite fragrances. It reminded her of her childhood in the Bavarian Alps. She welcomed the chance to walk with Wotan, the only German in O'Grady's group. Until now, she hadn't had the opportunity to talk to him one-on-one. Among other duties, he was the team's medic and had removed her stitches yesterday. She spoke in German.

"Where are you from, Wotan? In Germany, I mean."

"Ah, it is wonderful to speak German again. I was born in Dortmund, but when I was still a small boy my father moved the family to Hannover."

"Ah, so you're a northerner. I assumed as much from your accent."

"And you?"

"I spent my younger years in Bavaria, but my father and I lived in Berlin for several years, both before and during the war. Cyril has told the team what I did during the war—my time with Abwehr. What did you do during the war?" The rain still fell but had weakened to a sprinkle. Erika didn't mind that her clothes and hair were damp. The sun still shone.

"Like you, my name is included on the so-called 'war crimes' list. I was SS and served the Fatherland proudly with Einsatzgruppe 4A."

Erika nearly stopped in her tracks but shook off the surprise and kept walking. The Einsatzgruppen were mobile killing units that followed behind the advancing German troops on the Eastern Front. Their orders were to kill Jews, local Polish and Russian officials, and other undesirables. Einsatzgruppe 4A was particularly infamous for an atrocity near a place called Babi Yar where it murdered nearly 34,000 Jews by shooting or the use of mobile gas chamber trucks made deadly by diverting the truck's engine exhaust fumes into the enclosed truck bed.

"Yet you were a medic?"

"Yes, one of my duties included caring for our wounded soldiers, but my passion has always been flying. I learned to fly before the war, and I originally sought to join the Luftwaffe, but being in the Totenkopf-SS, my commanders assigned me to the Einsatzgruppen instead."

Erika left it at that; she didn't want to hear about his other duties with the Einsatzgruppen.

[later that morning—Denver]

Lunch at the Denver County Jail was served at 11:00 a.m. each day. A guard pushing a cart stopped at Axel Ryker's cell. Ryker was being held in the solitary confinement wing because of the heinous crimes for which he was under suspicion.

When the guard pushed Ryker's lunch of vegetable soup through a narrow slot in the cell bars, Ryker looked at it and said, "You gave that man across the corridor two bread rolls. Why do I get only one?"

"That guy isn't in here because he killed three people, so stick that roll where the sun don't shine, Ryker."

Axel Ryker had agreed to be placed in jail as part of the mission, but he would not forget the guard.

[two hours later]

Leroy Carr, Al Hodge, and Chris Singleton gathered in Singleton's FBI field headquarters office. Again, instead of Singleton taking his place behind his desk, the three men sat in chairs arranged in a triangle.

"Leroy," Singleton said, "as you know, the newspaper article you requested is out. I had to give Detective Bolles enough information to convince him that Ryker was the real killer, but he kept his word that the FBI wouldn't be mentioned in the newspaper article. It was treated as a one state crime, so this buys us a little more time before my superiors back in Washington find out about it. But Bolles will send Ryker's prints to the FBI print division as standard procedure. So we're on the clock."

"I doubt if the FBI has Ryker's prints on file, Chris," Leroy said, "but I understand what you mean. A suspect in three homicides will get the FBI's attention regardless."

"That's right," Singleton agreed.

"How long can Bolles keep Ryker in jail in this state?"

"Forty-eight hours," Singleton answered. "After that he will have to have Ryker arraigned or set him free."

Carr turned to Hodge. "Al, anything new on Ryker's prostitute?"

"Nothing. Ryker sticks to his story that he didn't harm her, but I don't believe him. I figure she's fish food at the bottom of some lake or buried somewhere in the mountains."

Carr returned to Singleton. "Chris, since we have only one day left before Ryker will have to be arraigned or released, let's just stand back and let him be arraigned. But let's make sure that information is in tomorrow morning's newspaper."

Chapter 60

Boulder, Colorado
Next day—Wednesday, 02 June 1948

In the warehouse was a small room that had apparently served as an office for the manager or owner of the building when it held plumbing equipment. In that room, Cyril O'Grady and Erika Lehmann spent the night together. O'Grady, tired after a night of passion, awoke late. When he emerged into the main area where his men stayed, Darragh handed him that morning's newspaper.

On the front page was a brief article noting that the suspect in custody for three recent murders would be arraigned before a judge that afternoon at the Denver courthouse.

This was good news for O'Grady. He now had an opportunity for revenge on the man who killed Lukus and Petros. He called the group together, including Erika, and had them all read the newspaper article.

"Erika, now is the time to prove you belong on this team," O'Grady said in front of everyone. "Your bodyguard betrayed you and us. It will be your job to kill him. Are you willing to do this?"

"I'm willing, but I'll need a sniper rifle."

"We have three, you can take your pick. We have a German rifle you'll probably recognize."

"If Ryker is being taken to the courthouse this afternoon," Erika said, "I have to move quickly."

"Dante will drive you and offer help as needed," O'Grady added.

As Erika walked away to look over the rifle choices, O'Grady gave Dante his order. "She's not going to kill her bodyguard. They are working together, either for the FBI or CIA. Your own reports from scouting the arsenal tell us the Americans have recently increased security. They must think we're fools. Before you get to Denver, pull over in a remote area. Make sure you bury the body, then come back here. The weather gods have finally smiled on us. The forecast for tomorrow is what we've been waiting for. We attack the arsenal tomorrow tonight."

[one hour later]

Erika had picked out her rifle, a Karabiner 98K with a Zeiss Zielvier 4x telescopic sight. O'Grady was right, she was very familiar with the German-made weapon, having trained with it at Quenzsee. Apparently, the German Wotan had chosen the rifle as part of the team's arsenal. Still, Erika wondered why she had yet to see or learn of any explosives. Roxanne told her she saw no explosives in the second cabin, and Erika had seen nothing after the move into the warehouse other than small arms.

The newspaper article failed to mention a time of Ryker's arraignment, simply stating 'this afternoon.'

Dante offered friendly small talk as they drove out of the Boulder city limits. "Looks like we might have a long wait this afternoon," he said pleasantly.

"Yes, we might," Erika replied. "Those courts usually take long lunch breaks, so we should have plenty of time to find a good vantage point. The wait will work to our advantage."

Between Boulder and the outskirts of Denver lie about twenty miles of woodlands or farmland. As they approached one of the islands of trees, Dante said, "I'm sorry Erika, I have to pull over here for a moment. Wouldn't you know it, nature always calls?"

Dante pulled off the road and drove a short way through the trees, the 1940 Dodge Deluxe bumping and jostling over the uneven terrain.

"I'll be just a moment," he said as he exited the car. He walked a few feet away and, with his back to the car, appeared to fidget with his pants zipper. He spun around quickly with his pistol in hand as he shouted, "Get out of the car!"

Those were the last words Dante would ever say. He saw Erika pointing her Beretta at him, her arm extended outside the car's rolled down window. The muzzle flashed and the bullet entered his head between his eyes. The gunshot sent a resting clamor of rooks squawking into the sky.

Dante had made the mistake of turning off the engine when he stopped.

Erika dragged Dante's body to the car and deposited it in the trunk. She jumped behind the wheel, started the engine, slammed the stick into reverse and spun the wheels until she was back on the road. She sped down the dirt road, leaving a cloud of dust in her wake until she finally reached a gasoline filling station. From there she called Lowry but Hodge was not in. Erika still wasn't aware that Leroy Carr was in Denver. She jumped back into the car knowing her best bet to reacquire Hodge would probably be at the Denver County Courthouse. Erika knew Hodge would be along for any transfer of Ryker from the jail.

[30 minutes later]

When Erika arrived at the Denver County Courthouse, she parked in a lot located in a city park that directly faced the courthouse. There were already several police cars and a paddy wagon parked in front of the large building. She relaxed in her seat and waited. This location would have served as a good spot to kill Ryker with the sniper rifle if she had ever intended to do that.

She sat there for over an hour. Finally, a large entourage of uniformed Denver policemen emerged from the building with a handcuffed Ryker and led him to the paddy wagon, the arraignment apparently over. Following them was Al Hodge, but the surprise for Erika was that walking next to Hodge was the FBI agent who had been chasing her since her mission in Evansville in 1943.

Instead of approaching Hodge, which was her original intent, Erika watched until the paddy wagon and escort of police cars pulled away to return Ryker to jail. She started the engine, put the Dodge in gear, and drove away.

Chapter 61

Denver, Colorado
Same day—Wednesday, 02 June 1948

Chris Singleton had just returned to the Brown Palace after a lengthy meeting with Leroy Carr and his CIA team. The plan concocted to draw out Cyril O'Grady had failed. Singleton had, on Carr's request, succeeded in convincing the Denver police to have the newspaper articles published, but O'Grady didn't bite. They ended the meeting with no one quite sure about the next step. Intentions were for them all to reconvene in the morning to devise Plan B. It was seven in the evening and Singleton had not eaten dinner. He was hungry, but the day had been exhausting and he decided to skip eating altogether. He'd make up for it with a hearty breakfast tomorrow morning.

He stepped off the elevator and walked to his suite. When he entered, it was the second time he saw Erika Lehmann sitting on the sofa waiting for him in his hotel room. Her Beretta was pointed at his chest. Her stiches had been removed and she no longer had a bandage on her arm, but her sleeveless blouse clearly revealed the fresh red scar from Marienne's gunshot wound on her arm.

"Close the door and lock it," Erika ordered.

After he did so, Singleton said, "It looks like you have the habit of showing up in men's hotel rooms."

"Funny," she said without laughing. "FBI humor; I didn't know it existed." She waved her gun at a chair. "Sit down. I was surprised when I checked the hotel registry to see your name, Agent Singleton. It's not good protocol to stay in the same hotel twice."

"Maybe not for the CIA," Singleton replied as he sat, "but the FBI doesn't have to skulk around like thieves in the night."

Erika asked, "Are you hungry? I'm starving. Let's order room service. Surely your FBI that doesn't have to skulk can afford it. I want a medium rare steak, soup, vegetables, and some hard bread with a lot of butter on the side. Just water to drink. What are you having?"

"I'm not hungry," Singleton said. It wasn't true, but he said it anyway.

Erika continued. "Then you can watch me eat. Pick up the phone and dial room service, when I've finished eating you can take me into custody. Are we agreed?"

"Fine by me," Singleton answered.

Erika could see in his eyes that the young FBI man was again not intimated by the gun she held on him. His fearlessness impressed her. She pointed the Beretta at the ceiling, un-cocked the hammer, and returned the gun to her belt.

"Then please order my dinner," she said.

Singleton stood up, walked over to the table where the phone sat, picked up the receiver, and dialed room service. He added a dinner for himself.

When Erika heard him adding his dinner she smiled. Singleton hung up the phone and sat back down.

"Please call me Erika. May I call you Chris?"

"I don't care, but if you think we're going to have a friendly reunion like old classmates you can forget it."

"It's still the death of Charlie Pulaski that is on your mind every time you see me, I know that. I'm so tired of getting blamed for his death. You have to know by now it wasn't me."

"Ryker pulled the trigger, but it never would have happened if you hadn't drawn him to the United States."

"Another thing I had no control over. Himmler sent Ryker to Evansville to kill me. Do you think I approved of that?"

Singleton had plans to deal with Ryker, but he wasn't about to tell her.

Erika continued. "Now you have joined forces with Al Hodge."

"How do you know that?"

"I saw you walk out of the courthouse this afternoon with Al and Ryker. I'm a bit surprised Ryker's hands were cuffed in front of him. I would think that would do little to keep Ryker at bay. His hands should have been cuffed behind his back."

"I can't disagree with you. Once we got Ryker back to the jail, he knocked out a guard on the way to his cell. When I asked him why, he shrugged and muttered something about a bread roll."

The door knocker banged and they heard, "Room service" from the hall. Two waiters delivered their meals. One pushed a cart, the other carried a folding table. After they set up, served, and departed, Erika asked, "Where do you come from, originally? Or it that subject taboo?"

"I was born and raised in Salt Lake City."

"Are you a Mormon?"

"Not everyone who lives in Utah is a Mormon," Singleton replied. "I was raised Catholic."

"So was I."

"I know."

"Yes, of course you do. Silly of me to forget that you probably know more about me than I would ever suspect. Since it seems our conversation will be limited, why don't you go ahead and call Al. I eat quickly. By the time he arrives, I'll be ready for you to arrest me."

◊ ◊ ◊

Twenty-five minutes later, Leroy Carr and Al Hodge walked through Singleton's hotel room door. Erika was finishing up her dinner. Singleton had eaten only half of his.

"Leroy," Erika said, "I didn't know you were in town. Chris didn't tell me."

"Chris?" Carr said more as an exclamation than a question. "Don't tell me you two are chums now."

"No, we're not chums," Erika answered. She got right to the point. "Was Ryker's arraignment authentic or just a set up to lure O'Grady?"

"The arraignment was real, but we set it up. I have the paperwork to get Ryker released into our custody whenever we need to get him out of jail."

"As much as I'd like to let Ryker rot in jail, we have to move against O'Grady tonight," Erika said to them all. "I know where he and his men are hiding. They're in an old warehouse in Boulder."

Carr asked, "Does he still have just three men since Ryker took out two?"

"Actually, he's down to two men besides himself. The body of one of his men is in the trunk of a car parked on the street out in front of this hotel. You need to have someone do something with it. I didn't leave it behind in case Al wanted fingerprints.

"There is something curious about all this, Leroy. In my time with O'Grady I never came across any explosives, only small arms. He's down to a three-man team, and with only small arms he has to know he has no hope of sabotaging the arsenal. We might as well take him out. We need to try to take him alive although it will be difficult. I think O'Grady will gladly die before allowing himself to be captured. If we can't capture O'Grady, we have to keep his second in command alive—a man called Darragh. I think he might be the only one besides O'Grady who might know the name of their employer. I know that's a key for you, Leroy, to find out who hired them."

Carr replied, "We're not moving against O'Grady tonight."

Erika Lehmann very rarely was dumbfounded, but this was certainly one of those times. In fact, she was stupefied at Carr's nonchalant attitude about everything she has just told him. Erika knew Leroy Carr as well as he knew her. She now realized her boss had a snake in the woodpile and he wasn't going to tell her.

Chapter 62

Denver, Colorado
Next day—Thursday, 03 June 1948

As soon as the rental dealer in Denver opened, Cyril O'Grady and his two remaining men were waiting. They rented a large stake-bed truck with a covered canopy. "My friends here are helping me move, and my wife doesn't want to get our furniture wet in case it rains," O'Grady told the owner in a very friendly tone. They would have to wait until the cover of darkness to load their real cargo.

◊ ◊ ◊

Erika Lehmann was having breakfast with Leroy Carr and Chris Singleton in the Lowry Air Force Base mess hall. It was at Lowry that Erika had stayed over the night. Carr had put the nix on Singleton arresting her.

She had loaded her plate in the chow line with a mountain of scrambled eggs, French toast, and linked sausages. Singleton watched this beautiful woman shovel the food into her mouth like a starving Gypsy. All this food after eating a large meal in his hotel room just ten hours ago.

Erika mumbled something with her mouth full that neither Carr nor Singleton understood.

"We can't understand you, Erika," Carr said. "You're talking with your mouth full again."

Erika took several bites and swallowed. "What is on the agenda for today, Leroy?"

"I'm not sure yet," Carr replied. "We play a waiting game right now."

"Waiting for what?" she asked before she took a sip of milk.

"The weather."

Erika dropped her fork. "Okay, Leroy. Tell me what's going on. I've done my job and told you everything I know. It's apparent that you know something I don't."

215

Carr also took a drink; his beverage was coffee. "Do I?"

Erika first looked Singleton in the eyes, and then Carr. "Are you saying you don't trust me?"

"I don't know, Erika," Carr answered. "Am I saying that?"

Erika sat back in her chair and gazed at Carr. Her overseer was being his usual ambiguous self.

"Why isn't Al here?" Erika asked.

"He's at the county jail getting Ryker released into our custody."

"Leroy, to be honest, I can't understand why this country would take in a man like Axel Ryker. If justice was served, Ryker would rot in jail if not get what he really deserves, a hangman's knot."

Carr returned her gaze and didn't respond. Singleton, on the other hand, replied, "Some people in the FBI would claim the same fate should befall you. You're looking at one of them."

[8:30 p.m. that evening]

Darragh drove and O'Grady and Wotan crowded into the truck's cab alongside him. O'Grady's second in command backed the truck up to a small storage barn in Wheat Ridge, a small community on the outskirts of Denver, just northwest of the city limits.

O'Grady had the key. He opened the padlock and opened the barn-style door. He and the other two men began carefully loading the aerial bombs onto the truck.

Three of Al Hodge's men watched through binoculars from a safe distance, something that Hodge's men had been doing for days. Agent Houchen, Hodge's right-hand man, happened to be on duty tonight. Houchen picked up his walkie-talkie.

[a half-hour later]

Leroy Carr, Erika Lehmann, Axel Ryker, and Al Hodge and his remaining men who were not surveilling the storage barn crowded into Carr's small Lowry Air Force Base barrack's room.

"Al, go ahead and start," Carr said.

"My men watched O'Grady pick up his weapons less than an hour ago from the barn Ryker found out about after his . . . interrogation of one of O'Grady's men." Hodge was, of course, referring to Ryker's torture of Lukus before he dispatched the man. Hodge then deferred to Carr. "Leroy?"

"O'Grady has to be planning the attack for tonight. He wouldn't retrieve his arsenal of bombs any sooner than he has to."

Erika interrupted. "Leroy, you need to clarify all this. What type of bombs? And why didn't you move in on O'Grady when he was loading them on his truck?"

"Never mind, Erika" said Carr. "You and Special Agent Singleton are flying out to Garden City, Kansas, as soon as we're done with this meeting. Two of Al's men will go with you. I don't want to hear any questions, Erika. Agent Singleton will brief you during the flight. For the rest of us, as far as O'Grady's attack on the chemical weapons arsenal, we won't interfere. We'll let it proceed as O'Grady has planned."

[less than an hour later]

Erika Lehmann and Chris Singleton had their seat belts fastened as the wheels of Leroy Carr's Hudson left the ground at Lowry. In the cockpit, out of earshot sat a pilot and co-pilot from the Air Force base. Hodge's two men, one who was Hodge's right-hand-man, Houchen, sat behind them.

As soon as the plane got airborne, Erika said, "Okay, Chris . . . or Agent Singleton, whatever name you feel most comfortable with, what in Heaven's name is going on?"

Singleton left her hanging for several minutes, ignoring her, then he finally began speaking.

Chapter 63

Denver, Colorado
Next day—Friday, 04 June 1948

By 3:00 a.m. O'Grady, Darragh, and Wotan had loaded four crates of small incendiary bombs onto a tan-colored Cessna 190 airplane that they had bought with cash shortly after arriving in Denver. The Cessna's 245 horsepower engine was powerful enough to lift the machine off the ground with the weight of three men and four heavy crates of bombs. The bombs were by necessity small. It would be necessary for O'Grady and Darragh to drop them by hand as Wotan flew the aircraft. The overhead wing would not be in the way of dropping the small bombs from the open windows and the plane's slow cruising speed would make it easy to hit targets. The compact size of the incendiary bombs, being only about the size of an American football, allowed many more bombs to be carried aboard and dropped. The explosive power of one of these bombs equaled that of about ten hand grenades, plenty of explosive energy to rip open the steel tanks that contained the chemical weapons at the Rocky Mountain Arsenal.

The airplane had waited for them all these weeks at a small airfield in Longmont, north of Denver, the grass take-off and landing strip used almost exclusively by crop dusting airplanes. Wotan had made several trips during that time, making sure the aircraft was in good working order, tuning up the engine, checking the timing and the hoses, and taking the plane up for test flights and scouting of the arsenal from the air. He was careful to not fly directly over the facility, which was forbidden; instead, flying by from a distance with either O'Grady or Darragh using binoculars.

The German mercenary started the engine and spent about fifteen minutes checking gauges. O'Grady and Darragh sat directly behind his seat with the bomb crates behind them.

With the unusual amount of weight onboard, the Cessna took nearly every inch of the grass runway before it could nudge its wheels off the ground, but finally the plane lifted into the night sky pointing directly at the full, dusty moon as if that were the airplane's destination.

It was the weather O'Grady had been forced to wait for: a bright moon and prevailing winds from the northeast thanks to a cyclone that had struck southwest Nebraska yesterday afternoon.

Wotan did not immediately fly over the arsenal, instead, he guided the plane in a wide arc around the facility. O'Grady's ground scouts had told him about the extra security. Those scouts had been Lukus and Petros until they turned up dead. O'Grady suspected Erika for this inflated security. He didn't know it was the CIA egg-head analyst, Mr. Beckman, who had uncovered the plot weeks ago.

That Dante had never returned to Boulder after being ordered to kill Erika was even further confirmation to O'Grady that Erika was a mole and had either eliminated the Italian or turned him over to authorities, but it didn't matter to O'Grady. His men knew the risks and had signed on without any illusions. What mattered was that O'Grady had done an exemplary job of hiding facts from her concerning any details of the attack, and after all, each man would now receive more money with less men to divide it up.

After several wide orbits of the arsenal, O'Grady gave Wotan the go ahead and all three men donned gasmasks.

The Cessna banked sharply and at a very low altitude, only 150 feet above the ground, flew into the heart of the Rocky Mountain Arsenal and headed toward were the tanks containing the toxic chemical weapons were held in railroad car-sized steel tanks.

Many of these tanks were clustered in tight groups. O'Grady and Darragh lifted the small bombs from their crates and began dropping them from the open fuselage windows on each side. The slow speed of the airplane allowed accuracy. Explosions erupted below, and white and yellow clouds spewed into the air, the wind directing the clouds toward Denver.

Chapter 64

Garden City, Kansas
Later that morning, same day—Friday, 04 June 1948

Garden City, Kansas was a mere two-hour flight from Denver. Erika, Singleton, and Hodge's men had been on the ground in that west Kansas town for nearly three hours. After Singleton had explained things to her during the flight, she understood why Carr wanted her to take along the Karabiner 98K sniper rifle.

After they landed, Singleton had reached Leroy Carr on the phone, told him he and Erika were on sight, then all four of them found a booth in the small, all-night café in the Garden City Airfield terminal.

[Denver]

After hearing from Singleton, Leroy Carr and Al Hodge drove to the Rocky Mountain Arsenal at dawn and walked among the exploded tanks. All the toxic chemical weapons at the arsenal were stored in a series of below ground bunkers. This had been the case since the bunkers had been completed a year ago. The empty above ground tanks were a top-secret decoy, photos of which had been released a year ago to publications such as *Time* magazine and *Life*. The military could not keep the arsenal a secret, but one thing they could do was supply spurious information about the operation.

Three weeks ago, Leroy Carr ordered the empty tanks filled with white flour and yellow cornstarch. Carr wanted Cyril O'Grady to proceed with his bombing mission. He had to find out the fuselage number of O'Grady's aircraft—information Lukus did not know during his brutal interrogation at the hands of Axel Ryker. Last night, the remaining members of Al Hodge's team had set up in the scrub bushes on the slopes of some gentle hills outside the arsenal. The high-powered cameras enabled them to capture photos of the airplane in the full moonlight.

[Garden City, Kansas]

At 7:30 a.m., the CIA/FBI team watched the tan Cessna with the fuselage number B515HC land on one of the two landing strips at the Garden City Airport. O'Grady had Wotan fly directly south to Pueblo, Colorado before banking east to Garden City. This extended their flying time from two to three and a half hours but added a layer of vigilance.

"Erika, take your station," Singleton said. They all rose from their seats in the diner. Between her legs sat the Karabiner wrapped in a blanket. Here again, they knew about the refueling stop in Garden City from Axel Ryker's torture of Lukus.

"Remember," Singleton said to Erika, "we want O'Grady alive."

When the Cessna came to a stop on the tarmac near the refueling trucks, O'Grady told Wotan, "Falsify your log. Tell them we're flying to Kansas City, then get this thing refueled as quickly as possible so we can take off."

The three men exited the plane: Wotan walked toward the small terminal to check in with his flight log and request refueling, O'Grady and Darragh stretched their legs but stayed near the plane.

Inside the terminal, Wotan walked up to the pilot's flight desk. The clerk didn't have time to hand him the flight ledger before three men appeared. One of Hodge's men, Agent Sutton, without warning grabbed Wotan around the neck from behind and wrestled him to the ground. Singleton and Houchen helped subdue the German. Singleton frisked him and removed the holstered handgun inside his light jacket. Houchen cuffed Wotan's hands behind his back.

The desk clerk reached for a phone to summon his supervisor, but Singleton showed the man his FBI identification and told him to hang up.

"Sutton," said Singleton, "stay with the prisoner. Agent Houchen, let's get to the refueling truck."

Fifteen minutes later, O'Grady and Darragh saw the refueling truck pull out of one of the terminal's garages.

"At last," said Darragh.

The truck made its way to the Cessna but when it stopped, the driver stayed inside the cab. Two men in suits emerged from the passenger-side door. O'Grady immediately drew his handgun and aimed it at Chris Singleton. Just before he pulled the trigger, a shot rang out from atop the terminal. A 7.92x57mm Mauser bullet from Erika's Karabiner slice through O'Grady heart, exited out his back and ricocheted off the tarmac. O'Grady fell dead. Darragh had also drawn his gun but raised his hands when ordered to do so.

"FBI! Drop the gun!" Singleton shouted at the lone standing man.

O'Grady's trusted lieutenant lowered his hands, put the barrel of his handgun in his mouth, and blew his brains out.

Chapter 65

Garden City, Kansas
Same day—Friday, 04 June 1948

Twenty minutes after the confrontation at the airplane, Chris Singleton was on the phone with Leroy Carr in Denver.

"Leroy," said Singleton, "we have O'Grady's pilot in custody."

"What about O'Grady?"

"He's dead, and so is the third man who flew in on the aircraft."

Leroy Carr rarely swore, but this time the words blurted out. "Jesus Christ, Singleton! You had strict orders to capture O'Grady alive. What the hell happened?"

"I don't appreciate your tone, Mr. Carr. I'm cooperating with you at your request but at my discretion. In answer to your question, Erika killed O'Grady and the other man killed himself."

Carr lowered the phone, covered the mouthpiece with his hand, and told Al Hodge who stood nearby, "Erika killed O'Grady."

Hodge threw up his hands.

Carr spoke again into the phone. "I apologize, Chris. Get the pilot to a safe place. My Hudson is back at Lowry. Have Agent Houchen at the Garden City terminal to meet me and Al when we arrive. We should be there in a couple of hours."

◊ ◊ ◊

Carr's time estimate was close. Two and a half hours after the phone call from Chris Singleton, the tires of his aircraft screeched down on the asphalt landing strip of the Garden City Airfield under a foreboding dark gray sky.

Singleton, Houchen, and Sutton had found a flea bag highway motel just east of Garden City and that's where they took Wotan. When they got to their room, Houchen returned to the air terminal to wait for Carr and Hodge to arrive. Erika stayed at the motel.

When Carr, Hodge, and Axel Ryker (a surprise to Houchen) stepped off the plane they crowded into a rusting taxi that Houchen had

223

summoned to the tarmac. With the presence of the cab driver, nothing could be discussed during the drive to the motel.

When Carr and the others entered the motel room, they saw O'Grady's man, Wotan, securely bound both hands and feet with a rag stuffed in his mouth and black electrical tape holding it in so he couldn't spit it out.

Like Agent Houchen, Erika did not know Ryker would be with them. Singleton, on the other hand, did not seemed surprised. In Ryker's hand was a satchel.

"Take the prisoner into the bedroom," Carr ordered. "Make sure his ears are muffled so he can't hear us talk."

Al Hodge pointed to his man Sutton for this duty. Sutton got Wotan to his feet and took him away to the other room and closed the door.

Carr turned sternly to Erika. "I stressed to you and everyone else how important it was to keep O'Grady alive. Why is he dead?"

"He was a second away from killing Agent Singleton, Leroy. How would you like to explain that to J. Edgar Hoover and the Justice Department?"

"Chris, is this true?"

"Yes. She saved my life."

Carr had to accept it. She was right; an FBI agent dying under Carr's watch would create a firestorm in Washington that could be disastrous for the fledging CIA.

"Al and I will talk to O'Grady's man first," Carr stated.

When they entered the bedroom, Hodge ripped off the tape covering both his mouth and ears. "Spit out the rag, but if you shout out it's going right back in."

Wotan spit out the rag.

Carr did the rest of the talking. "I want to know who hired your boss, Cyril O'Grady."

Wotan turned his head and spit on the floor, indicating his distaste for the question.

"It would be in your interest to cooperate."

"Why?" Wotan smirked. "What can you do—kill me? You know I'm a dead man already from the job we did, releasing poison gas over your city. If I die now or later it makes no difference."

"What was your next scheduled stop after leaving Garden City?"

"I know nothing. O'Grady didn't tell us anything about our escape plans. I didn't know we were coming here until after we were in the air last night."

"Very well," said Carr, "have it your way. Al, send in Ryker."

"When Al emerged from the bedroom and summoned Ryker, Erika stepped in. "Let me talk to Wotan first, Al."

"You'll have to ask Leroy."

Erika stepped into the bedroom and saw Wotan lying on the bed. "Leroy, let me talk to him before you turn him over to Ryker—alone, German to German."

"Waste of time, Erika. This is why Ryker is here."

"Just give me five minutes, please."

Carr sighed. "Five minutes." When he walked out the door, Erika closed it behind him.

She sat down on the bed beside him and spoke in German. "Wotan, is that your real name?"

"My real name is of little matter, Fraülein."

"Wotan, you have to cooperate with these men. If you don't terrible things will happen to you. There is a man waiting to come in and interrogate you who has no boundaries for cruelty and inflicting pain. Will you tell us what you know?"

The German stuck to his story. "I told the other man I know nothing."

"Then it will be as you wish," Erika said. "I feel badly for you." How badly she felt was metered. She found it difficult to feel sorry for a former member of the Einsatzgruppen, the death squads on the Eastern Front who had shot mothers as they held their children in fear, and then shot the babies and toddlers, or forced both mothers and their children into the gas extermination trucks. Erika found herself thinking that Wotan deserved the suffering she knew Ryker would deal out to him.

Erika left the room and shook her head at Carr, indicating she had no success.

Carr turned to Ryker, who took off his porkpie hat, picked up his satchel, then walked into the bedroom and closed the door. The first thing Ryker did was stuff the rag back in Wotan's mouth and reapply the tape. Then he opened his satchel. "Let's get started, my friend," Ryker said calmly as he started pulling out various items from the bag. "My supervisor wishes to know who hired your commander, and how you planned to escape this country. When you are ready to give me this information, I will remove the gag from your mouth and you can speak."

Among the items Ryker extracted from the satchel was a meat cutter's apron. He put it on and tied the string behind his back. Ryker first used a pair of sheet-metal tinsnips. He sliced off about a quarter inch of the tip of Wotan's nose. Wotan struggled violently but it was not hard for the grossly strong Ryker to keep him on the bed. Then Ryker snipped off Wotan's right earlobe.

"I commend your courage, but then you are German," Ryker said matter-of-factly. "I salute the Fatherland with you."

Ryker pulled down the man's pants and underwear. Ryker withdrew a cigar from the bag, lit and puffed on it several times to get the end orange hot. This hot business end of the cigar he pushed down against Wotan's scrotum.

Still, the tough German mercenary gave no indication that he was ready to talk so Ryker went back to the tinsnips and removed more small parts of Wotan's body—a couple of fingers, a big toe. Ryker was patient with his torture. He knew a job worth doing was worth doing well.

Chapter 66

Garden City, Kansas
Same day—Friday, 04 June 1948

Axel Ryker had been behind the closed bedroom door with Wotan for nearly an hour.

"I can imagine what's going on in there, Leroy," said Singleton. "I don't like it."

"Do you think any of us like it?" Carr said angrily. "This was the same as a state of war, Singleton. If there had been real poisons in those tanks it would have killed thousands of civilians. It would have made Pearl Harbor look like a slingshot fight. We don't have the luxury of taking O'Grady's man back to Washington and interrogating him for days."

"Leroy's right, Chris," Erika chimed in. "None of us like it but it can't be avoided. And Wotan murdered innocents during the war just like he was willing to do to innocent people in Denver."

Suddenly Ryker emerged from the bedroom with blood on his hands. His apron looked like it belonged to an employee of a slaughterhouse who had just butchered a steer.

"The man doesn't know who hired his superior," Ryker told them all. "If he knew, I would know by now. I did find out a few things. The team's next airplane stop was scheduled for Juárez in Mexico and their contact there is a man called 'Sedik.' That is all he knows, I'm confident of that."

"He's still alive, right, Ryker?" Hodge asked.

"My orders were to not cancel him. He is still alive. Now I wash." Ryker went into the bathroom.

The others walked into the bedroom. Blood was everywhere. The bed sheet was soaked, and blood had even splashed onto the walls. Wotan lay unconscious with his pants down, his three severed fingers and two toes at rest on a night stand next to the bed.

"Holy Mother of God!" Hodge exclaimed.

"Al, have Houchen and Sutton get him to the nearest hospital and guard him. When this 'Wotan' has been cleared by the doctors to travel,

227

have your men fly him back to D.C. and put in a lockdown unit at Walter Reed."

Hodge looked at Houchen and Sutton, both of whom stood right there. "You heard the man. Any questions?"

Both men understood their orders, approached Wotan, and went about doing what they could to staunch any more blood loss.

Carr continued. "The rest of us are flying out to Juárez. We'll leave the Hudson here for now and take O'Grady's plane. I'm sure my pilot will know how to fly a Cessna. Perhaps this 'Sedik' will have been informed of the call numbers of O'Grady's plane and he'll be there on the tarmac to meet it when we arrive. We need to get going now. It wouldn't have taken O'Grady this long to refuel his plane."

"What did you do with O'Grady's body?" Carr asked Erika.

"It's wrapped in a tarp in the back of his plane, along with Darragh—the other man."

"Lord!" said Carr.

She said, "We couldn't leave them on the tarmac, Leroy."

"When we get to the airfield, we'll have to smuggle the bodies onto the Hudson," Carr said. "Al, I'm going to have to leave you here with your men to take care of this situation. Contact Lowry and get another Air Force pilot down here as soon as possible. Leave Houchen and Sutton here in Garden City with Wotan. Have the pilot fly you and the bodies to Andrews Air Force Base. Call ahead and have people meet the plane and take the bodies for examination. After that, instruct the pilot to fly you and the Hudson back to Lowry in Denver. We'll check out this Juárez business."

Ryker walked out of the bathroom. The apron had been stashed in a paper bag that already had dark blood stains soaking through. Ryker smiled and held up his hands to show the others that his hands were clean.

"What is it you Americans say? . . . I believe it is 'Clean as a whistle.' Is it not?"

In his mind, Chris Singleton renewed his vow that someday he would bring this monster to justice.

Chapter 67

Ciudad Juárez, Mexico
Same day—Friday, 04 June 1948

Leroy Carr had been correct, his Air Force pilot had no trouble flying the Cessna 190 which was much easier to fly than the Hudson. The tarpaulin shrouded bodies of Cyril O'Grady and Darragh were no longer aboard, having been transferred by Ryker to the Hudson. Ryker carried both bodies in one trip.

The gray sky had opened over Garden City and the plane climbed from the ground of the Sunflower state into rain clouds. The jostled aircraft finally reached altitude above the lower clouds and the rain; nonetheless, much of the flight was a bumpy one.

Ciudad Juárez, Mexico, was just across the border from El Paso, Texas, and a mere three-hour flight from Garden City for the Cessna. Besides the Air Force pilot and co-pilot/navigator, onboard were Leroy Carr, Erika Lehmann, Chris Singleton, and Axel Ryker.

Erika sat looking out the window in deep thought. Two nights ago, she had made love to O'Grady. The act had been meaningless to her; it was exactly that—just an *act* done for the mission's sake, but today she ended his life with her forefinger and a squeeze of a trigger. *Life is so fragile.* Erika thought of her dead parents and contemplated what they would think of some of the things she had done since she became a spy during the early years of the war.

Behind her, Chris Singleton was forced to sit on the empty bomb crates alongside Ryker near the tail of the plane since the aircraft had only two seats behind the pilot and co-pilot. The Cessna's engine was not overly loud. A conversation was possible without shouting.

"Tell me," Ryker said to Singleton, "how do you like your work at the FBI? How much do they pay you?" Ryker recognized Singleton from Evansville and knew he had to carry a grudge for his killing of Singleton's partner.

Singleton looked at him. "You can keep your bullshit to yourself. You know I know who you are. You're living on borrowed time, Ryker."

A jackal's sneer appeared on Ryker's face. "Yet for now we are comrades. What would your dead partner think of that?"

Singleton had an urge to pull his handgun and shoot Ryker in the face, but the young FBI agent instead just turned away in loathing.

Ryker burst out in a ghoulish cackle.

◊ ◊ ◊

The sky cleared over New Mexico, and at seven o'clock that evening the Cessna sat down on a dry runway in Juárez. This time of year meant the landing took place with nearly two hours of daylight still lingering.

The man codenamed Sedik had grown up with Rafik Djebar; in fact, he was a cousin to the man who now sat on the throne as the opium king not only of the Casbah but much of North Africa. Now Djebar was Sedik's boss, and Sedik was Djebar's most trusted confederate.

Sedik brought two bodyguards with him from Algiers. His job was to maintain contact with Cyril O'Grady and notify Djebar of how things were progressing. Sedik did not have to risk entering the United States to confirm in person if O'Grady completed his mission. An event of this magnitude would immediately become worldwide news.

Sedik and his two men had been at the Ciudad Juárez airport for four hours. The last time he had heard from O'Grady was yesterday when O'Grady told him the mission was to be undertaken that night. O'Grady gave him an estimated time that he and his team would arrive in Juárez. When O'Grady and his men arrived, it was Sedik's job to aid the men in their escape. He had a plane waiting to fly them all back to Algiers where O'Grady would receive his final installment in gold.

The plane was late. According to O'Grady's estimate it should have arrived nearly two hours ago but Sedik knew delays sometimes happened and was not overly concerned. If it turned out that O'Grady and his men didn't arrive today, then that was the time for alarm.

One of Sedik's men had been watching the airfield from the windows of the terminal. He entered the airport café where Sedik and his other bodyguard sat with their coffee, which for them was almost undrinkable when compared to the Turkish-roast coffee of Algiers.

"The plane has landed," the man said.

They had already paid for their coffee. Sedik and the other man jumped up and walked briskly out of the café. From the terminal window Djebar's top captain confirmed the fuselage number—B515HC.

◊ ◊ ◊

Inside the Cessna, Leroy Carr was not optimistic.

"This is another reason we needed O'Grady alive. We could have forced him to step out of the plane and kept a gun on his back. None of us look anything like O'Grady. Singleton, you're the closest to him in age. You'll have to step out. Tilt your hat down low on your forehead. We have to hope this 'Sedik' will just assume you're O'Grady."

◊ ◊ ◊

Sedik waited until the Cessna's pilot had killed the engine. He then saw a man step out of the plane. From where he stood, he could not tell if it was O'Grady, so he turned to one of his bodyguards, a man named Izri. "Walk out and meet the plane, Izri. You have seen O'Grady, make sure that man who stepped off the airplane is him, or one of his men. If that is one of his men, confirm that O'Grady is on the plane. If so, signal us and we will join you."

◊ ◊ ◊

Chris Singleton saw a man approaching. He had his fedora pulled low on his brow and avoided holding his head up high. When the man reached Singleton, the man stuck out his hand. Singleton shook it. Izri could now see the face of the man he greeted and knew it wasn't Cyril O'Grady.

"We've been waiting for your airplane," the man said in heavily accented English. "You must be one of Mr. O'Grady's men."

"Yes, I am," said Singleton.

"Since you are here, we expect that you have completed the work you were hired to do."

231

"Yes, we were successful."

"I would like to confirm that Mr. O'Grady is onboard."

"You must be Sedik," Singleton stated.

The man looked at him rather quizzically and lied. "Yes, I am Sedik."

Singleton signaled that the fuselage door be opened. When Izri peered into the plane, the giant hand of Axel Ryker grabbed him and jerked him up and into the plane. Singleton jumped onboard and Erika slammed the door closed.

"Let's get out of here," Carr said to the pilot.

Singleton remarked, "This guy said he is Sedik but added 'we have been waiting for you.' He must have more men close by, maybe inside the terminal."

"As CIA we're in this country covertly," Carr replied. "We can't openly chase people around this town or in the terminal. We'll have hell to pay with the State Department and the Senate intelligence committee. The Mexican government was not fond of us when we were the OSS and it's not fond of us now."

"Let's get off the ground," Carr again told the pilot. "Don't ask flight control for permission, just go. Our border is only ten minutes away once we get airborne."

"I will question this man," Ryker volunteered.

"Forget it, Ryker," said Carr. "I can't stomach any more of your brand of questioning. Since O'Grady and all his men are dead except the guy you 'questioned' in the motel, the threat is over. We're taking this guy to Washington."

After the plane got airborne, Carr told the Air Force pilot to land in El Paso, just a few minutes away.

"Erika, I'm dropping you off in El Paso. From there, get a commercial flight to Denver and wait for Al to get back there after he drops off O'Grady's body in D.C."

"Why am I going back to Denver, Leroy?"

"Never mind that now. Al will bring instructions for you when he returns to Denver from Washington." He handed her some money. "This should be enough to pay for your flight, a couple nights at a hotel, and food until Al gets back there. When you get checked in, call Sheila and tell her where you're staying."

Carr then gave her a serious look. "Don't get in any trouble in Denver while you're waiting for Al, Erika. If you do, our deal is off."

No one else onboard knew what Carr was referring to other than Erika. She knew Carr was commenting on her citizenship.

◊ ◊ ◊

Inside the terminal, the real Sedik watched his man get dragged into the plane then the plane immediately began taxiing away. He turned to his other bodyguard.

"O'Grady has failed. I must notify Rafik immediately."

Part 6

It is essential to seek out enemy agents who have come to conduct espionage against you and to bribe them to serve you.

—*Sun Tzu*

Chapter 68

Denver, Colorado
Next day—Saturday, 05 June 1948

Yesterday evening, Erika was dropped off in El Paso too late to get a flight to Denver that day, or a flight that connected to Denver, so she was forced to spend the night. She found a late dinner at a Mexican restaurant within walking distance of her hotel, stayed after for one drink, then returned to her hotel room and retired for the night. She was determined to stay out of trouble. Erika wanted nothing to undermine getting the charges against her dropped by the Justice Department, which would open an avenue for her to become a U.S. citizen. When she became a citizen, Erika could bring her daughter to the States where she could at least try to be a real mother to her child.

She flew out of El Paso this morning and arrived in Denver in mid-afternoon after a stop in Albuquerque to disembark a few passengers and embark a couple of more for the leg to Denver.

During the last leg of the flight, a man boarded and sat down beside her. The plane had no sooner gotten off the ground when the man began to flirt. She let him down kindly with a white lie, telling him she was on her way to Denver to visit her boyfriend.

"I think he might be planning to propose," she added.

From Denver's Stapleton Airport, Erika hailed a taxi. "Oxford Hotel, please," she told the driver. Carr had given her enough money to stay at the expensive hotel for two nights.

"Where's your luggage, lady?" the cabbie asked.

"I don't have any." One of the reasons she chose the Oxford was because from her previous stay there she knew the hotel had a ladies' boutique where she could buy some clothes and other necessities.

After checking in at the registration desk, Erika paid a visit to the boutique. She was frugal with what she purchased, yet the clothes and other items in the swank hotel boutique cost her much more than she expected. She thought about Leroy Carr, *That's a typical man. He didn't take into consideration that I would need clothes.*

237

◊ ◊ ◊

After dropping off Erika in El Paso, Carr made a phone call from that terminal to Sheila Reid in Washington. When the Cessna arrived in Dallas, Texas, a C-47 and a Lockheed Electra were waiting for them. Carr put Axel Ryker on the Electra and ordered the CIA pilot who had a co-pilot and two armed CIA agents onboard to fly Ryker back to Fort Huachuca in Arizona. Carr could no longer stand to look at Ryker. He would keep the fiendish brute in Arizona until the unwelcomed time came that he would need him again.

The large, twin engine C-47 transport flew on to Washington with just Carr, Singleton, and their shackled prisoner onboard.

◊ ◊ ◊

[7:00 p.m.—Denver]
When Erika walked into Gaetano's she greeted Mirko and asked, "Are the boys upstairs?"

"Yes, they're having dinner. The game hasn't started yet."

"I'll go on up if that's okay, Mirko."

"Sure. There's plenty of food up there if you're hungry."

At the top of the steps she was frisked, as always. This time she had her Beretta on her and the guard took it from her.

When she entered the upstairs room, most of the men she was accustomed to seeing there sat around the table eating. When they saw her they all stopped chewing, surprised to see her.

"Erika," said Checkers, "we thought you might be dead. Mirko said he saw you get shot on the walk in front of the restaurant. We all ran down after we heard the gunshot, but you were nowhere to be seen. What the hell happened?"

"I don't know, Checkers. I think it might have been my crazy ex-boyfriend. It looks like he followed me to Denver. Lucky for me his aim was off." She raised her blouse sleeve and showed them her scar.

"Where is the fuck? We can make sure he doesn't bother you again."

238

"I have no idea, Checkers, and I can't say for certain it was him. No one saw who did it. Whoever it was used a rifle from a rooftop across the street. Even if it was him, I'm sure he's long gone from this town."

"You need to protect yourself. Do you know how to use a gun?"

"Yes, I have a gun. Aldo took it from me at the door."

Checkers looked at the teenage boy who always sat off in a corner. "Donnie, go get her gun from Aldo and give it back to her. Then get Erika a plate." Erika was still standing. The mob boss looked at Paulie. "Move your fat ass over and make room for another chair."

As Fat Paulie scooted his chair, he asked Erika, "Where is the big ugly fuck who broke my damn hand?" He was asking about Ryker, of course.

"He's long gone," she answered. "You won't see him again."

"I hope the cocksucker is dead."

Donnie returned with her Beretta and then set her up a plate and silverware from extras sitting on a table against a wall.

"That's a peashooter, Erika," another man at the table commented when he saw her handgun. "You need one of these." He took out his Browning semi-auto called the Hi-Power and showed her.

"That's a good weapon, Gino. A 15-round magazine of 9mm Parabellum. But it's large and heavy. Women have a harder time concealing a handgun than men. We don't have the luxury in the summer of wearing a shoulder holster under a sport coat. In the warmer months the only place we have to hide a gun is on a thigh holster under a dress or at the back of our belt under a loose-fitting blouse. My .32 Beretta is light, small, and accurate."

The men looked around at each other, surprised at her knowledge of handguns, then just shrugged and went back to eating.

In the center of the table was bread, a large bowl of rigatonis in marinara sauce, and a big plate of Italian sausages and fried green and red peppers. Three bottles of red wine had already been opened. Erika poured her wine, took bread, scooped a man-sized portion of the pasta, and stabbed two sausages and some peppers with her fork.

Fat Paulie gave her a compliment. "I like a broad that don't eat like a bird."

"Checkers," Erika said before she began eating. "I need some money. I don't have enough to live on right now. I'm staying at an expensive hotel." The Oxford was indeed expensive, a small suite cost $40 per night.

The Smaldone boss didn't blink. He reached in a pocket without comment, took out a thick roll of bills, and thumbed off five $100 bills. She was hoping to get $200, less than half that amount. "Let me know if you need more," Checkers said, then he turned to Gino. "Quit hogging the Parmesan, asshole. Pass it to Erika."

Gino passed her the block of cheese and the grater.

Then to her, Checkers said, "Erika, remember, there's no such thing as too much Parmesan on your pasta."

She might have gotten up and kissed his cheek in thanks for the money, but she thought it might embarrass him in front of his crew. "Thank you, Checkers, for everything."

"Fuck that. We take care of our friends. It's part of our thing that we do. Dig in and enjoy your meal. My mother is the cook here and everyone in the kitchen is family. You can tell from looking at Paulie's fat belly that my mother is a good cook."

Erika knew that 'our thing' translated to Italian was 'Cosa Nostra.'

Chapter 69

Washington, D.C.
CIA Headquarters on E Street
Next morning—Sunday, 06 June 1948

As Leroy Carr waited for Al Hodge to arrive, he stared out of his office window. He had slept little since Garden City and the torture of O'Grady's man, and the sleep he had gotten was fitful. He second-judged his decision to bring a man like Axel Ryker onboard the CIA. Recruiting ex-Nazis for clandestine service was not uncommon for the Americans or the British after the war ended, but still he had a hard time with his decision to save a man like Ryker from the gallows he so justly deserved. Erika had warned him about this abomination of a man, yet he had ignored her advice. But it was Carr's and the CIA's job to protect America, even if by doing so the intelligence organization had to occasionally make an accord with an insalubrious creature like Axel Ryker.

Both the C-47 that flew Carr, Singleton, and the prisoner back to Washington; and the Hudson that brought Hodge and the bodies of O'Grady and Darragh, landed at Andrews Air Force Base yesterday afternoon, two hours apart.

Carr scheduled their meeting for this morning, knowing both he and Al needed sleep. He hoped Al had gotten some rest last night, even if he hadn't. Carr's only relief was seeing his wife, Kay. They had enjoyed a pleasant dinner at Jocko's where Carr had, however briefly, put what had happened in the Garden City motel room out of his mind. The brief respite ended as soon as they left the pub.

Hodge arrived shortly before eight o'clock carrying two large paper cups of coffee. He sat one on Carr's desk then sat down. Carr walked away from the window and sat down behind his desk.

"Did you get any sleep last night, Al?" Carr asked.

"Yeah, I slept okay. How about your?"

Carr shrugged.

Hodge immediately picked up on that. He knew his old friend well.

"Look, Leroy. You did the right thing with Ryker considering the seriousness of the situation. I can't stand the sonuvabitch either, but he played his part in helping us stop a horrendous attack within our country. Don't blame yourself." Hodge then tried to steer the conversation to a happier angle. "I bet Kay was glad to see you."

"We ate at Jocko's last night."

"Good. And other things are looking up, Leroy. Ryker is trapped back at Fort Huachuca, Lehmann's out of my hair, and most importantly the threat is over. 'Wotan' is at Walter Reed in the lockdown wing. Beckman will supervise his questioning." Beckman was the CIA analyst who had given them the lead about O'Grady.

Hodge continued. "Where is Lehmann, by the way? Is she back at the Farm?"

"No, I had our pilot drop her off in El Paso and told her to return to Denver."

Hodge looked surprised. "Why?"

"There's something we still have to wrap up there, Al. I told her to stay out of trouble and wait for you to return. You need to fly out at dawn tomorrow morning. With the refueling stop you should still get there in the early evening. Take the Hudson."

[that evening—Denver]

Erika Lehmann had attended Sunday Mass this morning at the Cathedral of the Immaculate Conception.

Now, she puffed on a cigar as she scraped another pot of poker chips toward her. She was on a hot streak at Gaetano's and quickly counted her winnings.

"Checkers," Erika said, "I can pay you back $250 of the money you gave me."

Checkers looked at her as if he were insulted. "Don't ever offer to do that again, Erika," he said sternly. "You won that money fair and square."

She didn't quite know why, but she felt at home in this crowd. She had no clue to why Leroy Carr sent her back to Denver, but she loved this town at the base of soaring peaks.

Back at the Oxford Hotel, the switchboard operator got a call from a Leroy Carr asking to be connected to Erika's room. After two tries and several long rings, he was told there was no answer. He left a message.

Chapter 70

Denver, Colorado
Monday, 07 June 1948

After the all-night poker game at Gaetano's, Erika didn't return to her suite at the Oxford until 7:00 a.m. She returned with $350 in winnings to add to the $500 Checkers Smaldone had given her. Besides the money, she also returned with a hangover from over imbibing on wine. When she asked for her key at the desk, she was also given the message from Leroy Carr. It was nine o'clock in Washington, so Erika called Leroy's office. She got Sheila Reid on the phone.

"Hi, Sheila. It's Erika. I got a message from Leroy to call."

"How are you doing, Erika?"

"Fine."

"Good. Leroy is in his office. I'll put you through."

After the connection, Carr said, *"Erika, where were you all night?"*

"I was playing poker at Gaetano's, Leroy. The game lasted all night. I didn't break orders. You didn't tell me I had to remain in my hotel room all the time."

"I hope you had fun," Carr said impatiently and with more than a hint of sarcasm. He immediately knew he wasn't being fair. Carr was more upset with himself because of the Ryker situation than he was with her. *"I'm sorry, Erika. Al is in the air on his way there. He should set down at Lowry around six or seven o'clock this evening. Be there to meet him. He'll have your instructions."*

[7:30 p.m.—Lowry Air Force Base]
The Hudson landed a bit late.

"We fought a head wind half the way here," Hodge told Erika after she met him on the tarmac.

"What's going on, Al? Why am I back in Denver?"

"Lehmann, can I get my feet on the ground before you start grilling me? I'm starving. The only thing I've eaten today was an egg salad sandwich I bought at the concessions counter at Fort Leonard Wood during the refueling and fluids check. I'll fill you in over dinner. Where should we eat? It's too late to eat here on the base. The mess hall closed an hour ago. I've stayed here enough, I know the schedule."

"I'd say Gaetano's where you and I ate once before, but Italian restaurants in this town close on Mondays."

"Sheila's assistant got me a room at the Oxford where you're staying. We'll eat there."

Erika had taken a taxi to the base. Hodge had a covered Jeep and MP driver waiting.

◊ ◊ ◊

Erika ordered the rainbow trout that the bow-tied waiter said had been caught wild the previous day in Colorado, more specifically in the Gunnison River—a high altitude, cold river on the western slope of the Continental Divide. Hodge ordered a large Porterhouse steak and all the accoutrements.

As they waited for their meals, Erika couldn't wait any longer. "Spill it, Al."

"We have to remove the files on both you and Ryker from the Denver Police Department." Hodge waved over a waiter and ordered another Scotch on the rocks. "Do you want another brandy?" he asked Erika.

"No, thanks. I drank too much wine last night."

The waiter left to get Hodge's drink.

"That's why Leroy sent you back here," Hodge said.

"How am I supposed to do that?"

"What do you mean? You stole your file from FBI Headquarters. Surely getting a couple of files from a city police department can't be tougher than that."

"I had Ryker watching my back."

"That won't be the case this time. Leroy hasn't decided what he wants to do with Ryker and that goon is staying at Fort Huachuca until Leroy decides. I'm here to help; I can bring in some of my men if we need them. Tomorrow morning we'll take a taxi to Lowry and I'll requisition two cars, one for each of us."

"And if I get caught breaking into the Denver police station, what then?"

"Then you're screwed, Lehmann. The CIA will disavow knowing anything about you. It was Singleton, an FBI guy, who got you out of jail and took you into custody after you got your butt arrested in that stupid brawl at that dive bar. The Denver police know nothing about CIA involvement. So, my advice is don't get caught."

"Leroy told me that when the threat from O'Grady was eliminated, he would give me a path to citizenship."

"He didn't say that Erika. I was in the room. He told you 'when the mission is over.' It's not over."

Chapter 71

Denver, Colorado
Next day—Tuesday, 08 June 1948

This morning, Al Hodge and Erika took a taxi to Lowry where Hodge got them each a loaner sedan. Automobile production had been halted after Pearl Harbor when all the Detroit car makers retooled factories to make military vehicles and other matériel. Although civilian car production had restarted after the war, spotting a new car on the roads was still the exception. Erika's car turned out to be a 1939 Ford.

Detective Bolles of the Denver Police Department had spearheaded both the cases against Erika and Ryker. Erika told Al Hodge her next move when they gathered for a pow wow in his hotel room after lunch.

"Al, first thing I have to do is find out more about this Detective Bolles. I might know a way to do that, but you'll have to trust me."

"Lehmann, every time you tell me I'll have to trust you I get a bad case of diarrhea. What are you planning? And don't give me the runaround."

"I'm going to Gaetano's tonight. The men there might be able to tell me something about Bolles."

"That's the mob headquarters, right?" Hodge didn't wait for an answer. "You're not going there anymore, Erika."

"Yes, I am. And you're going to stay here at the hotel. It's my neck in the noose, Al, not yours. Call Leroy."

"You're damn right I will."

Twenty minutes later, Hodge hung up his hotel suite's telephone. Both he and Erika had spoken with Carr with Hodge being the last one on the phone.

"Alright, Lehmann. My instructions are to let you loose. But know this, Leroy sent me here to help but if you refuse that help everything is on your head. That's according to Leroy, not me, and if things fall apart, the CIA never heard of you."

◊ ◊ ◊

[that evening]

Tonight, Erika's poker luck at Gaetano's wasn't as good. After just an hour, she had lost $90.

As Gino shuffled the cards, she blurted it out. "Do you men know a Detective Bolles of the Denver Police?"

Gino immediately stopped shuffling and everyone around the table looked at her.

"Why do you want to know about Bolles?" Checkers asked.

"He has something I need, Checkers, or I guess I should say the police have it."

"What's that?"

"A file on me and another file on someone else."

"Who else?"

"Axel Ryker, the man who came here with me one night."

"What's in the files?" Checkers asked.

"We're both on the run. We're accused of some crimes back east." It wasn't a lie.

"What crimes?"

"Murder."

The men looked around at each other. After a pause, Checkers asked, "Did you two do it?"

"Ryker, yes. I didn't plan on killing anyone, but a man died who was attacking an innocent woman after I stepped in to help her." This was also true and had happened in Cincinnati. She stopped there, not saying anything about charges of espionage during wartime that hung over her head.

Checkers took a drag on his cigar. "So, what is it exactly that you want from us, Erika?"

"I'm hoping someone here knows this detective and can tell me something about him. Maybe where he lives."

Checkers smiled. "What are you going to do? Take him a bouquet of posies?"

The other men laughed.

Now Erika was irked. "Forget I said anything. Deal the cards, Gino—please."

Checkers signaled Gino to hold the cards.

"I didn't say we couldn't or wouldn't help you, Erika. What did I tell you the other night?"

"That you always help friends," she answered. "That's why I asked, Checkers. Instead, you make jokes. Fuck you. You know what, cash me out. I've come to the wrong place."

Fat Paulie interjected. "Woah! Lady, you've got some balls talking to the boss like that. Guys have woken up in dumpsters with broken legs for less."

"It's okay, Paulie," Checkers said. Then he looked at Erika. "How much have you lost tonight?"

"About ninety bucks."

"Your luck has just changed. Twenty percent of the Denver cops are on the take. Bolles is on our payroll."

Chapter 72

Denver, Colorado
Next day—Wednesday, 09 June 1948

By nine o'clock this morning, Al Hodge had Leroy Carr on the telephone.

"She didn't come back to the hotel last night, Leroy."

"That doesn't mean anything with Erika," Carr said from Washington.

"True."

"She'll get this done, Al. She wants citizenship too badly to let anything stand in her way. When she surfaces, call me immediately."

"ROGER that."

[same time]

Erika sat eating a late breakfast (for her) that had just been served by Paulie's mother. Fat Paulie, the leg-breaker, didn't live with his mother but he brought Erika here after Checkers tasked him with finding a safe place for her to stay the night. After the poker game ended at two in the morning (early by Smaldone standards), Paulie brought Erika here and left. He had yet to reappear.

Mrs. Villano was a traditional Italian mother, and a widow who desperately wanted grandchildren.

"You and my Paulie, you like each other, yes?" she said with a heavy Italian accent.

"Yes," Erika said as she cut a slice of cheese from a block on the table. "We're friends."

"Friends? Perhaps you will be more than friends soon. My Paulie will be a good husband. He has a good job selling stocks and bonds."

Erika was skilled enough not to laugh.

"I'm sure your son would be a good catch for any girl, Mrs. Villano, but he and I are just friends."

"I will talk to Paulie about a proposal. A nice girl like you should have a husband and children by now."

[noon]

Across the street from a restaurant in downtown Denver named *Leonard's,* Gino sat behind the wheel of a new Cadillac. It took extra money under the table to get a new Cadillac, but then that was just business. Checkers Smaldone sat in the passenger seat next to the driver. In the back seat sat Fat Paulie and Erika.

"Gino, you said Bolles is supposed to meet us here, right?" Checkers asked.

"Yeah, I called him at his house this morning. I told the fuck to be here by noon."

Checkers looked at his watch. It was ten minutes after.

Finally, they saw Detective Bolles pull over and get out of his car.

"Gino, go get him and bring him to the car," Checkers ordered.

Gino jumped out of the car, ran across the street, and returned with Bolles. Fat Paulie got out and Bolles ended up sitting in the back seat between Erika and Paulie.

Bolles looked at Erika. "What are you doing here?"

Paulie interrupted. "Never mind what she's doing here. Keep your trap shut and listen."

Checkers took over. "We need you to hand over to us a couple of files, Bolles. Erika, give him the names."

"Erika Lehmann and Axel Ryker." She handed him a paper. "Here are the spellings."

"I know how to spell the names. I booked both you and that creep, Ryker, remember." Then Bolles redirected to Checkers. "This is bullshit, Checkers; pulling me off the street like this is dangerous for all of us."

"Yeah," Checkers replied, "especially for you if you don't come up with those files."

"It will cost you extra," Bolles said boldly.

Paulie jabbed his pistol into Bolles side. "We pay you plenty already Bolles for the little we get out of you. The only person it will cost is you if you don't deliver. And it won't be money—get my drift?"

"Alright, alright . . . Jesus. Give me a day. We'll met tomorrow."

"Do you think we're fucking retards," said Checkers. "Give you a day for what, so you can have a secretary type copies? You're going back to headquarters right now. Once you enter, you have ten minutes to come out with the files."

"I'm supposed to walk out of headquarters and hand you the files? Are you nuts?"

"Get in your car and drive to the parking lot of Saint Anthony's Hospital. We'll follow you and get the files there. Now get the fuck out of my car."

Chapter 73

Denver, Colorado
Same day—Wednesday, 09 June 1948

"Leroy, it's me," Al Hodge said into his hotel room telephone.

"I know it's you, Al," Carr said from Washington. *"Sheila told me before she connected us."*

"Right. I always forget that. Lehmann handed me the Denver police files on her and Ryker twenty minutes ago."

"What?"

"I said I have the files on Lehmann and Ryker."

"How did she do it without your help?"

"Beats me. When I asked her, she clammed up tighter than a midget's underwear on a cow."

"Get her on the Hudson tomorrow morning. I'll see you when you get here."

"Do you want me to destroy the files?"

"Does it look like anything might be missing?" Carr asked.

"No, the files look in order."

"Don't destroy them. I want to take a look at them."

"Has Beckman gotten anything out of that Sedik guy, Leroy?"

"Only that he's not Sedik."

"Huh?"

"This isn't for the phone, Al. I'll fill you in when you get home."

"Okay, I'll call you when we land at Andrews."

[that evening]

Aldo didn't bother taking her handgun this time; he opened the door for her at the top of the stairs at Gaetano's.

The card game hadn't started. The men were still eating. Tonight, it was Italian sausage sandwiches with fried green peppers and melted provolone cheese.

"Erika, there you are!" said Checkers loudly.

Erika had talked to Al Hodge and knew she was leaving in the morning.

"I just stopped in to say thank you." She didn't concern herself with mob etiquette this time. She went around the table, hugged each man, and gave them a kiss on the cheek. "I'm leaving town tomorrow morning. I might never see you again, so I wanted to thank you for all you did for me."

She started to leave.

"Where the fuck are you going?" Checkers asked. "Sit down and have something to eat." Then he added, "We'll fire up the poker game when we're done. You're not going anywhere until you give us a chance to win back some more of our money."

Erika paused on her way out, smiled, and turned around. She took a seat between Gino and another man named Frank 'Blackie' Mazza. There was no place she'd rather be, other than with her daughter.

"Donnie," Paulie bawled at their teenage gopher. "Quit playing with your cock and get Erika a sandwich."

Chapter 74

Washington, D.C.
Next day—Thursday, 10 June 1948

The Hudson landed at Andrews Air Force Base at 6:00 p.m. Two hours later, Leroy Carr, Al Hodge, and Erika Lehmann sat in a secluded table at Jocko's Pub in Annapolis.

"Erika," said Carr, "Al and I have both looked over the Denver police files on you and Ryker. All seems to be in order. It looks like nothing is missing. Al told me he asked you again on the plane how you got the files and you wouldn't say. How did you get them, Erika?"

"Leroy, do I have your word that it won't go any farther then the three of us?"

"Yes."

"The Smaldone family helped me."

"That's the crime family in Denver, correct?"

"That's them. The detective that covered the cases is on their payroll. Apparently, police corruption is a big problem in Denver."

Carr looked quickly at Hodge, then took a drink of his gin and tonic.

Erika asked, "Where's Chris Singleton?"

"Hoover fired him for joining forces with us."

Erika looked at Carr for a long moment. "You need to offer him a job, Leroy. Singleton is smart, and a good man."

"I already offered him a job, Erika. He said he needed some time to think it over."

"So what now, Leroy? Is the mission over?" she asked.

"It's over, at least for now. Beckman is still interrogating the prisoner who claimed he was Sedik, which it turns out he's not. I should know more in a day or two. That 'Wotan' guy hasn't yet recovered enough to be grilled."

"I hate Ryker's guts," she said, "but he gets information a lot faster than that."

"I don't want to talk about Ryker," Carr said firmly.

"I understand," she said. "So now, since the mission is over and successful, you will keep your promise to get charges against me dropped and help me gain citizenship?"

"My promise was that I will do everything I can, Erika, and I will keep that promise. It will be a process and it won't happen overnight. I was clear about that."

Hodge cut in. "What's next, Leroy?"

"Erika will return to the Farm. After Beckman gets what he can out of the prisoners, I'll call everyone in for a meeting."

"May I see Nick?" Nick was a bartender in Williamsburg, Virginia, that she had seen from time to time when she was stationed at the Farm at Camp Peary.

"You're not a prisoner, Erika," Carr answered. "If you have a weekend furlough you can do what you want. Just stay out of trouble."

[two days later—Saturday, 12 June 1948]

Erika had few duties at the Farm since her return yesterday. Her last battery, the one she had to leave with another instructor when the Denver mission began, had finished up last week. Another class would not start until next week. For these past two days, Erika kept herself busy with her own training—hours spent on the firing range, swimming, judo classes and other close-quarters combat skills.

[that evening]

Tonight it took the bus twenty minutes to drive from Camp Peary to Williamsburg, Virginia. Normally it took only ten or twelve minutes but tonight the driver was slowed by a pouring rain. Erika had remembered to bring an umbrella.

When she stepped off the bus it was a quick walk of two blocks to reach Lane's Tavern where Nick worked at his family run bar and restaurant. Erika waited to come until tonight. She hadn't called ahead, but knew Nick always worked Saturday evenings, the busiest time.

Their time together in the past had been sparse, but they enjoyed each other's company. They had never made love. Their physical relationship had progressed no farther than kissing and petting. Nick seemed very taken with Erika and had at one time even volunteered to move to Texas where, before leaving for an assignment overseas, she told him she was being transferred to Fort Hood. He thought she worked as a civilian secretary/file clerk for the Army at Camp Peary— at least that's what she had told him. Of course, both Texas and her secretary job had been covers and she talked him out of leaving his family's business.

Erika walked in the front door, folded the umbrella, and spotted an empty seat at the bar. The crowd was large tonight. Most of the tables were taken. The voice of Hank Williams escaped the jukebox. Two couples danced.

Nick stood at the far end of the bar, wedging off the caps of two bottles of Yuengling beer. When he spotted Erika, she smiled. Nick quickly sat the beers in front of the men who had ordered them and walked over to her.

"Erika," he seemed surprised.

"Hi, Nick. I just got back to Camp Peary. It's wonderful to see you."

"It's nice to see you."

She felt the tone in his voice a bit reserved but didn't comment. "What time do you get off tonight?"

"Listen, Erika, it's great to see you, but it's been so long, and you told me the last time you left that you might never return."

"Yes, I did say that, didn't I."

"You told me to move on with my life."

He was right again. Suddenly a woman approached Nick and leaned on the bar.

"Darling, my father would like another beer. I'll take it over and save you some steps."

"Uh," Nick stuttered out, "Francey, this is a friend of mine, Erika. Erika, this is Francey, my fiancée."

Francey was small, perhaps around 5'3". She was a pretty brunette with a sweet smile.

"Hi, Erika. Nice to meet you."

Erika noticed the small diamond on her left ring finger. "Nice to meet you, Francey."

Nick asked, "What are you drinking, Erika? It's on the house."

"Nothing tonight, Nick. I just stopped in to say hello. I have to get back to Camp Peary. I wish you and Francey the best of everything. Truly." She got off the stool and gave Francey a hug.

Erika quickly walked out into the downpour, this time not caring to open her umbrella.

Chapter 75

Washington, D.C.
E Street Complex
Two days later—Monday, 14 June 1948

At mid-morning, Leroy Carr sat behind his desk. Yesterday, Al Hodge had driven to Camp Peary and picked up Erika Lehmann. She spent last night at the Mayflower Hotel and now sat next to Hodge across from Carr.

"How's your guy . . . Nick?" Carr asked Erika for etiquette's sake; he monitored and vetted anyone Erika Lehmann decided to date. Al Hodge had vetted the Williamsburg bartender when the two first began seeing each other. Nick was a WW II Navy veteran and they had found no red flags.

"Nick has moved on, Leroy. He's engaged to a sweet girl. It's the best thing for him. We have no future together, you know that, don't you?"

"It's tough for a clandestine field agent to have a successful private life, Erika. You didn't learn that from us. You learned it during your time with the Abwehr when you and Kai tried to make a life. It seldom works out."

Erika knew he was right.

Carr added, "Nevertheless, I'm sorry things worked out as they did, but it's best for the young man."

Time to change the subject as far as Erika was concerned. "What's the situation with my citizenship?"

"Erika, we just talked about this a few days ago. First, we have to get all charges against you sanitized. I'm going to start working on that process this week. Recovering the FBI files and the Denver police files will certainly help, but as I said, it will take time.

"Now, let's get to the business at hand. I sat down with Mr. Beckman earlier this morning. Beckman hasn't had a chance to really question 'Wotan' yet, but my guess is he's doesn't know any more than what he told Ryker. The man who at the Garden City airport claimed he was Sedik is not, as we all now know. He is one of Sedik's men. Beckman and his interrogation team are still working on this guy. A link to North Africa has been established because of an article of clothing he was wearing, but not much more than that at this time."

"O'Grady was hired by someone in North Africa?" Erika asked.

"Possibly," Carr answered.

"Why?"

"That's the question, Erika. If I knew I'd tell you. As I said, Beckman is still working on him."

"So what now, Leroy?"

"Back to your citizenship situation. We need to get Singleton onboard, Erika. Even with the FBI files on you now safely locked away here at E Street, Singleton still has all the details in his head. Not only would Singleton be a fine addition to the CIA, if he worked here he would be under oath to never divulge classified information to a Congressional or Department of Justice committee. Do we understand each other?"

"You want me to convince Singleton to join the CIA."

"I set up a meeting between you and him for tomorrow morning at nine o'clock on the steps of the Lincoln Memorial. I didn't elaborate about the subject of the meeting and he doesn't know the meeting was my idea. Singleton thinks you asked to see him; that way you can play it anyway you think will be most effective."

Chapter 76

Washington, D.C.
Next day—Tuesday, 15 June 1948

Chris Singleton parked his car in the parking lot of the Federal Reserve building off Constitution Avenue and walked to the Lincoln Memorial. As he neared the Memorial, he saw her sitting on the steps, about half way up to Honest Abe.

As he approached the steps he noticed she was reading something. She didn't acknowledge him until he sat down beside her.

"Good morning, Chris."

"Good morning."

She had been reading a tourist brochure about the Lincoln Memorial.

"It says here the columns are made from Colorado marble," Erika said. "Isn't that ironic? We just left there. And there are thirty-six columns denoting the number of states in the union when Lincoln was assassinated in 1865."

"Erika, why did you ask to see me? Don't tell me it was for a history lesson."

"Do you still hate me?" She finally put down the brochure.

"No, I don't hate you. I know you didn't kill Charlie. I guess I should thank you for saving my life, so thanks, but still, Charlie would be alive if Ryker hadn't been sent to the States because of you."

"Leroy told me you lost your job."

Singleton said nothing.

"He also told me he offered you a job with the CIA."

"I haven't told Mr. Carr yet, but I could never be part of an organization that employs a man like Axel Ryker."

"You need to accept Leroy's offer, Chris."

"I just told you my reasons, Erika. I'm going to bring Ryker to justice if it takes until my dying breath."

"How are you going to do that? You're no longer with the FBI or any official justice organization. What are you going to do, become a game warden and hope you catch Ryker over his fishing limit?"

"I'll find a way."

"I can suggest a way."

Singleton looked at her. She looked deep in thought, staring out across the reflecting pool toward the Washington Monument.

"What is that?" he asked.

"Not now. Let me take you to dinner tonight. It's on me."

"What?" Singleton was taken aback and not just because women didn't ask men for a date. Any man would be offended if a woman offered to pay. "That's insulting, Erika. Do you think I'm flat broke because I lost my job?"

"Why should men always have to pay, and why can't a woman ask a man to dinner? And no, I don't think you're broke. I won a tidy sum of money playing poker in Denver and I want to splurge a little. What's your answer? Yes, or no?"

"The answer is no if you plan on paying."

Erika pulled a quarter out of her pocket. "Call it in the air. Heads you pay; tails I pay." She flipped the coin up into the air.

Singleton called heads.

She caught the coin in her right hand and flipped it onto the back of her left hand. "Tails. Dinner is on me fair and square."

Singleton shook his head. He would never figure out this woman.

"Where and when should I pick you up?" he asked.

"I'm staying at the Mayflower. They have a very fine restaurant there called The Senator. I'll make reservations in my name and meet you in the restaurant at seven."

"I've never eaten there. Is it black tie?"

"No, a sport jacket and any tie will do."

[an hour later]

Erika called Leroy Carr from her hotel room.

"Leroy, you told me to call you after I met with Singleton."

"How'd it go?"

"He told me he's going to turn down your offer but I'm going to work on him tonight. We have a dinner date."

262

"Singleton asked you on a date? I thought he blamed you for his partner's death."

"I asked him to go to dinner. I'll report in when it's over. It might be late. Do you want me to call you tonight at home or wait until tomorrow morning and come into your office?"

"Call me at home as soon as it's over."

[that evening]

Singleton was waiting at the table when Erika entered The Senator. He stood and held her chair for her.

"Thank you," she said as she sat.

When he returned to his seat he said, "That's a lovely dress. Very classy."

"Thanks, Chris." She wore a modest light green dress with half-sleeves to cover her still fresh scar courtesy of Marienne and her Garand rifle. The dress revealed only a modest amount of cleavage. She wasn't trying to seduce him. Her blonde hair was pulled up and pinned using metal 'chopsticks.'

Singleton got right to the point. "Erika, you mentioned you had a suggestion on how I can bring Ryker to justice. What is it?"

"Do you think we can avoid shop talk until after dinner? I'd appreciate it."

Singleton was trapped without a response, so they picked up menus.

The freshly made dinner took time to prepare. For the next hour and a half, they drank wine, ate dinner, and talked of small things.

"I know to become an FBI agent, an applicant has to have either a law degree or an accounting degree. Which one do you have?" Erika asked.

"I started out as an accountant, but when the war broke out I applied to join the FBI."

"Do you have family, Chris?"

"Yes, a large family."

"Any sweethearts?"

"Not since about six months ago. How about you, Erika?"

"My parents are both gone. I have an uncle and a couple of cousins in Germany, but I haven't seen them in years."

"A boyfriend somewhere? You asked me, so the question seems fair."

"I'm a widow. My husband died in battle." She would let him think she was referring to the war, even though Kai died on a mission for the CIA after the war.

"I'm sorry to hear that. That must be tough, even now."

"We have a daughter. She's seven years old now and living in London with my maternal grandparents."

"You have a daughter?"

"That surprises you, I'm sure."

Singleton decided to be honest. "Yes, I guess it does surprise me somewhat, but I hope your daughter is doing well."

After dinner they walked up one flight to an outdoor veranda at the front of the Mayflower. In the waning twilight, Singleton offered her a cigarette. She took it and he lit it for her.

"Okay, Erika, dinner is over. What is your suggestion you told me you had concerning Ryker?"

Erika blew out a puff of smoke and looked at him. "You sound like dinner was an assignment you couldn't avoid. Was it really that bad?"

"I'm sorry," he said. "Dinner was very nice and thank you for paying. I've never had a lady pay for my dinner, so that was something new, although I still don't feel it right that the woman pays. But I didn't consider it a chore by any means. You're smart, and a fine dinner companion. I enjoyed our conversation." Singleton didn't want to admit it, but against his will he found himself attracted to this very singular woman.

"Chris, you told me this morning that your ultimate goal is to make sure Ryker gets what he deserves."

"That's right. That's why I could never be part of the CIA."

"Your thinking is all wrong," Erika replied. "The only way you have any chance of getting to Ryker is from within. Take Leroy's offer, Chris. That's my suggestion. Now I'll say goodnight. I enjoyed our time together."

Without touching him she walked away, leaving him on the veranda. Once back in her room she followed orders and called Leroy Carr. She then changed into slacks and a blouse. An hour later she was sitting in the half-empty Majestic Theater watching the late night showing of Hedy Lamarr's latest film, *Let's Live a Little.* She knew Hedy personally. Erika and her fellow Shield Maidens, the team of four female agents that Leroy Carr had disbanded after a mission to South America last summer, had rescued Hedy after the movie star/scientist was abducted by the Russians. In this film, Robert Cummings was her co-star.

The daughter of Karl and Louise Lehmann ate her popcorn and drank her Orange Crush soda alone.

Chapter 77

Washington, D.C.
E Street Complex
Next day—Wednesday, 16 June 1948

As ordered, last night after her dinner date with Chris Singleton, Erika called Leroy Carr at home before she went to the movie. She told Carr the truth: Singleton was noncommittal, but time would tell. Before they ended the call, Carr told Erika to be in his office at ten o'clock this morning.

Carr had said last night, "I have a meeting with another team early tomorrow morning, but I should be finished by ten. If not, wait for me in Sheila's office."

Now that morning, Erika and Sheila Reid had just started catching up when Carr buzzed in and asked Sheila to send Erika into his office.

When she entered, no one else was in Carr's office, not even Al Hodge.

"Where's Al?" Erika asked after she sat down.

"He and I had a briefing with another team this morning, Erika. Believe it or not, you're not the only field agent in the CIA. We do have assignments for others."

"I see you're in a good mood this morning, Leroy," Erika said sardonically.

"I *am* in a good mood. I don't know what you said to Chris Singleton last night, but he called me this morning and accepted my job offer. That should make you very happy, as well. Once Singleton is sworn in, he can't divulge any information about you to anyone outside the CIA, and even then, only to people within the CIA with proper clearance."

Erika knew why Singleton had taken the job—so he could get to Ryker. Erika didn't elaborate to Carr; nevertheless, she felt she owed him a warning.

"Leroy, that's great news. I think Chris will make a fine agent, but I would recommend keeping him away from Ryker. Chris knows Ryker killed his partner in Evansville."

"I'm aware of that, Erika, but let's not get ahead of ourselves. Singleton must still complete training at the Farm. I'll make sure he's assigned to your battery. You'll be in charge of overseeing his fitness for CIA duty, which, as you know, is much different from the qualities that make a good FBI agent."

[later that day]

Leroy Carr and Al Hodge both had a busy day with various business. It was late that afternoon before they got a chance to sit down together. Hodge already knew that the fired FBI special agent, Chris Singleton, had accepted Carr's job offer.

"At least that was good news this morning when Singleton called and accepted your offer, Leroy. What are your plans for him?"

"He still has to go through training at the Farm. I told Erika she would oversee his training."

Hodge chuckled. "That should be interesting. What's the latest from Beckman concerning his interrogation of the fake Sedik?"

Beckman got us the name of his boss—Rafik Djebar—and a motive. This guy is apparently the biggest opium czar in North Africa and has plenty of money. He hired O'Grady to avenge the death of his wife and children who apparently got caught up in a battle between American Army troops and someone with the Vichy French. It was early in the war, before the free French joined the Allies."

"We're not going to send Lehmann to get this joker, I hope," Al commented.

"No, another team."

Hodge breathed a sigh of relief.

"Houchen and four or five good men should do it," Carr said. "It's a capture or kill mission. That last part makes it easier, but we'll capture him if we can. Hillenkoetter sent this all the way up the flag pole to the White House. The order comes from Truman himself. This Djebar waged what could only be classified as war against the United States. We need to get this guy, and the sooner the better. We can't spend months on this mission, Al."

"Okay, Leroy. I'll put some preliminary plans together and bring them to you ASAP. I'm just glad I don't have to deal with Lehmann and her hijinks."

Chapter 78

[One Month Later]
Camp Peary, Virginia
Friday, 16 July 1948

This was one of the hottest and muggiest Virginia summers in recent memory. Biting and stinging insects set up their encampments in the forests of Camp Peary, intent to Blitzkrieg any human invading their territory.

Chris Singleton had just completed the obstacle course, his last task of the day, in a secret area of Camp Peary known as the 'Farm.' At the Farm, the CIA trained prospective agents.

Finishing the obstacle course under the time allotted meant he had just completed his fourth week of an eight-week course at the Farm. After that, it would be on to another location for advanced training.

The CIA agent in charge of training his battery (a group of eight prospective agents) was Erika Lehmann who was, for all intents and purposes, the reason he got fired from the FBI.

When the day's training finally ended, Erika walked her flock of seven sweating and exhausted men and one woman plebe back to their barracks after a long day in not only the obstacle course but calisthenics, handgun target practice, elusive automobile driving techniques, hand-to-hand combat, and a grueling swimming competition in the Farm's lake on a full stomach right after breakfast to start the day off. As the group walked back to their barracks, eager for a shower and dinner, Erika called Singleton aside.

"Come to my quarters after chow," she told him.

[two hours later]
Chris Singleton didn't know what to expect as he knocked on the door of Erika Lehmann's quarters. At times, it almost seemed that she was flirting with him during his time at the Farm. Then, after that she had changed demeanors as easily as flicking a light switch and became a grueling (to the point of being an abusive) taskmaster who made it a

point to be harder on him than any of the other recruits. He reasoned all this was a part of a head game she played.

A half minute passed after his knock, then the door opened.

"Come in," she told him.

The CIA trainers at the Farm had private accommodations. Even though their rooms were small, no larger than a prison cell, they enjoyed a measure of privacy unlike Singleton and the other trainees in his battery who all bunked together in Army basic training style. Only the single woman in their battery was not in their barracks; she was billeted in the women's barracks, yet like the men, her bunk was in a large communal room with women in other batteries. The fledging CIA needed additional agents badly and the Farm ran at full capacity because of all those there currently training, few would make the grade as possible field agent material.

Erika's tiny room was only large enough to house a single bed, a small writing table, and two chairs. The common latrine was down the hall.

"Sit in a chair," she told Singleton. "I'll sit on the bed."

Singleton didn't say anything as he sat down.

"You're doing well, Chris. You're the top scorer in my battery in all categories except foreign languages."

"That's good to hear, I guess. Is that why you ordered me here, to give me my report card so I can take it home to my parents?"

Erika smiled. "More FBI humor. No, I brought you here to tell you today is my last day with your battery. Starting Monday, another instructor will take over. I've been recalled to Washington. Leroy wants me in his office Monday morning."

Singleton shrugged. "Okay, thanks for the update."

"You're half way through your initial training and doing well," she told him. "You'll be fine."

Singleton couldn't help but think the next training instructor would be less demanding than her; although, he didn't care. He had never feared a challenge.

Erika stood and flashed him a disarming smile. "That's all I have to tell you."

When Singleton stood, she moved close to him (nearly brushing her body against his). Erika gave him a sultry look as if she might kiss him, then suddenly slapped him hard across the face. "You may return to your quarters now."

She modeled her coaching techniques after the severe training she had received during her plebe days with Abwehr in Nazi Germany.

Chapter 79

Washington, D.C.
E Street Complex
Monday, 19 June 1948

Sunday afternoon a driver picked up Erika at Camp Peary and drove her the four hours to Washington. She didn't bother trying to milk the driver for information about her recall; Erika knew the driver would know nothing. After she arrived in D.C., her room was already reserved for her at the Mayflower.

Now it was eight o'clock the next morning and, as she had done so many times before, sat across the desk from Leroy Carr in his E Street office.

"How's Singleton doing?" Carr asked, even though she sent him weekly reports.

"Fine. In fact, he's the best recruit in my battery."

"Doesn't surprise me," said Carr. "He's already completed FBI training. That training is far from a walk in the park."

"Leroy, I assume I'm here about a mission to find the man in North Africa who hired O'Grady. Can we cut to the chase?"

"That's not why you're here Erika. We sent a team to Algiers a month ago. Rafik Djebar, the man who hired O'Grady, is dead. Our goal was to capture Djebar but it didn't work out as we had hoped. We did, however, capture his right-hand man, Sedik—the real Sedik this time. Al picked up his team and the prisoner in Casablanca. They landed at Andrews last night. I turned Sedik over to Beckman in case we can pry anymore information out of him."

Erika was surprised. "Why didn't you send me along? French is one of the languages of Algeria. I speak French."

"I have another assignment for you."

Erika looked at him intently. "I'm listening, sir."

"You're going on a mission with Kathryn and Zhanna Rogova—that is if we can convince Rogova to leave the convent in Honduras."

"Zhanna?"

"Yes, Zhanna."

"I know Kathryn won't hesitate, but I'm not sure about Zhanna. Send me to Honduras, Leroy. I'm the one with the best chance of convincing her."

"Thanks, but no thanks. I remember the last time you and Rogova were together in South America. That little episode aged me ten years. Especially after you disappeared with my wife. Fetching Rogova will be Al's job. He'll fly out to Honduras on Wednesday."

"What does Al say about bringing Zhanna back in?" Erika could imagine.

"I haven't had a chance to speak with Al about it yet. We're meeting later today."

"When do I get a briefing about the mission?"

"I need you to do something first."

"What's that?"

"You're leaving for Los Angeles tomorrow morning, Hollywood to be more specific."

"Hollywood! Why?"

"Your job is to convince your old buddy, Hedy Lamarr, to be part of your team for this next mission. It will be a one-time deal for her."

Erika gave him a perplexed look. "You're talking in riddles, Leroy. You're not briefing me now and yet I'm supposed to convince Hedy Lamarr to agree to do something I know nothing about. You know she'll have questions; how will I answer?"

"Your assignment could not be simpler, Erika. You and the other Shield Maidens saved Lamarr's life. I'm sure she feels obligated to you. All you have to do is get Lamarr here in my office so I can talk to her. I'll take it from there. After she hears what I have to say she is free to accept or decline. That's all the information you need at this point, and it's all you're going to get for now. Your flight leaves from Andrews at 0715 tomorrow."

[that evening—Annapolis, Maryland]

Carr and Hodge sat over drinks at Jocko's Pub.

"That Denver mission was a rough one, Leroy. I'm glad it's over.

"Don't get too comfortable, Al. You're not going to like what I have to tell you."

"What kind of shit did Lehmann stir up now? Did she do something while I was in Africa?"

Carr chuckled at his old friend who was never hesitant to say what was on his mind. "Nothing like that." Then Carr became serious. "I'm sending you to Honduras to fetch Zhanna Rogova."

Hodge had just taken a swig of his Laphroaig. He choked and coughed.

"Come on, Leroy! Why? Don't tell me that Rogova and Lehmann will be back together. Mixing those two is like drinking gasoline mixed with rat poison. Hell, if we're going to do that we might as well bring all those wild broads back together," Hodge said as a mordant joke. "Let's throw Kathryn Fischer in the witch's caldron and stir up more whammies."

"Kathryn will have to be included for a very important reason, Al. We have no choice but to bring the Shield Maidens back together. We'll send Sheila along to keep an eye on them."

Hodge burst out in a belly laugh. "Sheila is professional at E Street, but when she gets around those three weirdos, she changes. Lehmann, Rogova, and Fischer are gangsters who wear lipstick, Leroy. You remember when Sheila got thrown in a Bamberg clink with those other three and it took you two weeks to quiet things down with our embassy in Munich."

Carr took a drink and didn't reply. He refrained from smiling. He knew it was sometimes best just to let his old friend get things off his chest, even if it wouldn't change anything.

"Well, thanks for telling me this," Hodge added. "I'm going to get shit-faced now."

Without even asking about details of the mission, Hodge immediately rose from the booth, walked to the bar, and ordered another Laphroaig—this time a double.

"Keep the Scotch coming, Joey," Hodge told the bartender. "When I'm lying on the floor, just have someone cart my ass out and dump me in the alley."

Epilogue

Denver's Smaldone Crime Family

Checkers and Clyde Smaldone established themselves as Denver's most prolific Prohibition bootleggers. Both of these men, along with their younger brother, Clarence "Chauncey" Smaldone, took the family business to even greater heights in the 1940s. Even though the escapades of the eldest brother, Clyde, received more press, it was Checkers who was considered the patriarch and Don during the time I knew the family.

Denver Police Corruption Scandal

In the mid-20th Century, one of the most infamous police corruption scandals in the history of the United States unfolded in Denver, Colorado.

Not only were many Denver police officers taking bribes and payoffs from organized crime, the Denver police had their own burglary ring. Denver cops stole money and valuables from businesses they were charged to protect. Police cars would close down a few blocks of a business area then burgle and steal safes and valuables from businesses along the closed area. Denver cops would take the loot, then respond to the alarms and take the reports from the victimized business owners.

Finally, it came to a crashing halt when a stolen safe fell out of the trunk of one of the crooked cop's police cruiser. He testified against his fellow officers and over forty-seven officers lost their badges or went to jail.

Times have changed. Today, the Denver Police Department is routinely recognized as one the finest departments of any major city.

Former Nazis Working for the CIA after the War

Neither the American nor British intelligence communities displayed any qualms about bringing Nazis into their clandestine societies after World War II.

During the Cold War, both the CIA and British MI-6 made use of Nazis (some who were boldly unrepentant). Furthermore, records show both organizations went out of their way to recruit Nazi agents, especially if the Germans could offer experience or expertise in working against the Russians. The CIA not only maintained a close working relationship with Reinhard Gehlen, they helped him set up shop. During the war, Gehlen served as the German Army's intelligence chief for the Eastern Front. With protection from the United States after the war, Gehlen assembled a large intelligence organization staffed with numerous ex-Nazis and known war criminals—at least 100 of Gehlen's operatives were former SS/SD officers or Gestapo agents. Gehlen's organization eventually became the official West German intelligence agency—the BND.

Records from the National Security Archive of George Washington University show that at least five associates of the notorious Nazi Adolf Eichmann worked for the CIA, and over 200 other Nazis were recruited by the United States government and brought to America.

– Mike Whicker

Acknowledgements

I have to thank my weapons expert in Ohio, Gary Klemens. Gary never fails to have the answer to any questions I ask him about weapons of the 1940s.

Thanks to Rich Eisgruber, retired from the FBI, who was kind enough to write the back-cover review for this book.

To my proofreaders, Erin Whicker and Tim Heerdink—thank you.

Thanks to Zach Whicker, Jenna Meyer, and Carla Boyles for all their work.

My friend, Dr. Susanna Hoeness-Krupsaw, always checks my sometimes-dubious German translations.

Another thanks goes to Josh Whicker, a professional historian. Josh gave me valuable information for several historical scenarios in the story.

And as always, many thanks to David Jones, my friend and attorney who is also quite an historian himself. David always supplies me with constructive critiques.

I must cite the former Denver newspaper, *The Rocky Mountain News,* along with *Colorado Life Magazine,* and the website *AmericanMafia.com* for certain information about the Smaldone family and the Denver Police corruption scandal. Another source of information about the Smaldone family was the excellent book by former *Denver Post* writer, Dick Kreck. His book *Smaldone: The Untold Story of an American Crime Family* is packed full of history, not only of the Smaldone family but of other Colorado crime figures, as well. You can find Dick's book on Amazon.

All those sources were helpful to authenticate my own personal knowledge of members of the Smaldone family who I knew personally and was on friendly terms with for many years when I lived in Denver. To this day, the best Italian meals I have ever eaten were prepared by Checkers Smaldone's mother, Mamie, at Gaetano's. Although now under different management, Gaetano's is still open today and continues to serve delicious food. The restaurant is located on the corner of West 38th Avenue and Tejon Street in northwest Denver. If you're ever in the Mile High City I highly recommend it if you enjoy authentic Italian fare.

– Mike Whicker

A New Valhalla

Erika Lehmann will return in:

Shield Maidens Return

(available in the summer of 2019)

A New Valhalla

The author welcomes reader comments.
Email: **mikewhicker1@gmail.com**

Mike Whicker is also on
Facebook and Twitter

A New Valhalla

CPSIA information can be obtained
at www.ICGtesting.com
Printed in the USA
LVHW09s0058190918
590615LV00001B/97/P

9 780999 558218